CHAPTER ONE

Anno Domini 1360

He came over the rise, the bag of tools weighing heavily on his shoulder. The track snaked away in front of him, down the slope, with the soft promise of water at the bottom of the valley. Over in the woods a magpie chattered to its mate as it swooped through the branches.

The August sun was already fierce, even though midday was still four hours away. He shaded his eyes with a hand and squinted. In the distance he could make out the low roofs and the church tower of Chesterfield. Another hour and he would be there, with a dry throat and a hunger the size of England. The chantry priest in Dronfield had let him sleep on a bench the night before, but the man had possessed precious little food to share.

He strode out, stopping to drink at the stream and wet his head then cross himself for luck before striking out along the road into the town. There were few people about, but that was no surprise. Coming down from York he had often gone half a day or more without seeing a soul, his tongue and his heart aching for conversation and companionship.

When he was a child, before the great pestilence came and swept away most of the world, he felt he remembered people everywhere, a welter of conversation that filled his ears all day. He had helped his father then, beginning to learn how to make the wood do what he wanted, shaping and shaving it. But then his father was gone; his life withered to nothing in two brief days, and all John had left was the man's satchel of tools and a mind that tumbled with memories and confusion.

He could recall the crops rotting in the fields at harvest time, not enough people still alive to bring them in, and the cows lowing until they died, their carcasses stinking and covered with flies.

He had taken to the roads that autumn, not wanting to cling to the few folk still alive in Leeds. He had the beginnings of a trade and it had served him well in the twelve years since. By God's good grace he had a feel for wood. He could run his hands along the grain and understand how it should be, how to use its strength, where to cut and where to leave it.

A cart passed, going the other way, the horse plodding slowly between the traces, and he exchanged greetings with the driver, asking about the town ahead, eager for any gossip or information he could use. By the time they parted with a 'God be with you' he had learned there was work for a good man building the spire for the church, and the names of two places where he might find food and ale. Smiling, he walked on into Chesterfield, easing his way up the hill that climbed towards the church.

He glanced around with a curious eye, taking in the marketplace close to the building, then the construction of the spire itself. Groups of men were at work, the masons up high on the scaffold, laughing and joking as they laboured away, joiners busy under the shade of trees in the yard; it seemed a good site, with everyone busy enough.

He passed through, taking a turn around the town. Houses were packed tight along the streets and there was a sense of money about the place. Not wealthy, perhaps, but a comfortable little market town, and a growing one at that. The rich iron tang of blood hung in the air in the crowded streets of the Shambles, where the animal carcasses were suspended and goodwives haggled loudly with butchers over the price and quality of meat.

A few yards further, where the ginnel ended, stood another market place, the largest he had seen, bigger even than the one in York. Astonished, he stood and gazed over the space, imagining it full of traders.

He was still wide-eyed when a high voice close by said, 'You need to see it tomorrow,' and he turned quickly. The boy was no more than twelve or thirteen, not even any down on his chin yet, but he had a warm, guileless smile. His dark hair was awry around his face and he wore a cote of good cloth that was too short, as if the lad had grown too quickly.

'The market's Tuesdays by the church, Saturdays here. People come from all over for it. You're new here, aren't you?'

'Aye,' he agreed. The boy seemed harmless enough, but he still felt to make sure his purse was still attached to his belt. 'It looks like a fair town.'

'Wait until the morning,' the lad inclined his head at the square, 'you won't believe it then. You've never seen so many people,' he said, his eyes wide, then nodded at the man's satchel. 'What do you do?'

'I'm a carpenter,' the man replied. 'I thought there might be work at the church.'

'I'm sure there will be,' the boy laughed. 'They always seem to want people there.'

The answer didn't surprise him. The death had carried off so many skilled men that a craftsman could earn good money these days, before he moved on when he wanted, safe in the knowledge that there would be work ahead of him.

'I'll go over there soon,' he said.

'I'm Walter,' the lad told him and cocked his head questioningly. 'What's your name?'

'I'm John.'

Walter smiled happily and nodded once more. He started to leave, but then looked back.

'Do you need somewhere to stay John?'

'I do,' he replied. 'Do you know of a place?'

'Ask for Widow Martha on Knifesmithgate.'

'Thank you, I'll do that.'

And with that Walter waved and ran off, moving across the empty marketplace with the effortless grace of the young.

John tried to pat the worst of the dirt and dust from his cote and hose, then made his way back to the church. He watched the workmen for a minute before asking one of the masons for the master carpenter.

'Over there,' the man pointed, staring at the stranger with open curiosity while he drank from a mug. 'They say he's not easy to work for.'

John grinned.

'I'll survive; I've had hard masters before.'

The master carpenter was bent over, planing down a length of oak, sawdust and small curls of wood caught in the sweat and hairs of his broad forearms. He was stripped to shirt and hose, the skin on the back of his neck red and angry.

'What do you need?' he asked without glancing up.

'I'm looking for work,' John said.

'You and a hundred others lad,' the man answered.

'I'm a carpenter.'

'Oh aye? Where did you apprentice?' He ran the plane along the beam again, then felt the surface delicately with his fingertips.

'I started with my father in Leeds,' John explained, 'then the sickness took him. I've been on my own since then.'

The man stood up and faced him, assessing him coolly. He was small but with the breadth and thick strength gained from a lifetime of labour, his short hair heavily flecked with grey, his lips clamped in a thin line.

'Let me see your hands.'

John held them out, palms upright to show the callouses of work.

'Turn them over.'

He did as he was ordered, displaying the many small scars that stood out on his skin.

'What's your name?' the man asked.

'John.'

'And where did you work last?'

'York. At the Minster.'

'Oh aye?' The man said doubtfully and ran a hand across his chin. 'No shortage of jobs up there for them as is willing.'

'Could keep busy till Judgement Day, most likely,' John agreed.

'So why did you leave?'

He reddened. 'A lass's father thought I ought to marry her. We had words.'

'Anyone hurt?'

'No.' He shook his head. 'I left in the night on Lammas Eve. It was best to move on.'

The man nodded then inclined his head at the satchel.

'Let me see your tools.'

John lifted the flap. The leather was old and scarred, and over the years he had mended the strap more times than he could count. But he had never been tempted to replacc it. He remembered his father carrying it, the sound of it banging against his hip as he walked, looking down at his son and smiling.

'Old but good,' the master carpenter said. 'Now let's see what you can do with them.' He gestured at a pile of offcuts thrown into a corner. 'Make me a mortise and tenon.'

'Can I have a drink first?' John asked. 'Been a long walk in the heat.'

The man chuckled. 'Go on, then. The barrel's there. I'll come back in a few minutes.'

He slaked his burning thirst with two mugs of the small beer then set to work. He picked up a piece of the wood – good, well-seasoned oak – and caressed it tenderly, rubbing along the grain before setting it aside. Within a minute he'd selected the pieces he wanted, knowing they'd fit together well.

He worked quickly. The wood told you what it wanted, if a man knew how to listen. That was what his father had always said, and John had learned the lesson well. He made his marks carefully then worked with chisel and saw, each stroke deft and sure. He forgot all the sounds around him, absorbed in the task until it was done and he stood up, coming back to the world.

He watched as the man inspected the joint, easing it apart then pushing it back in place, checking how closely the two pieces fitted together before nodding.

'It's fourpence halfpenny a day and all your ale. A penny less in winter, if you last that long.' He extended his hand and John took it, shaking it to give his agreement. 'You can call me Will. But I'll give you a piece of advice, lad.'

'What's that?' John asked as he rubbed the tools with an oiled cloth before putting them away.

'Keep your pizzle in your braies round here and don't get any of the lasses with child. They have a temper on them, do Chesterfield men.'

John grinned. 'I'll remember that.' He cast an eye over the building. 'What church is this, anyway?'

'St Mary's, dedicated to Our Lady. Right, you start at daybreak and – ' before he could say more there was a loud cry from the other side of the yard. Will ran towards the sounds, fast and agile. John slung his bag over his shoulder and followed, curious.

Two men were facing each other, one holding a knife, the other with a long cut along his forearm that dripped blood onto the grass. Will strode between them, pushing them both back. John came up quietly behind the man with the knife, clamping his hand around the man's wrist, tightening his grip until the weapon fell from his hand. The man turned with pure fury in his dark eyes. He had thin, bony features; his lips were curled in a sneer, the heat of anger boiling off him.

'Get him bandaged up and send him home for the day,' Will ordered, as two of the workers led the injured man away. He turned to the one who'd wielded the knife. 'And you, you've been nothing but trouble since I took you on.'

'He went for me.'

'I don't give a rat's arse what he did.' Will stood close, his spittle landing on the man's face as he spoke. 'I'll not have you here anymore. And you'll not be paid for today.' The man opened his mouth to speak but Will cut him off. 'Get yourself away from here and you'd better just hope Stephen there doesn't swear out a complaint against you.'

The man stood defiantly for a moment, then bent to retrieve his knife and walked away.

'Is it often like that?' John asked.

Will shook his head. 'They're good lads, for the most part. Loud when they've been paid, but that's life. There's always one, though. Anyway, start at daybreak, work until sunset. Be here in the morning and not a slug a bed like some of this lot.'

'I will,' John promised.

'You did well there,' Will added quietly. 'Where did you learn that?'

John shrugged, 'Around.'

CHAPTER TWO

All of Chesterfield knew Widow Martha, it seemed. The first man he asked readily gave him the direction to her house, taking time to praise her as a good Christian woman.

'I'm told she takes in lodgers,' John said.

'One or two, maybe.' The man looked him up and down, eyes taking in the plain russet cote, old hose, and dirty boots that had covered too many miles in recent days. 'But she's choosy.'

'Well, happen she'll choose me,' John answered with a broad smile. 'God be with you.'

The house on Knifesmithgate was the only one with its ground-floor shutters closed tight against the day. All along the street, cutlers had their wares on display, windows open to the day, the sound of grinding metal and voices spilling out into the light.

He knocked on the door, licking his fingertips and running them through his hair to try to tame it as he waited.

Widow Martha was a small, stooped woman, not even reaching to his shoulder. Her hair was hidden neatly under a crisp, clean wimple, a green wool dress over her round frame, and she was wearing a dark surcote in spite of the warmth. But it was her eyes that he really noticed, pale blue and calm, as clear and sparkling as any young girl.

'Good day to you, Mistress,' he said politely. 'I am told you take lodgers.'

She gazed at closely him before she replied, 'And who told you that?' Her voice was light, teasing, a touch of music in her words.

'A boy called Walter.'

Her glance moved to his satchel. 'Are you working on the church?' she asked.

'I am, Mistress. Just arrived here and hired.'

'How long do you intend on staying?' A smile played across her lips. 'I know you young men, you're here one week, gone the next.'

'As long as the work lasts,' he told her, 'and it seems like there's plenty there yet.'

'So they say,' she agreed. 'There's still the spire to go on the tower.' She paused. 'What's your name?'

'John, Mistress.'

She nodded. 'And do you keep the gospels, John?'

'Not always,' he admitted wryly, although she had likely guessed it already.

She stepped aside, holding the door wide. 'Come in,' she said, 'you're welcome enough. There's a place for you here, if it suits you. Call me Martha.'

He stepped through an empty workshop, to a small, neatly kept hall with two benches against the walls, and a well-polished table and small joint stool in the middle of a floor covered in fresh rushes and lavender. A rough wooden staircase led up to the solar. The back door stood open, trying to draw in a cool breeze, looking out on the long burgage plot of the garden, heavy with vegetables.

'How do you know Walter?' Martha asked, sitting calmly on the settle.

'I met him near the marketplace,' he told her, nodding his approval at the house. 'Are there really enough traders to fill all that space?'

'You should go down one Saturday and see for yourself,' she told him with a smile. 'Walter must like you. He wouldn't have recommended you here if he didn't think you were trustworthy.'

'He'd barely met me two minutes before,' John protested.

'Don't you underestimate that boy,' she chided gently. 'He might have young shoulders, but there's a wise head on top of them and a good heart inside. He does jobs for me when I need them. He only lives round the corner with his mother and his sisters.'

'What do you charge for lodging, Mistress?'

'It's threepence for a week, tuppence more if you want your food too. I keep the sheets clean and changed regularly. The food's filling, even for a working man.'

'I'll stay,' he said, digging in his purse for five small silver coins.

'It's a good house, if I say so myself,' Martha said, closing a small fist around the money. 'I've been here nigh on thirty years now. My husband was a cutler – God rest his soul – and I couldn't bear to leave after he died.'

• • •

The room was small, tucked away at the back of the house, with an unglazed window looking over the garden and out across the long valley to the north. He sat on the bed, feeling the firm straw and the sheet crisp against his touch. A small chest stood open against the wall; he placed the satchel carefully inside it before using a small cake of lye soap to wash his hands, face and feet in a ewer, enjoying the delicious coolness of the water then drying himself on the scrap of old linen Martha had given him. There was ample daylight left, time enough to go and explore Chesterfield properly. Instead he stretched out, hands behind his head, and let sleep carry him away.

• • •

The morning was a thin, pale band on the horizon when he woke. He pulled on his boots, picked up the tools and tried to move quietly through the house. But Martha was already there by the front door, fully dressed, her face half-lit by the flame of a tallow candle.

'Here,' she said, passing him a small package wrapped in old fabric. 'You had no supper, so there's something for your dinner.'

'Thank you, Mistress,' he answered in surprise. 'That's a kindness.'

'Oh, get on with you,' she told him kindly. 'And I told you to call me Martha. Everyone else does. There's a market today, just tell me if you want me to buy you anything.'

'Bread and cheese, if you would.' He began to open his purse but she just shook her head. 'Pay me tonight.'

As he walked down the street he could hear people moving around behind their doors, the day already beginning. Over in the churchyard small groups of men stood together, some going over to the barrel to fill their mugs with ale.

He looked around in the gloom, finally spotting Will by the church, staring up at the tower.

'Good morning, Master,' he said. 'What do you want me doing today?'

'There's work up there,' Will told him. 'We need to finish reinforcing the ceiling in the top room. Next week we start work on the spire.' John followed his gaze, trying to picture it. Already it seemed tall enough. 'It'll be more than two hundred feet high when we've finished. People will see it for miles around.'

'What's going to hold it in place?' He couldn't even start to imagine what would be needed to keep a structure like that sturdy.

Will grinned broadly. 'That's the beauty of it, lad. It'll be heavy enough that its own weight will keep it there.'

'What?' John looked up again. It seemed impossible. Any strong wind would topple it if it wasn't attached. But if it worked, if it could stay, it would be one of the wonders of the world.

'That's what the engineers tell me, any road.' He scratched at the dark stubble on his chin. 'And they're the ones who are paid to know. So that's why we need the ceiling strong. Good cross-bracing.'

The dawn had lightened enough for John to make out Will's features and see the glimmer of doubt that flickered across his mouth and troubled his eyes. If anything went wrong it would be the master carpenter and his men who would take the blame first. Will drained the mug in his hand.

'Right,' he said, 'off you go. One of the engineers will tell you what to do. Can you read a plan?' John shook his head. 'Then just do exactly what he tells you. There'll be some others up there. I'll come by later and see if you're as good as you think you are.' He gave a wink and strode away.

John entered through the porch and made the sign of the cross. The stairs were close to the screen, and he stopped for a moment to look around. It didn't compare to the great Minster in York, but nothing could; that was a building as large as any castle. This church had a pleasing symmetry in its shape, though, and he ran his hand along one of the decorated pillars, feeling the sharpness of the mason's cut in the stone before climbing the winding staircase.

The room stood open to the sky, tall enough to catch the faint morning breeze. Already there was the scent of heat in the air, and he knew that in another hour he'd be covered in sweat and stripped to his shirt. He put the satchel carefully in a corner and examined the area. Some beams were already in place, a basic structure that was solid when he pushed against it.

He heard footsteps and turned. A man in a cote of expensive wool topped with a dark blue surcote entered, followed by three others. He carried a piece of vellum rolled in his fist, while one man carried a bag, the others were empty handed. They were big men with thick hands and muscled arms.

'You're the new carpenter?' the man asked without any real interest. He was short, with a hawk nose and weary eyes, carrying his air of self-importance like a crown as he unrolled the plan. His fingernails were clean, his hands as smooth as if he had never used them more than was needful.

'I am.'

'Have you done any cross-bracing before?'

'Aye, some,' John said. He'd done most everything in his two years in York, but he listened closely as the man explained everything in his haughty voice, his mind's eye seeing each piece go into its place to ease the weight and spread the stress of the spire.

He set to work with the other carpenter, a thin, dour man named Robert who spoke little, and with hair the colour of iron cropped close against his skull. The labourers did the hardest work, shifting the heavy beams and helping to keep them steady.

By the time the bell sounded for dinner the linen of his shirt was soaked through. The sun burned down hot, not a cloud in the sky, the room trapping the warmth like an oven.

Outside, he found a place in the cool shade of a birch tree and took a long draught of ale and began to eat. He had almost finished when Will came by. John had watched him going around his men, talking to them, asking interested questions. A good master, he decided, one who cared about the job and those under him.

'How are you getting on up there?' he asked.

'Slow but steady. It'll take a few days to have everything secure.'

'There's time yet. Just make sure it's right. What do you think of the engineer?' John turned his head and spat. Will roared with laughter. 'Aye, he's an arrogant streak of piss, but he knows what he's doing. That's more than you can say for some of them.'

John nodded and watched idly as Will passed a moment with a group of men. He stood and stretched before returning to the room at the top of the tower.

They worked hard all day, never as fast as the engineer wanted, but John didn't care about that. If he was going to do a job he had do it properly and at his own speed. He had pride in what he did; no one would ever need to go over it.

He finished as the shadows fell and it became too difficult to see. Carefully, he wiped the tools with the oiled cloth, slung the bag over his shoulder and walked down the stairs, the leather rubbing noisily against the stone as he moved. His arms ached, but that was a good feeling. Along with the others he lined up to be paid, making a mark with a quill before slipping the coins into his purse.

The dying of the day had always been his favourite time, the sounds muted, the night scents appearing on the air, a suspicion of magic in the sky. He leaned against the wall of the churchyard, looking down the slope towards the river that moved sluggishly in the distance and felt the satisfied weariness of labour done well. A man was his work, and the ache in his muscles felt as rich as any full coffer.

It was full dark when he returned to the house on Knifesmithgate, opening the latch quietly in case Martha was already asleep. But a rushlight burned bright and she was seated on the bench, her back straight, eyes bright and alert. She had a needle and thread in her hand and a small pile of sewing at her side.

'Good evening, Mistress,' he said, then corrected himself with a smile as she gazed steadily at him. 'Martha.'

'There's ale on the table for you,' she told him, 'and a coney for dinner tomorrow, if you've a mind.'

'I'd like that. Thank you.' He drank and settled himself on the joint stool. 'I'm surprised you don't have a servant here. I thought all women did.'

She chuckled and shook her head. 'Shows how much you know. Most of the ones I've had couldn't do anything right, I always ended up doing it myself anyway.' She caught his grin.

'Besides, if I had a servant, what would I do all day? You men have your work, but what do I have?'

'You don't have any children close by?'

'There's only one still alive,' Martha said with a gentle sigh, 'and she's up in Sheffield with a brood of her own. Married to a cutler, of course, and he's doing well in his guild. They come twice a year to see me.' She paused, as if she was embarrassed to tell him so much. 'I left the bread and cheese in your room.'

'Thank you.'

• • •

The next morning was Sunday, and John escorted Martha to the church as the bell rang, leaving her to stand at the side along with the widows and crones, where they could exchange gossip behind their hands. He took his place at the back among the workmen, nodding a greeting to the few faces he recognised.

Close to the front he spotted the lad Walter, there between women he assumed were his mother and sisters. The boy smiled to see him and leaned over to whisper to one of the girls. She turned to look, a promise of mischief and flirtation in her eyes and a bold smile on her bonny face.

He hurried away after the service, glad of his own company to wander around Chesterfield on the quiet streets, taking a path down to the marshy area around the river and staring back up to see the church tower standing proud and tall. What would it be like with the spire on top of that, he wondered.

He made sure he was back at the house on Knifesmithgate for his dinner, an edge to his hunger, ready for the tender rabbit that Martha had cooked in a heady pepper sauce with other spices he couldn't name. He ate slowly, relishing each mouthful, spearing the food with his knife and chewing slowly, trying to remember when he had last had a good meal in someone's home. For so much of his life his food had come from cookshops or charity as he walked between towns.

In the afternoon he did some small jobs for the widow, adding a thin shim to a joint in the settle to stop it wobbling, then planing down the bottom of the back door where it stuck on the stone of the step. It took no more than a quarter hour and it was repayment for the woman who had just fed him so well.

• • •

He entered the churchyard in the half light, pausing for a quick drink of ale from the barrel before climbing the stairs to the tower. The stars stood bright, clear in the still sky. He had heard once how some men claimed to understand them and what they meant, but he knew nothing of that and never would.

He started to ease the bag from his shoulder then halted as he breathed in. The room stank of decay. He coughed, tasting the bile as it rose in his throat, then put a hand over his mouth.

In a few moments he could make out enough to see the shape on the floor. It was large enough to be a man – a corpse. He took the steps at a run, gasping for clean air, and rushed out of the church.

'In the tower, quick!' he shouted. 'Someone's dead up there.'

CHAPTER THREE

Men dashed from across the churchyard, pressing into the building and up the stairs to the tower. John stayed outside, leaning against the stone, breathing in the clean air deeply and letting the sweat of fear cool on his skin. He had seen too many bodies before, many of them with the agony of the plague on their faces; he had no wish to see another.

He could hear the hubbub of voices, then the sharp, distinctive sound of someone striking a flint to light a candle.

'Christ's blood, it's Will,' a voice said, the words carrying in the dawn. 'The crows have been at him, too. Go for the coroner.'

John slid down the wall, resting on his haunches and sighing. With the coroner coming and the inquest in the tower there'd be no work done today. And as first finder he would have to give his evidence then pay a fine to make sure he stayed in the district.

It was full morning before the coroner finally appeared, a tall man with thick, pale hair, wearing polished boots, red hose and a blue cote buttoned up tight, a monk for his clerk limping behind him and carrying a small, portable desk.

The man must have selected his jury on the way. Six men trailed along, some looking around curiously, others try to hold back, reluctant to be there but knowing they couldn't refuse.

'Where's the body?' the coroner asked.

'Top o' there,' someone told him, pointing to the tower.

'Who's the first finder?'

John stood slowly.

'I am,' he said.

'You come too, then,' and motioned for the jury to follow him.

The room seemed cramped and airless, the stench more powerful than before. Men were packed together in the space, gagging and retching; two went to the corner and vomited. John stayed back, hating all this but unable to keep his eyes from the body.

It was Will, no doubt about that. Enough remained of his face to be sure of that; the birds and rats had taken the rest and now flies were thick on his skin. He lay crumpled in the middle of the floor, so much smaller in death than he had seemed in life. A lake of blood had bloomed under him, dried now to a thick, dark stain on the wooden boards.

The coroner turned Will over gently with his boot, an expression of distaste on his mouth. Maggots crawled around the deep wound on his back; the shirt soaked a deep red.

'I'll hold the inquest in the nave,' the coroner announced, then turned to the monk. 'Arrange for some of the women to prepare him for burial.'

The jury assembled near the font, the clerk sitting with the desk on his lap, quill ready.

'Who was he?' the coroner asked.

'His name was Will,' John said. 'He was the master carpenter.'

'English?'

'As much as you and me, aye.'

'You found him?'

'I did,' he answered with a brisk nod.

'And who are you?' the man wondered. 'You're not from here.'

'I'm John. Will hired me on Friday. I'm staying with Widow Martha on Knifesmithgate.'

He felt the coroner's pale eyes on him.

'What were you doing in the tower?'

'Getting ready for work. We're putting cross-bracing in there for the spire.'

'Who told you to go up there?'

'No one.' John took a breath. 'I'd been working up there on Saturday and there was still plenty to do.'

'What did you do when you found him?'

'I came down to raise the alarm.' The memory came back to his throat and he swallowed. 'I could smell him, but it was too dark to see who it was.'

'When did you see this Will last?'

'Saturday evening, when he paid the men. All the men,' he added.

The coroner turned to the clerk.

'Fine him a shilling as first finder.'

Head bent, the monk nodded.

'What do you think, jury?' the coroner asked.

'Someone killed him,' a man at the front said. 'Knifed him in the back. It's obvious to anyone.' He turned to glance at John. 'Could have been him for all we know.'

'Anyone else?'

'He's been there a while,' an older man added thoughtfully. 'A man don't end up like that in an hour, stinking and pecked to buggery.'

The coroner nodded.

'I pronounce Will unlawfully murdered.' He looked around the men. 'I charge the jury with finding his killer.' Finally he turned to the clerk again. 'Take their names before you let them go.' Then he strode off, gesturing to John to follow him.

They stood in the porch, looking out at the groups of men gathered in the yard.

'How well did you know him?'

'Not at all,' John answered.

'Do you know of anyone who'd want to kill him?' the coroner persisted.

He thought back to Friday and the fight Will had broken up.

'I saw him dismiss a man just after he had hired me.'

'What happened?' The coroner stared at him curiously, his pale eyes intent.

'A couple of the workers were fighting. One of them cut another.' He shrugged. 'From what I heard, the man with the knife had been a troublemaker and Will sent him on his way without his wages.'

'Was it reported?'

'I don't know,' John told him, seeing the doubt on the other man's face.

'Do you know the man's name?'

John shook his head. 'Stephen, I think. He was the one who was hurt.'

'Where is he?'

John inclined his head. 'He'll probably be out there somewhere. Look for someone with a bandage on his arm. He can tell you more.'

'You're not a helpful man,' the coroner said, his voice bemused. 'Didn't you like Will?'

John was slow to reply. 'He seemed liked a good master, he looked like he cared about the people working for him. But like I said, I didn't know him.'

'Go and pay your fine. You're a stranger here; that makes you a suspect in the death.'

He had known those words would come. No one knew him here; there wasn't a soul to speak for his good character.

'Most of the people working on the church aren't local,' he countered.

'They didn't find him,' the coroner said firmly. 'You did.' He turned and strode away, out of the churchyard.

John sighed. He leaned against the wall, waiting until the jurors had filed out, their faces set, two of them glancing angrily at him as if they blamed him for their task. Then he returned to the nave, the flagstones solid under the sole of his boots, to the clerk slowly packing away his vellum and ink.

'My fine,' he said, counting out coins from his purse and passing them over. He hated to lose the money, but knew he had no choice. He was better off than many; he had worked steadily for a long time and spent little of his wages. Most of his small wealth he had painstakingly sewn away in his cote, safe from the eyes of thieves and cutpurses.

The monk took the money with a nod, sliding it into the scrip that hung from his belt. He had a long face with all the lines of age but a lively mouth that twitched into a smile.

'Don't worry,' he said, 'he doesn't think you did it.'

John raised his eyebrows. 'How do you know?'

'If he'd had any doubts about you he'd have arrested you straight away. I've seen him do it before.' The man stood, smoothing down the black habit that had been patched and mended many times. A shaft of sunlight through the window of the church shone on his tonsure.

'How long have you clerked for him?'

'Five years come Michaelmas. He's a good man, is Richard de Harville.' He picked up the small desk wearily and put it under his arm. 'He's thorough in his duties.'

'You need a strap on that,' John told him. 'That way you could carry it on your shoulder. Find some leather and I'll put one on for you.'

'That would be a kindness,' the monk said, inclining his head. 'I'll do that.'

'How does a Benedictine come to work as a clerk?'

'There's a tale in that, right enough,' the man said with a grin. 'I taught Richard his letters when he was little, before he inherited the manors from his father. When the king appointed him coroner around here, he asked the abbot for my services. So I was called to God but I end up serving man once more,' he finished with a sigh.

'And do you like living back in the world?'

'Not so much, to tell you the truth.' He walked towards the porch with the slow gait of an old man who had traipsed too many miles. 'The monastic life chose me, I was happy in it. I've asked to go back, but the Master says he needs me.' At the porch he straightened a little. 'God go with you, John Carpenter,' he said.

• • •

The men clamoured around, eager for the gossip and the verdict. John told them briefly, his eyes moving around, searching for someone. Finally he saw Stephen, standing by the barrel of ale, a dirty bandage wrapped around his forearm.

Soon enough the questions faded, men wandering off to spread the word of Will's murder. John strolled across and poured himself a drink.

'How's the arm?' he asked.

'Well enough,' Stephen answered with a small shrug. He was tall, with a thick growth of beard on his sallow face and his hood pulled back to show long, stringy hair. 'I can still work, if there's anything for us today.'

'There won't be,' John told him. 'Not with Will dead.'

'You're the one who found him?'

'Aye.' He took another drink, trying to wash the taste of death from his mouth.

'How did he die?'

'Knifed, by the look of it.' He let the words sink in for a moment. 'That one who attacked you, who was he?'

'Mark?' Stephen shook his head. 'He was just one of the labourers. Turned up drunk most days, when he showed up at all. Always with a temper on him too, just itching to pick a fight.'

John knew the type all too well; there were one or two like that on every site, never happy, never satisfied, their anger lying too close to the surface.

'What happened on Friday?' he asked.

'He tried to push in front of me for the ale. I wasn't having that. He pulled out the knife and cut me.' His voice turned boastful. 'Another minute or two and I'd have put that blade up his arse.'

'This Mark, is he local?'

Stephen shrugged. 'I never asked.'

John put down his empty mug. 'God be with you. Maybe we'll all be able to earn some money soon.'

He was scarcely ten yards down Knifesmithgate before Walter was at his side, all gawky limbs and questions.

'Did you really find him?' he asked, walking quickly to keep pace.

'Word travels fast here,' John replied, smiling inwardly at the boy's eagerness. 'But I did.'

'What was he like?'

He stopped, put a hand gently on Walter's shoulder. 'He was dead, lad. That's all you need to know. It's not a sight anyone wants to recall, believe me.'

The boy's face fell for a moment, but then brightened again. 'Do they know who did it?'

'Not yet.' He smiled sadly. 'The coroner thought it might be me. I found him, and I'm a stranger.'

'You?' Walter looked shocked. 'You'd never hurt anyone like that.'

'No,' he agreed. 'But don't be so trusting. You don't know me.'

'But I can tell,' the boy protested.

'Then I thank you for that,' John said graciously, and asked, 'Do you know of someone called Mark? He was dismissed from the job on Friday.'

'I don't go near him,' Walter replied cautiously, and he could see fear in the lad's eyes. 'Keep away from him, John.'

'Where does he live?'

'Over by West Bar, the far side of the marketplace. Why?'

'It's nothing,' he said. 'I just wondered.'

'Be careful if you see him. Please, John.' The boy's voice was serious and pleading, his gaze steady and worried. 'He's a bad man.'

'I'll do that,' John assured him, wondering what Mark had done to the boy.

Walter started to lope away, then turned his head as he ran. 'My sister says you look handsome,' he called back with a grin. 'She thinks you look like a rogue.'

He was still smiling when he entered the house, expecting to find Martha there. Instead the place was empty, only the ghosts of family life there in the marks on the walls and the scuffs on the furniture.

He settled in his room, removing his hose to darn a rip in the knee with the needle and thread he kept packed deep in his satchel. He'd barely finished and dressed again when he heard the door open and emerged to see the widow with a large, heavy bag.

'Let me take that,' he offered, removing the weight from her arms.

'Bless you,' she said, settling herself on the bench. 'Just leave it on the table, I'll put everything away later.' She flexed her fingers. 'Thirty years ago I'd have thought nothing of carrying that.' She paused and reflected. 'Even twenty.' Martha raised her eyebrows at him. 'So everything they're saying is true, then?'

'Everything?' John asked. He went into the small buttery, returning with two mugs of ale.

'Thank you,' she said gratefully, and drank. 'They say that someone's been murdered at the church.'

'Aye, that's true enough. The master carpenter.'

She eyed him carefully, running her hand over the rim of the cup.

'Folk are saying you were the one who found him.'

'They're right,' he admitted, 'and the coroner made me pay a fine for the privilege.'

'All the goodwives at the baker's are wondering if I have a murderer in my house.'

He leaned against the table.'Do you think you have, Martha?'

She smiled and shook her head.'If I believed you were capable of that you'd never have had a bed here,' she told him.'I'm sure you've done things you'd rather not talk about, but murder's not one of them.'

He laughed loud and for a moment the tension of the day left him.'That's one way of saying it. Even the coroner doesn't think me guilty, according to his clerk.'

'Brother Robert told you that?'

'A Benedictine with a desk under his arm and a face as long as death? If that's his name, then yes.'

'He's the one. He was just Robert when we were young. We used to dash up and down the street there with no more sense than a pair of buttons. His parents lived over on Saltergate. Then he had his calling,' she cocked her head,'and now we're both old and he's back where he began,' she sighed.'It's strange how the wheel turns, John Carpenter. Whenever I look at him I still see the boy who had to keep pulling his hose up as he ran.'

'He seems like a pleasant man.'

'He is, he is,' she agreed.'And if anyone knows Richard de Harville's mind, it's him.'

'What do you know about a man called Mark? He lives over by West Bar.'

'What would you want with someone like him?' she asked with the same wariness he had heard in Walter's voice.

'The master carpenter broke up a fight between him and another man on Friday and dismissed him.'

'Leave him for the jury, then,' Martha advised seriously, looking up at him.'They'll know who he is right enough, and no one would put murder past him. The good Lord knows he's spent enough days in the stocks for his fighting.'

'Walter warned me to keep away from him.'

'And well he might,' she said sadly. 'A year or two back, Walter said something. It was nothing at all, just a little joke or whatever. But Mark overheard, took it the wrong way and beat the poor lad bloody before anyone could haul him away.' She lowered her eyes and took a small drink. 'The boy's never been quite the same since.' The silence hung deep in the air. 'Stay away from him, John,' Martha told him quietly, 'for your own sake.'

He grinned, trying to cheer her with his charm. 'I'm not after a fight with anyone, you don't have to worry.'

'Don't I?' she asked wryly. 'I've been in this world long enough to know what a man's thinking, even if he believes he's not showing it.'

'You're a wise woman, Martha.'

'I'm an old woman,' she corrected him with a gentle pout. 'That doesn't mean the same thing. But I've known enough men in my life.'

'You've had sons?' he asked.

'Three of them.' She gave a long, sorrowful sigh. 'One of them was a John, too. He'd have been about ten years older than you if the great death hadn't taken him. It took two of them, God rest them both. The other one drowned in the river when he was small. Then one of my girls died when she was giving birth, so there's only Agnes left now.' She paused. 'It's hard to know you've outlived your children.'

He said nothing; he didn't have any words to comfort the woman. His memory slipped to his father, a strong, kind man who did his best to look after a lonely boy, then further back to the woman who had died when he was three. Her face was no more than a blur in his mind, but sometimes, on those long, empty nights when sleep was an enemy, he could hear her voice in his head. It was just her tone, never the words, as if the wind had whipped away meaning, but still it brought comfort.

John put the mug on the table. 'I think I'll take a walk. Explore the town a little. There's nothing else for me to do today.'

Martha stared at him shrewdly. 'And the walk will take you to West Bar?'

'Only if my feet take me there.'

'Be careful, John. That's all I can say.'

He nodded and took his leave. At the door he loosened the knife in his sheath. It was better to be prepared.

The streets were livelier than he had expected, with folk bustling hither and yonder, faces determined as they went about their Monday errands. Servant girls dawdled to gossip and stare at apprentice lads who worked under their Masters' eye, still finding time for a wink or a yelled comment that caused outraged, flattered laughter.

This was a town where a man could feel comfortable, he decided. Small enough to know all the folk around but still large enough for there to be work. And if he stayed until the spire was complete, he'd be here a while yet.

In the broad square of the market place he tried to imagine the space filled with the noise and cries of vendors, and all the items they had to offer. One Saturday he'd find the time to come down here and take it all in, maybe even buy a small gift for Martha.

She had known where he was going just as certainly as he had, he thought, as he headed to West Bar. He wasn't even sure why he was doing this; it was none of his concern, it was the business of the jury to find Will's killer.

It was the work of a moment to ask the direction to Mark's house, a small, tumbledown building out beyond the town, on the road to Bakewell and the green country beyond.

The thatch on the roof was old, heavy with mould and rotting in places. A shutter hung loose on the window, leaning like a drunkard away from the opening. He stood and stared, hearing no sounds from within, wondering if the man was even there and what he might say to him.

'John Carpenter.'

He turned at the sound of his name to see Richard de Harville coming towards him, striding out with serious purpose, and Brother Robert struggling to try and keep pace, balancing the small desk awkwardly under his arm, a grimace of pain on his face.

'God be with you, sir,' John said.

'And with you,' de Harville said without thought. 'What brings you out here?'

'I'm not sure,' he admitted. 'To see what this man Mark says.'

'Why would that interest you?' he asked with a dark look.

'I don't know,' John answered truthfully, then gave a small laugh. 'Maybe because I'm under suspicion. Maybe I'm too curious for my own good.'

In the full light de Harville looked older than he had in the church. There were lines etched in the pale skin around his mouth and eyes, his shoulders slumped slightly, as if he carried too many cares in his head.

'When I questioned you, you should have told me that Mark was the man dismissed for fighting,' the coroner reprimanded him.

'I didn't know his name then. But it seems as if you had no trouble discovering it.'

'Not too difficult to find,' the man admitted. 'He's someone the town wouldn't miss if he died. Most of them would probably come out to watch him hang.'

'I've heard a thing or two.'

'I'd wager they're all true, too.' He noticed that de Harville kept a hand loosely on the hilt of his dagger, watching alertly. 'He had reason to kill Will, then?'

'Possibly,' John said. 'I was the one who disarmed him. He probably has just as much reason to wish me harm.'

'How did you do that?' The coroner eyed him with deepening curiosity. 'There aren't many here who'd try that with Mark.'

'I didn't know who he was. It was just a little pressure on his wrist. There's no magic in it.'

'Maybe you'll be a good man to have by me while I question him.'

'If you like,' John agreed.

'Stay close and use your knife if you need,' de Harville instructed. He turned to Robert. 'Are you ready, Brother?'

'As much as I'll ever be, Master,' the monk replied in a low, weary voice.

'Dame Martha sends her regards,' John told him mischievously and watched a small, astonished look come into Robert's eye before he said,

'And return mine to her, if you please.'

De Harville knocked hard on the wood then moved back a pace. Moments passed before the door was flung open.

Mark wore old hose with holes on the thighs and calves and a dirty, threadbare tunic that was too short for him. There was the madness of drink on his face, and John felt the same heat and intensity he'd experienced close to the man on Friday, the anger that was ready to flare in a heartbeat.

'You,' he said to de Harville.

'I want to talk to you about the murder of the master carpenter.'

'Dead, is he?' Mark leaned against the jamb. 'Good riddance to a bad soul.'

'We can talk in the street or in your house. It's your choice,' de Harville said coldly.

'Out here is fine,' Mark told him. 'Let the gossips have their fill.' He hawked and spat, the phlegm landing close to the coroner's boots. 'They're all tosspots, anyway.'

'Where were you Saturday night and Sunday?'

Mark chuckled. 'Ask in the alehouses. I daresay they'll tell you. Or I was maybe here, sleeping. Does that tell you what you want?'

'Do you want me to arrest you for murder?' de Harville asked.

'You'll do whatever you wish, Master,' the man replied with a mocking, exaggerated bow. John watched him carefully. His breath was full of stale ale, but there was a wire edge of danger to him.

The coroner glanced at John and raised his eyebrows in a question. He gave a minute shake of his head in return. Mark was too cocksure, playing with them.

'Let me see your knife,' John said, and the man looked at the coroner in surprise.

'You let your dog ask questions now?'

'Do as he says,' de Harville ordered.

Very slowly Mark removed the knife from his belt. John kept his eyes on the man's hand. He presented it blade first, daring John to take hold. Then, in a quick, flowing motion, he gave the dagger a small flick, letting it turn swiftly in the air before taking it between his thumb and first finger close to the tip.

John took hold of the handle, pulling the knife free of Mark's hand. He examined the metal. It was rusted and uncared-for, although the edge was sharp when he ran it against his thumb. But there was no blood to see, and it was thinner than the cut he'd seen on Will's back.

He returned the knife, carefully watching Mark's face.

'Anything?' the coroner asked.

'No blood that I can make out, and it doesn't look as if he's cleaned it in a long time,' John told him.

'I'll still be checking.'

Mark turned and stared at de Harville. 'Aye, you do that. Folk know me around here.'

'And hate you. We might be back if there's cause.'

The man nodded. As they walked away John glanced back and saw Mark examine the weapon, a look of black fury on his face.

De Harville led them to an alehouse on Low Pavement, the branch over its door showing its trade. It was nothing more than a small room, but clean and tidy, fresh rushes and thyme on the floor bringing a sweetness to the air.

The men settled around a bench, Brother Robert off to the side, lowering his old bones carefully. The alewife bustled over, wiping her hands on a leather apron and opening a mouth empty of teeth to ask their pleasure.

Once she'd brought the ale, the coroner drank slowly then asked, 'Why don't you think it was him?'

'He knew full well where he'd been,' John answered slowly, building the ideas in his mind. 'And he knows you can discover the truth easily enough. If h'd been guilty he would have been more wary.'

'You don't know him.'

'No,' he admitted. 'But I've seen enough like him. And there's something else.'

'What's that?'

'I barely saw Will's wound but it looked wider that Mark's blade.'

De Harville nodded. 'Aye, you might be right there.' He turned to the monk. 'What did you think?'

'Mark's one whose blood is always hot,' Robert said after deep thought. 'He could commit murder, right enough, but he'd never have the wit to plan it.'

The coroner nodded. 'That's worth considering.' He supped more, looking thoughtful. 'And you, you're a strange one, John the carpenter.'

'Me?' John asked, bemused. 'I'm just a man who works with wood, nothing more than that.'

'And one who notices things, who can think, and understands men.'

He shook his head. 'That's nothing more than life, Master.'

'Maybe,' de Harville allowed. 'But you're a rare one, nonetheless. I'll remind you to stay around Chesterfield until we find the killer.'

'I'll be working again tomorrow, God willing,' John told him. 'Is the body gone?'

'Aye, but you can still see the blood on the floor.'

'We'll scrape that clean first thing. When's the burial?'

'This afternoon at the church.'

'I'll be there,' he promised.

• • •

Martha rose as he entered the room, her face blossoming into a smile. A small lock of white hair peeked out from her wimple.

'You went, didn't you?' The words rushed from her mouth. 'I prayed God would turn you away from there.'

'I went,' he admitted. 'But I had the company of the coroner and Brother Robert. He sends you his greetings.'

'Does he now?' She glanced at him curiously then chuckled lightly. 'You're trying to distract me. Did you talk to Mark?'

'We did, and there was no violence,' he assured her.

'Did the coroner arrest him?'

'He didn't kill Will.'

'Then who did?' she asked. It was the question he'd been pondering as he strolled back to the house, and it was likely he would never be the one to find the answer. He knew nothing of Will, whether he had any enemies in the town, not even where he lived.

'I don't know. I'll leave that to the coroner and the jury.'

She nodded gratefully.

'There's dinner left if you want some.'

He realised he had eaten nothing that morning and felt the hollowness in his belly.

'I'd like that. Thank you.'

She bought two trenchers in from the cookhouse at the other end of the burgage plot, where a fire could heat food without danger to the home. It was the remains of the coney, with strong ginger added. He poured ale for them both and moved the bench to the table.

'Where did you come here from, John Carpenter?' Martha asked as they ate.

'York,' he told her, spearing a small piece of the meat with his knife.

'York!' she said in surprise. 'I've heard so many tales of that place. Is it really as big as they say?'

'As big as a county, and more churches than the eye can count. There's everything a person could want in the city.'

'I'd have loved to have seen it and prayed in the Minster,' she sighed.

'It's a glorious place,' he said, his voice soft as he saw it in his mind. 'The light through the windows is so beautiful with all the colours in the glass. From the top of the towers you feel like you can reach out and touch the stars.' He stopped, seeing the wonder on her face. 'It's not too late for you to visit.'

She tapped the back of his hand lightly. 'Be off with you. God might have spared me this long, but He doesn't want me to go traipsing halfway across the country at my age. How long were you there?'

'Two years.'

'Did you worship at the Minster?'

'I worked on it,' he said, watching as her eyes widened. 'But I worshipped at St Saviour's.'

'If you loved the placed so much, why did you leave it?' She cast a shrewd glance at him. 'A girl?'

He felt himself redden but said nothing. Some secrets were best kept close.

'I have to go to the church,' he announced after finishing the meal. 'They're burying Will this afternoon. Someone should be there.'

'Would you like me to come with you?'

'No,' he said, gratitude in his smile. 'I knew him a little, I'll go on my own.'

• • •

The grave had been dug, the dark earth mounded on either side of the hole. A pair of shirtless diggers leaned on their spades in the shade of an oak, passing a flagon of ale between them.

Someone had assembled a coffin, the boards planed smooth, the lid nailed down cleanly. John stood by it and made the sign of the cross. Precious few people had come, just three of the workmen, the engineer, and a woman who stood alone, off to the side, her head bowed; the widow, he guessed. She wore a dark gown, shapeless in the old style, and gathered at the waist with a girdle, a deep blue veil covering her hair.

The sun beat down hard on the churchyard as the priest intoned the service in his rough Latin, the words consumed by the heat in the air. Then he nodded to the diggers, who lowered the coffin into the grave.

John tossed a sod down onto the wood, crossed himself once more and found a place in the shadow of the church wall. The woman was the last in the line, letting the earth slip down through her fingers, lingering to gaze down. Finally she slipped away through the weekday market place and along the road to Holywell.

He walked behind her, coming up close before he said,

'Mistress?' She turned in alarm, pulled from her thoughts and her grief. He could see the tracks tears had made on her face and the redness that clouded her eyes. 'I wanted to offer my sorrow.'

She tried to smile, but it was weak and wan, her heart lost from the effort.

'Did you work with him?' she asked.

'Only for a day, but I liked him. He was your man?'

'For ten years,' she told him, her voice aching with sadness. 'We moved down here when they hired him on at the church.'

'The men seemed to respect him,' he offered.

'Aye,' she sighed. 'Folk liked Will. What's your name, Master?'

'John,' he replied. 'John the carpenter.'

She nodded. 'He mentioned you on Friday. You're the one with a talent with wood.'

'That was just kindness on his part,' he told her. 'Did he come home after work on Saturday?'

A small brightness of memory lit her plump face. 'Back for his supper, same as ever. Then he was out in the town for a drink, and that was the last I saw of him.' The light in her eyes faded and the tears began again. She rubbed at them with her hand.

'Might I escort you?'

'God bless you and thank you, but I'd rather be alone.'

'Of course.' Before he turned to leave, he asked, 'Do you know anyone who might have harmed him?'

'No,' she answered simply, 'and I've thought hard enough these last hours.'

'If there's anything I can do at all, any task, send word to me at the church,' he said.

'I'll do that. Good day to you now, John. God be with you.'

'And with you, Mistress.'

He watched her slow, hopeless walk away from the town until the road turned and she was hidden from sight. Deep in thought, he took his time returning, pausing by the churchyard. The grave had already been filled in and all that remained of Will was a small hump of earth rising from the grass. Over by the wall the engineer was in deep conversation with another man dressed in the finery of a lordling or a merchant, worn with the casual grace of money and power. The engineer bowed low before the other man left, his face dark and thoughtful.

• • •

Down by Beetwell Street John saw a girl pausing for breath, a basket of washing heavy in her arms, water dripping down her old grey gown.

'Might I help you Mistress?' he asked impulsively. As she raised her head to answer, he saw it was Walter's sister, the girl with the lively glance who'd noticed him in church and called him a rogue, if her brother was to be believed.

She lowered her eyes modestly as he spoke, but moved her head quickly from side to side to shake her dark hair loose.

'Bless you for your thoughts, sir, but I'm just carrying this back from the river.'

'Let me take it for you.' Gently, he lifted it from her hands and was rewarded with a broad smile. He fell in beside her, matching her easy pace with his long legs.

'You know my brother, Walter.'

'I do,' he told her. 'I like the lad.'

'He says you're a good man.'

John grinned mischievously. 'And he told me that you think me handsome, so perhaps neither of us should believe all we hear.'

She blushed, the colour rising quickly from her neck, and she turned away so he couldn't see her expression.

'I'm sorry,' he said. 'I shouldn't tease you.'

'And I should learn to hold my tongue around him, or all of Chesterfield will know what I'm thinking.'

'I'll keep your secret.'

'I'll box his ears when I see him.' But she was smiling again, the start of a giggle on her lips.

'One thing he didn't tell me was your name.'

'I'm Katherine,' she answered, her voice suddenly shy again, as if her mood changed moment by moment with the wind. 'And you're John.'

'I am. John the carpenter.'

'Is it true what all the goodwives have been saying, that a man was murdered at the church?'

'It is, and now he's in his grave.'

'Do they know who killed him?' It was no question for a girl, perhaps, but still a natural one to ask.

'I don't think so.'

At the corner of Saltergate he stopped and held out the basket.

'It wouldn't be seemly for me to walk you to your door, Mistress Katherine. People would talk.'

She tossed her hair again, her eyes sharp and bright with delight. 'The gossips will have seen us by now, Master John, have no fear of that. They'll already be wagging their tongues and planning the betrothal.' She offered a small, formal curtsey. 'Thank you for your help, sir.'

He bowed.

'God go with you, Mistress.'

He strode back to Knifesmithgate feeling lighter inside; the girl had given some brightness to a dark day.

CHAPTER FOUR

The morning came too quickly. He slept deeply, waking with a start before rushing to dress and cram bread and cheese into his satchel. By the time he reached the churchyard most of the men were already there, gathered in small, expectant groups.

Orders came with the dawn. With the other carpenters, he moved to a corner of the yard where an older man was waiting. He looked as if his best years were past, the sleek hardness gone from the long muscles in his arms and his belly bulging under his plain brown cote.

'You all know what happened to your master,' he said, his voice loud and carrying easily in the still dawn air. 'He was a good man, and God will punish the one who killed him. Say your prayers for him. But I'm Joseph, and I'm the new master carpenter. I'll expect you to work hard and earn your pay, and above all I'll want you to do as I tell you.' He glanced around the faces, looking for questions. 'You remember what you were doing on Saturday, go back to that. You all lost a day's pay yesterday so make up for that today.' With a brisk clap of his hands, he dismissed them.

John had feared the stench of the tower room, but the stink of death had gone, only the bloodstain on the floor a reminder of what had happened. By the time the engineer arrived, his footsteps slow and tired on the stone stair, much of the blood had been scraped away, the last vestige of a life vanished into sawdust.

John and the other carpenter worked hard all morning, hearing the sound of the Tuesday market in the space beyond the yard. Beyond the engineer's instructions there was little conversation. It was difficult labour, demanding fierce concentration and when the dinner bell rang he was glad of the break outside.

There was a small whisper of a breeze to cool his face as he sat under the tree and ate. A few of the men came by to ask about Will's body, but for most it was already old news and he was grateful; he had no desire to keep seeing the body in his mind.

He took a long drink of ale, stood and stretched slowly.

'You're John?'

He turned to face Joseph, the man staring at him with an unreadable face, thin lips pursed, no expression in his brown eyes.

'Yes, Master,' he replied.

'I've just been up looking at your work. It's good.'

'Thank you.' He nodded briefly.

'But you need to go faster. We lost a day yesterday and we need to make it up.'

'We're going as fast as we can,' John protested. 'That cross-bracing needs to be exact and secure.'

'Aye,' the master carpenter agreed. 'I know that. You can do that and still work more quickly.'

'I'll try,' John said meekly. It was easier to give in, to mouth the words and then go back to what he had always done. The job went as fast as it went. Rushing only meant mistakes and there could be none of that here, not when the weight of the spire would rest on this bracing.

'You do that,' the man ordered. 'You were first finder, they told me.'

'I was, and the coroner fined me for the honour,' John answered wryly.

Joseph shook his head sadly. 'They'll always have their money from us every way they can. They don't suspect you?'

'No,' he said. 'I'm still here, not in gaol.'

The master carpenter looked at him coldly. 'Let's hope it stays that way, then. I'll not have any murderer working for me. You understand?'

'Yes, Master.'

'Right, get yourself back to work. The sooner you finish, the sooner we can start on the spire.'

He worked at the same, even pace as the day progressed. Everything needed to be exact, each measurement and angle precise, the ends of each beam carefully shaved to fit perfectly flush.

By the shank of the afternoon the heat in the room was wearing. He had taken off his shirt, but still the sweat ran freely, and he tied a rag around his head to keep it from his eyes. Even the engineer had removed his cote as he examined and checked each piece before giving his approval.

Finally the sun began to set. He wiped his tools with the oiled rag, running his eye over them for any damage or rust before putting them away. He took the stairs slowly, happy to have his freedom for a few hours. He loved his work, but a man needed his rest too. His muscles ached and his throat was dry from all the sawdust in the room.

He poured a mug from the barrel, downing it quickly, then another not quite as fast, as the evening air slowly cooled his skin. The darkness was rising in the east, the stars visible if he raised his head and looked.

Finally he pulled the shirt over his head, hung the satchel from his shoulder and took the path out of the churchyard. Most of the men had already left, just a few small groups scattered around, talking and laughing, off to the alehouse soon enough to drink away their pay, he thought.

The shadows were long in Knifesmithgate, just a few splinters of candlelight showing through chinks in the wooden shutters. Soon enough all would be dark and sensible folk asleep in their beds. He kept his hand close to his knife; there were always dangers in the night and it was better to be ready. But there were no quick footsteps behind him. No face appeared from nowhere to threaten him. He lifted the latch on the house and entered, a slow weariness coming on as he closed the door behind him.

He could hear Martha moving around slowly up in the solar as he took bread, cheese and ale from the buttery and settled in his room. He threw the shutter wide to draw in some air and looked out to the distance.

Who could have killed Will, he wondered. His widow said he had no enemies, but how much might she have known about his life? More than that, why had his life ended in the tower room? That was the strangest thing of all. If there'd been a fight after an argument when he was out drinking he would have died in an alehouse or out on the street where folk would have seen it happen.

There was no reason he could imagine for Will to be wandering round the church in the night, nothing he could have seen up there in the darkness. He tried to think it through, to find the answers to his questions, but it was impossible. It left his mind abuzz and frustrated. He didn't know enough to understand anything.

He finished the last of the ale, considered another mug, then set down the cup, stripped to his braies and went to sleep.

• • •

He could smell the faint promise of rain as he rose. The farmers needed it. Coming down from York he'd seen the fear on their faces of a season dry as bone before the harvest. In the tower they'd need to keep an eye on the weather and a canvas close at hand.

The work seemed to flow from his fingers. Every touch, every cut was sure and right. It was one of those perfect mornings that came so rarely. He always trusted his instinct with wood, but today the timber answered him faithfully. By dinner he felt happy, a satisfied smile on his face as he sat and ate.

He'd cut a piece from a loaf and a slice of cheese when Stephen sat on the ground beside him. The bandage had gone from his arm, leaving a livid red scab that was healing slowly.

'What do you think of the new master?' he asked, taking a bite from a cold pie.

John shrugged. 'Hard to tell yet. He'll want to push us for a while so we know who's in charge. And I suppose he has his masters to please too.' He'd given no more thought to the man after they'd spoken the day before.

'He's been on me three times already,' Stephen complained. He counted them out on his fingers. 'Found fault with a joint, then he said a cut wasn't square, and complained about splinters on a surface I'd planed.' He shook his head. 'I've half a mind to leave.'

John turned to look at him.

'What would you do? There's precious little else around here from what I can see.'

'Move on.' The man brightened, smiling to show brown, broken teeth. 'There are plenty of other towns. It might be good to see somewhere new, I've been here since before last winter.'

'Give him time,' John advised, 'he'll calm down in a few days.'

'Maybe,' Stephen returned to his dinner.

'Did you know Will?'

'Not well,' Stephen answered as he chewed. 'He was off home to his woman once work was done. I drank with him a few times in town on a Saturday night.'

'What was he like?' John asked.

'Pleasant enough.' He reached dirty fingers into his mouth to pick out a lump of gristle. 'Better company the more he supped.'

'Did he ever get into any fights?'

'Not that I saw.'

'Was he a good master?'

'He was as good as any I've worked under, I suppose,' Stephen replied after some consideration. 'Once he saw you knew what you were doing he'd leave you to get on with it. He would check on you, of course, but if you had his trust he'd let you be.'

'No enemies?'

The man hawked and spat.

'You know what it's like. There are always people who don't get along in a place like this. You saw what happened to me.' He held out his arm to display the wound. 'Nothing serious enough for murder, though, if that's what you're thinking.' He paused. 'Mind you, there was a man in the spring who swore he'd come back and kill Will when he was dismissed. But it was just words.'

'What was his name?'

Stephen thought then shook his head. 'I can't even remember now. You'd best ask Thomas over there.' He pointed, and John followed the finger with his eyes. 'The tall, bald one. He's been here longer than me and has a mind for things like that.'

He marked the face, a quiet man he'd noticed before who kept himself to himself; and when the day was done he'd seek him out.

The afternoon passed as swiftly as the morning. A few clouds rolled in to take the sting from the heat, but the rain he'd sensed at dawn never arrived. Finally he put the tools in his satchel and walked into the yard.

Thomas was alone under the oak, sipping slowly at his ale. John poured himself a mug and joined him.

'A good day?' he asked.

The man turned his head slightly. 'Good as any,' he said slowly, 'bad as most.'

'They tell me you knew Will.'

'Not really.' He was thrifty with his speech. A worn bag of tools lay between his feet, and there were scars on the back of his large hands.

'I heard he dismissed someone in the spring who threatened to come back and kill him.'

Thomas gave a short laugh. 'Anyone can be brave with words.'

'What was his name?'

'Geoffrey,' the man answered without hesitation. For a moment it seemed as if he might say more, then he closed his mouth again.

'Is he still in Chesterfield?'

'Not that I've seen.' With a curt nod he picked up the bag and walked off.

John finished the ale and began to make his way home. The evening was quiet and thoughts filled his head, but he remained alert, catching the quiet footfalls that followed him and easing the knife blade from its tight sheath.

He waited until he could hear the man breathing, then stepped aside and turned quickly, drawing the weapon and holding it in front of him.

'I wondered how long it would take you.'

CHAPTER FIVE

John held the knife loosely, jabbing forward a few inches to make the other man move back. The man held a thick cudgel, his eyes flickering between the blade and John's face, the hood drawn up over his hair.

'If you want to hurt me you'll have to do better than that, Mark. Or is it your way to attack from behind?' He took a single step forward, watching carefully, keeping his voice low and calm. He was close enough to smell the sour ale on Mark's skin and see that the drink that had given him courage had been replaced by fear now he was facing a weapon.

Mark tried to feint to his left, but John saw it coming, swinging the dagger in a small arc to cover it.

'Go home,' John told him. 'Sleep it off, pretend you just dreamed this.' He advanced another pace. Mark fixed him with a look of terror and fury mingled, then hared off down the street, stumbling at first before gathering speed, his footsteps echoing off the buildings.

He'd known the man would come, understood that he'd want revenge for the humiliation John had inflicted on him after the fight with Stephen. But that was done now, and Mark wouldn't return. No one else had seen, none had heard. What had happened had been purely between the two of them. He sheathed the knife, surprised to find he was breathing hard and his hands shaking a little.

'You made him run away.'

He turned quickly, his hand slipping back to the blade, then stopping as Walter crept out from the shadows. 'How did you do that?' the boy asked in awe.

'He hurt you, didn't he?' John asked and the lad nodded slowly.

'But I don't know why he did it,' Walter told him.

'People like Mark have madness in them,' John explained quietly. 'It drives them. But they'll only fight if it's against someone weaker or they can surprise them and win.'

'He didn't surprise you.'

'No,' John admitted. 'I went with the coroner to see him about the murder. We had some words. After that and the churchyard I expected he'd come for me sometime.'

'You weren't afraid.'

John shrugged. 'He's only a man. He preys on fear.'

'I'm scared of him,' Walter admitted in a small voice.

'I know,' John said. 'I know.'

'I thought you were going to stab him. I wanted you to.'

'There wasn't any need for that. He was scared. That's why he ran away.'

'But …' He saw the boy's jaw working, his fists curled in frustration at words he didn't possess. 'Will you be my friend and teach me to do that?'

He smiled. 'I'm already your friend, Walter.'

'But will you show me, John? So I'm not afraid.'

'I don't know if anyone can teach that,' he answered.

'Then teach me to be like you, John,' Walter said.

He gave a small, sad laugh. 'I'm not sure you want to be like me.'

'I do,' the lad insisted.

'Then if I can, I will,' he promised. 'Why are you out in the night, anyway?'

'I like walking in the dark. It's quiet then. When there's no noise I can think properly.'

'Aye, it's a good time for that,' John agreed. 'I tell you what, come after church on Sunday. We can talk then.'

'Do you mean it, John?' he asked eagerly. 'People say things they don't mean, I know that.'

'I mean it.'

• • •

Martha was waiting at the foot of the stairs. She glanced up at him, her mouth turned down in concern, her hands clasped together, clutching her paternoster beads.

'Is something wrong?' he asked with worry.

'I was in the solar,' she said finally. 'I heard a voice outside.'

'It was just a drunk,' he told her, trying to keep his voice light. 'I sent him on his way.'

'There's a good moon tonight, John. Don't lie to me.'

He smiled. 'It was nothing, Martha, I promise you; someone who thought to try his luck by robbing me. There wasn't even a need to spill his blood.'

'I might be old but my eyes are clear enough,' she continued. 'It was Mark, wasn't it?'

'Aye,' he admitted with a sigh. 'It was.'

She reached out and stroked his cheek. It was a gentle touch, a mother's caring touch. Her face softened and she said, 'I told you he was a dangerous man.'

'There was no harm done in the end. He left and he won't be back.'

'I saw that. I saw what happened after with Walter, too.' She moved to sit on the bench, adjusting an embroidered cushion behind her back. Her gown rustled as she walked, and he noticed the sheen of the fabric and the dark blue colour. 'Do you like it?' she asked as she saw his glance, her lips curling girlishly.

'I do. It suits you.' It was more than a mere compliment, it was the truth. The deep indigo of the silk set off her clear blue eyes.

'My husband loved me to wear this. He picked the material for me.' Sorrow flickered across her eyes. 'It's eight years ago today that he died.'

'I'm sorry.'

She shook her head.

'Don't be, John. God's blessing is that the pain fades but the good remembrances stay strong. That's why I wear this every anniversary. It makes me feel closer to him.'

'He must have been a good man to have your love.'

'We were well-suited, even though the marriage was one to please our parents. He left me well provided-for, and our daughter will want for nothing after I'm gone.' She arched her eyebrows. 'But don't you go thinking a little flattery will make me forget what I saw tonight.'

'I'm sorry,' he told her, ashamed of himself even though he'd only tried to spare her the truth.

'Did Walter see it all?'

He nodded.

'He'll look up to you now, you know,' she warned him. 'He's terrified of Mark after what happened.'

'He's a good lad. There's kindness in him.'

'There is that,' Martha agreed, then her voice turned harder, 'although most folk around here think he's a bit simple.'

'I don't pay much mind to what folk think,' John said.

She chuckled softly. 'It shows.'

'He asked me to teach him.'

'Teach him what?'

'I don't know,' he answered with a small shake of his head. 'I don't know what I can offer him.'

'If he wants to be like you, he could choose worse things in the world,' she said. 'But I'm only telling you this once. My husband never lied to me and I won't let any other man do it, either. I don't even know why you're involving yourself in this murder.'

'Truth to tell Martha, I'm not sure myself.' He hesitated, searching for the right words. 'But Will took me on, he seemed a fair man; perhaps because I was the one to find him?' He ran a hand through his hair. 'I don't know.'

'There's a flagon of wine in the buttery,' she said, 'and two goblets beside it. Would you fill them and bring them in, John?' He did as she bade him, noting the elaborate work on the York pewter cups. 'I'd be glad if you'd drink with me to my husband's memory. He'd have approved of you.'

He drank slowly, sipping at the dark red liquid and letting it roll over his tongue before swallowing it. He knew nothing of wine, but he could taste the cost in its smoothness and the deep ruby colour that glittered in the light.

'This is excellent,' he said. 'I thank you for your kindness, Martha. God grant you health.'

'The pleasure comes in having someone to share it with. But you'll be out of that door if you tell me less than the truth in future. I'm not a fool, John.'

'I promise.' He paused. 'How would I send a message to the coroner?'

'You should ask Walter,' she suggested. 'He'll do it for a coin.'

'I'll be at work before he's awake.'

'I can ask him for you,' she offered.

He dug into his purse. 'I'd like to meet the coroner tomorrow evening at the church.'

'I'll see he remembers properly and passes it on. I still think you're a fool, John.'

'Most like I am,' he agreed with a sad smile, 'but this seems to have chosen me.'

• • •

The heat remained sullen and brooding all day, so heavy that at times he believed he could almost taste it. The sweat ran off him in rivers, down his chest and back and soaking his hose. No matter how often he stopped to drink, a thirst raged through him, and his muscles tightened with cramp.

The others in the tower room were the same. At dinner they sat together outside in the shade, scarcely talking in the close air. Late in the afternoon a small breeze came out of the west, enough to make them all stop working and raise their heads to the sky, breathing deep and feeling the wind on their flesh.

He packed up the tools, wiping each one carefully, wearied beyond measure. The satchel felt heavy on his shoulder as he descended the stairs and walked through the nave, as if someone had filled it with stones when he wasn't looking.

The coroner was pacing just outside the church porch, looking clean and crisp in brown hose with a thin cote of sweet Lincoln green. He fell in beside John as he headed to the ale barrel, Brother Robert trailing a few steps behind, still awkwardly carrying the small desk under his arm.

'You wanted to see me?' de Harville asked. 'I hope it's worth my time, carpenter.'

'I do, but let me drink first.' He downed two mugs one after the other, the small beer like balm on his throat. Finally he put the cup aside and wiped a hand across his mouth.

'Mark came looking for me last night.'

The coroner cocked his head in curiosity. 'What did he want?'

'What do you imagine?' John asked in a tired voice.

'From the look of you he didn't have any joy.'

'In the end he ran off.'

'Wounded?'

John shook his head. 'Untouched.'

De Harville said nothing for a few moments, stroking his chin lightly. 'You didn't ask me here just to tell me that, did you?'

'No, there's more.'

'Let's go to the alehouse, then.'

The tiny place on Low Pavement was busier than on their last visit. They had to crowd themselves onto the end of a bench, Robert leaning against a wall close by. The harried alewife had someone to help her, a girl who bantered with the customers, slapping their exploring hands away from her skirts.

Finally the coroner was able to order ale and a bowl of pottage. They waited until it arrived, and he pushed the food across to the carpenter.

'You look like you need it.'

'I'll not say no,' John said, stirring it with the wooden spoon then tasting the liquid, a mix of flavours that teased his tongue and went down easily, filling his belly so he sat back with a contented sigh when he finished.

'Now…' de Harville began with a smile.

'I asked a few questions at the church yesterday. It seems that back in the spring Will dismissed a man who threatened to come back and kill him.'

'Does this man have a name?' the coroner asked with interest.

'Geoffrey,' John told him.

'What else do you know about him?'

'Nothing really.' He drained the mug and raised his arm to signal for more. 'I don't even know if he's still in Chesterfield.'

De Harville glanced quickly at the monk. 'We can discover that,' he said. 'If he's here I'd look at him for the killing.'

'Odd that he had wait so long,' John said, then shrugged. 'But maybe not. According to his widow, Will had no enemies he ever told her about.' The girl arrived with the ale and he paid her, smiling and winking as he placed the coins in her hand.

The coroner raised his eyebrows.

'You've been busy,' Brother Robert said quietly. 'I wonder why.'

John looked at him. 'Not because I killed him and I'd have someone else seen as guilty.'

'I believe that,' de Harville told him quickly. 'And your help's useful, no matter the reason.'

'I'd like Will to have some justice.'

'He will, if I have anything to do with it,' the coroner promised.

'God thank you for that.' John tilted the mug and downed it in one before standing. 'It's been a long, hot day. I'll try to find out more for you at the church.'

'You do that, carpenter. Find out what the people are saying.'

Before he could push his way out, he felt a light touch on his arm.

'Master,' Brother Robert said, 'you said you'd help with a strap on the desk.'

'Of course,' John replied.

'I found some leather.'

'Come to the church at dinner tomorrow,' he said with a broad smile. 'I'll attach it for you.'

'Thank you.'

• • •

The hour had turned late, and his body was tired and dirty. There was no sound from the solar and he walked quietly through to his room to bathe his face, hands and feet, then soap his chest and back before lying down to sleep.

An hour later he was awake again. He had ridden the nightmare, and now the images of death were etched behind his eyes. He rose, hoping to walk them away, to clear his mind, but they refused to leave, lingering in snatches, flickering as elusive as smoke. He drank a little more ale and settled again, hoping for sleep, but rest wouldn't return to him.

It had happened often enough before, coming without rhyme or reason to torment him and steal his nights. All he could do was count the hours, each minute stretching like a long, treacherous week. It had begun after the plague took his father, when it seemed as if God had taken His love from the world and all would die in pain during that never-ending devil's season. Cast on his own devices, he'd been afraid to seek out anyone, scared that they too would disappear from his life – that he had death in his touch. He'd been eleven then, a boy with no sense of the world, with nothing more than the bag of tools that had belonged to his father and the clothes he wore.

He slept in woods and hedges, took food from the houses that stank of decay, and tried to convince others that he was a carpenter. Times were desperate, men with any kind of ability scarce on the face of the earth, and he found work here and there. He earned a little money, enough to keep body and soul together. The jobs lasted a day or two, then a week, a fortnight. He grew taller and stronger and began to understand the wood, to feel it, to work with it rather than use it.

His feet took him around the kingdom. He had laboured on the high magnificence of Lincoln Cathedral, lying far above the nave to fit roof trusses and bosses in place, where the touch of each breath seemed to echo forever. He had worked on the colleges in Oxford and Cambridge, watching the scholars process like kings down the streets. But each time, from every place, he'd moved on, finding fault with the town, with the master, even with the weather, his soul restless and unsatisfied.

York had been different. There he'd come closest to the happiness he'd known as a child and the dreams hadn't come to him. He had stayed two years, relishing his work on the minster, making good friends among the other workmen there. He'd even courted a girl; she had been eager enough to jump into his bed – and many others, too, he learned later – turning shrewish and demanding as soon as she had his affection. The child she was carrying might have been his, but might well not, as he'd been told, although her father insisted otherwise. But he knew he couldn't trade brief moments of nightly pleasure for a lifetime of misery. Instead, he'd collected his wages and stolen away on a summer's night while the city slept, taking the road out past Monk Bar with no destination in mind beyond where the wind might carry him.

And now the dark visions had returned. The thought came that they might be death's reminder of his own mortality, the cold hand that could touch his shoulder at any time.

He dressed as the first smudge of light lifted over the hills. His body and his spirit ached and he scuffled his way along the empty street to the churchyard. The air had cooled, but even that gave him no pleasure. The day would wind out before him like an endless road, dusty and drear.

Nonetheless he worked hard, keeping his mind on the job to avoid the stupid mistakes of tiredness. By dinner all he wanted to do was eat and then snatch a few minutes of sleep in the open. He had taken one bite of the cheese when Brother Robert arrived, his face hopeful and his shoulder sagging under the weight of the desk, and John recalled his promise with a sigh.

It was the work of a few heartbeats, simply measuring and cutting the length of leather then fixing it in place with a pair of nails. The old man's face broke into a smile as he placed it on his shoulder, giving a blessing and heartfelt thanks as he left. It was no more than a tiny act of charity, but it brightened his mood enough to feel the rest of the day might pass well.

He was drinking a last cup of ale before returning to the tower when someone appeared at his side, a squat, round fellow with a deep white scar along his cheek and the little finger missing from his left hand.

'You were asking Thomas about Geoffrey,' he said as he poured himself a cup.

'Someone said he might know the name,' John explained. He'd seen the man around the site, impossible to miss, but had paid him no mind, just one of many working on the building.

'There were plenty of us breathed happier when Will turned him away.' He took a drink and gazed upward at the pale sky. 'Always late, arriving with some excuse or another, and if anything he did was wrong, it was always someone else's fault.'

'I've met the sort before,' John sympathised.

'Mondays he always arrived with a head like a hammer and you could never get much work out of him,' the man recalled, shaking his head. 'It never got much better during the week, either.'

'How long did he last?'

'Too long,' the man answered sharply. 'If I'd been in charge he wouldn't have stayed a month. But Will finally had enough, paid him what he was owed and told him never to come back. We were stood there cheering.'

'He threatened to kill Will?'

'He did, right enough. All he got for his words was a kick up the arse and the sound of our laughter. It's been a better place here since he left, too.'

'Did he leave Chesterfield?'

'So I heard.' He paused. 'It's a funny thing, though. I was out having a drink with some of them last week and I thought I saw him walking past the alehouse. Not seen hide nor hair of him since, mind. It's just that ...' He shrugged.

'You think he might have come back?'

'What do I know?' the man replied with a rueful sigh. 'I was so deep into a bellyful of ale by then that I could have imagined him. Paid for it the next morning, too.'

'What did this Geoffrey look like?'

'Hair as red as his temper and ugly as a bishop's sin,' he laughed. 'None of the lasses here would go anywhere near him, for all he boasted of his successes. They'd more sense.'

John slung the satchel over his shoulder. 'What's your name?' he asked.

'James,' the other man replied.

'If you see him again, James, you should tell the coroner.'

'Nay, lad, I'll not be doing that,' the man answered firmly. 'I stay as far away from the likes of him as I can. I'll tell you and you can pass the word, if you like.'

'I'll do that. God go with you.'

The heat of the afternoon gathered thick as a pool in the tower room. He tried to keep his thoughts firmly on the work, to concentrate, but they fought him, desperate to drift loose. He yawned, feeling a drowsiness that covered him like a blanket, blinking to bring everything back into focus. The chisel slipped in his sweaty palm and sliced open a cut on his finger.

Usually he was aware of everything around him, alert to all the accidents that could so easily happen. But the weather and the lack of sleep had dulled his mind so that when one of the labourers dropped the end of a beam he couldn't move back quickly enough.

It came down hard on his left arm, pinning it against the floor. He heard the quick, sickening snap of bone. For the briefest moment he felt nothing, then the pain coursed through his body and he screamed.

CHAPTER SIX

They lifted the timber off him carefully, easing it away as gently as a baby. Someone was sent running for the bone-setter. John lay, teeth clenched hard, gaze fixed on his left forearm. It was useless now, the break obvious under the swollen skin. He tried to move and a wave of agony flooded through him, leaving him nauseous. A labourer brought ale, pouring it slowly through his lips. He swallowed gratefully, draining one cup, then another, turning his head away from the limb.

The bone-setter was an old man, his long hair all grey, his cote a pale, peaceful blue. He had a calm, soothing face and large hands that moved with surprising lightness over the arm. After he finished his examination he smiled at John.

'It's a clean break. Once it's healed it'll be as strong as ever.'

He felt the relief. Without two good arms his skill would be gone. He watched curiously as the man delved into the deep bag he carried, bringing out two piece of thick bark, its roughness all smoothed down, a roll of cleaned linen, a bowl and a stone jar.

'Are you ready?' the man asked, and John nodded. It was a single moment of pain, not as intense as the break, but the sharpness made him cry out. 'Keep still,' the man ordered, fitting the bark around the forearm and cutting it to shape with the knife from his belt, adjusting and altering it until he judged the fit exact. He nodded to himself, then poured some of the liquid from the jar into a bowl. John wrinkled his nose at the rancid smell of animal fat and other things he couldn't identify.

'What's that for?'

'Watch,' the bone-setter said quietly, his voice soothing, as he unrolled the linen and passed it through the liquid before wrapping it around the bark. 'It'll dry and harden to keep the splint in place.' He worked deftly, trained fingers pulling at the cloth until he'd covered the whole forearm and he nodded to himself in satisfaction. 'You'll need to keep this on for six weeks.'

John shook his head. 'I can't work with this on,' he protested.

The bone-setter sighed. 'If you don't keep it on you'll never use that arm properly again, I can promise you that,' he said firmly. 'Tell me carpenter, which is the better bargain?'

John gave in with poor grace, angry at himself for his carelessness and stupidity. As soon as the mixture had dried and stiffened the cloth, the bone-setter drew a larger piece of linen from his bag and fashioned it into a sling.

'Keep your arm in that during the day,' he ordered. 'Don't try to use that arm and it'll mend without any problem.'

John reluctantly nodded and gave his thanks before climbing to his feet. Awkwardly, with just his good right hand, he paid the man then packed his tools into the satchel and rested the strap on his shoulder. The arm ached dully, a slow throb that pulsed through his body.

He trudged through the yard, seeking out Joseph the master carpenter. The man was in the corner, berating two men sawing at a log.

'I heard,' he said, his face still dark. 'A clean break?'

'That's what he told me.'

The master frowned. 'So now I'm a man short. How long?'

'Six weeks.'

Joseph ran a hand through his thinning hair. 'I can't keep a job for you. If there's something when you've healed I'll have you back.'

John nodded his understanding; it was what he'd expected. He'd have to take his chances. If there was nothing he'd move on elsewhere. There would always be another road with another job at the end of it.

He walked back slowly to the house on Knifesmithgate. There was no hurry about anything for a while. His skin was already beginning to itch under the bark splint, an irritation he couldn't reach. All it did was increase his fury at himself. He knew better, he should never have let his attention waver.

He'd seen enough broken limbs, and worse, to understand how dangerous any site could be. And now he was paying the price for his own stupidity. For the next six weeks he'd be useless.

He lifted the latch on the door and entered, leaving the satchel of tools in his room then pouring a mug of ale in the buttery. Every action was going to take longer and need more thought, he realised.

He drank slowly then went out into the garden. A light breeze had stirred from the north and the soft air began to cool his temper. In his heart he knew he'd been lucky. If the beam had fallen the other way it could have crushed his head and they'd be putting him in the ground.

He set the cup aside and bent over to pluck a few weeds around Martha's plants. With each glance he noticed more and knelt, the dry earth harsh against the thin fabric of his old hose. Methodically he moved along the row, pinching the weeds between the fingers of his right hand and easing them out of the ground. It was a way to pass the hours, and there were enough of them lying ahead of him.

He was still working when he heard the footsteps. He stood quickly, wiping the dirt from his good hand on his hose.

Martha gave him a wan smile.

'There was talk in the shops that someone had been hurt. I prayed to God it wasn't you,' Martha said.

'He didn't hear you this time,' he answered, raising the sling.

'Will it mend properly?'

'With His good grace,' he said with a nod.

'How long will it take?'

'Six weeks.'

Martha opened her mouth to speak, then hesitated.

'What is it?' he asked.

'If you don't have the money …' she began, then blurted out, 'I won't charge you for your board.'

He bowed and patted his purse.

'You're a generous, Christian woman, but I have coins here. I can last six weeks. All I need are things to fill my time.' He thought of the days stretching bleakly away.

'You've made a good start here,' she said, nodding at the pulled weeds wilting on the ground. 'There's plenty more, if you've a mind.'

'I might.'

'I won't complain. Just be sure you stay out of the alehouses.'

'That's never really been my way,' he answered with a grin. 'A pretty girl's a different thing, though.'

'I saw Katherine looking at you in church. The gossips said you carried her washing back from the river, too.' Her words were part tease, part question, and he grinned.

'The gossips will make something out of nothing.'

'She's pretty enough for any man.'

'For any man who's courting,' he countered.

A smile played across Martha's mouth. 'Every man's ripe for courting if the girl's right and she sets her eye on him. You'd better watch out for her.'

He shook his head in bemusement. 'She'll find little joy with me, then.'

'We'll see, John, we'll see,' she told him, her voice light and full of good humour. 'Katherine can be a determined lass; she might have you wed before the year's out.'

'No one's managed it yet.'

'There's always a first.'

They passed the last hours of the day in gentle banter. She heated pottage in the cookhouse and they ate outside, sitting on a bench in the garden as evening fell. The sounds of the town died away, and he saw a nightjar soar and dive while the low breeze softly shook the leaves on the trees. The shock of the fracture had passed, and the sleepless night had caught up with him. He stood awkwardly and yawned.

'I'm away to my bed,' he said. 'I wish you God's peace in the night.'

'And to you John.'

He removed the sling in slow, difficult movements, and washed as best he could. The cast restricted his movements, leaving him shifting around until he found a comfortable place in the bed. Then sleep came, deep and blissful.

• • •

By habit he woke before dawn, his mind already alert and urging him out of bed. Dressing was a long, awkward chore of balancing and pulling. He glanced longingly at the satchel in the corner. In all the time since his father taught him how to handle the tools he'd never gone a single week without using them, let alone six. He sighed, easing his arm into its sling.

He raised the latch softly, careful to make no noise that would wake Martha, and walked lazily down the street. His feet impelled him to St Mary's, where he shared a mug of ale with some of the other men. They joked about his arm, but he saw the relief in their eyes that the injury was his, not theirs. As they drifted off to their work he returned to the town. The streets were busy as servants shopped for their mistresses, eagerly talking to each other, a few looking him full in the face with challenging smiles that brought his sly wink in return.

He strolled through the tiny streets of the Shambles, watching a butcher expertly slice a beast apart, tossing the guts out into the street for a waiting pack of dogs, then another bring a cleaver down briskly, his cut clean and sure, showing the meat for a goodwife's inspection.

In the square, traders were setting up their trestles for the market, the space already bustling with people. He saw the coroner emerge from a grand house on the High Street, with Brother Robert just behind him. It was a rich man's dwelling, with three storeys jettied out one above the other, the limewash fresh and bright in the early sunshine, the timbers cut clean and straight. Without thinking, he quickened his pace until he reached them.

'Does the strap help, Brother?'

The monk turned with a smile that became shock as he saw the sling.

'God be praised, it does. But what happened to you?'

'My own fault,' John admitted.

'I wish you well of the healing,' de Harville said. He patted his left leg. 'I broke this once. With God's grace and a good bonesetter I was fine.'

'I'll pray for you,' Brother Robert promised.

'Have you learned anything more about Will's death?' John asked the coroner. The man shook his head and frowned.

'I can't find sign of this Geoffrey. People remembered him, but no one's seen him since spring. Your friend must have conjured him up when he was drunk.'

'What now then?'

'I don't know,' de Harville said brusquely. The light caught his hair, showing it almost white, a contrast to the deep blue of his cote and hose. 'We're off to attend a farmer dead in his field at Newbold. I bid you good day.' He swept away.

'Pay him no mind,' Brother Robert whispered. 'He argued with his wife last night. He knows he can never win with her. Then he drinks and it always leaves him in a foul mood.' He hefted the strap. 'I thank you again. God be with you.'

He hurried after his master as fast as his old legs could carry him.

John stopped at a cookshop and bought a pie, leaning against a wall to eat it, the meat deliciously hot in his mouth.

'I heard you'd broken your arm. Does it hurt?' He looked up to see Walter standing there with Katherine.

'It did when it happened,' he answered with an easy smile. 'Now it just aches a little and itches.' He bowed his head and added, 'Good day, Mistress,' gratified to see a blush rise from her neck into her face.

'I'm sorry for your distress,' she said. 'May God give you ease.'

'I'm sure He will.'

'How did it happen John?' Walter asked intently. 'Mark didn't come back, did he?'

'No, nothing like that' he assured the boy. 'Don't worry yourself, he won't be after me again. It was an accident at work, pure and simple. I was to blame.'

'How long before you'll be back at work?' Katherine wondered.

'Six weeks,' he told her with a sigh. 'That's if there's still a job for me there.'

'Surely they'll have something for a skilled carpenter,' she said, and for a moment he imagined he heard a hopeful note in her voice.

He shrugged. 'They need to do as much as they can before winter. They'll want to start the spire by then if they can.'

'They need craftsmen,' she said confidently.

'Aye, Mistress, but they need them now.' He lifted his arm. 'There's not the time to wait until I'm whole again.'

'What are you going to do, John?' Walter asked.

'I don't know,' he told the boy, glancing at his sister and catching her watching him, her eyes full of some deep thought he didn't understand. 'For now I'll walk home with you, though, if you don't mind the company.'

'We'd welcome it,' she said, and he fell in beside them. 'You should walk beyond the town, Master,' she suggested. 'People say it's very restorative for the soul.'

'Perhaps I will.'

'Walter knows all the country hereabouts, don't you, Walter?'

'I do,' the lad agreed with a quick nod of his head.

'He'd be an excellent guide,' Katherine suggested.

'Then we should do that tomorrow,' John agreed. 'I'd enjoy that.'

They halted at the corner of Saltergate.

'Walter, could you go on without me? I need to speak with Master John.'

The boy looked at them with guileless eyes.

'Of course. Tomorrow, John?'

'Yes,' he agreed, and watched the boy loping away before turning to the girl. 'You'll have the gossips flapping their ears to hear us,' he began before seeing the serious look on her face. 'What is it, Mistress? Have I offended you in some way?'

'You know Walter's hardly spoken of anything else since he saw you make Mark run.'

'He's making more of it then it was.'

She shook her head and pursed her mouth. 'I've lived here all my life. He's not the only one in Chesterfield who's scared of Mark. You heard what happened to my brother?'

'Martha told me.'

'Walter says you're his friend.'

'I am.'

'Words are easy, Master John,' she told him hesitantly. 'Deeds are harder. If you're going to be a friend to him, make sure you're a true one. Please.'

'I gave him my word, Mistress,' he replied seriously. 'I don't go back on that.'

Katherine's face softened. 'The boys his age don't want to know him. Other folk just ignore him or take advantage of him. He needs someone. He'd value your friendship, truly.'

'He has it.'

She looked up at him, her eyes suddenly playful. 'You'd have my appreciation, too.'

'Now how can I refuse that?' he offered gallantly.

'There's not an ounce of malice in him, Master John. He wouldn't hurt anyone. Please, don't let him down.'

'I don't make my promises lightly,' he replied. 'And I'd rather you called me John.'

She smiled broadly. 'John it will be then, but if I do that you'll have to call me Katherine.'

'With pleasure,' he agreed quickly, 'no matter what the gossips think.'

She started to giggle then stopped abruptly, as if she realised how childish it made her seem, and started again.

'I should go home,' she said, dashing off quickly. He lingered long enough to see her glance over her shoulder at him.

He'd turned to go back to Knifesmithgate, wondering what to make of the girl and whether Martha could be right about her, when out of the corner of his eye he spied a flash of red hair as a man rushed along the street.

CHAPTER SEVEN

John hurried after the man, trying to keep him in sight. He ducked between people, muttering his apologies, squeezing between a pair of women bowed under the weight of their baskets. All he could see was the man's back, the shoulders broad and rounded, and the bright shock of red hair. Just as he believed he was gaining ground, that he might reach him soon, the man turned the corner and vanished.

He ran, trying to keep his left arm pressed close to his body. But by the time he had made his way to the turning, there was nothing to see. He went down the street, into the Shambles, peering into the shops and the small alleys that led through to the ruined tumbledown houses of the poor. Breathing hard, he cast around, asking the butchers and goodwives if they'd seen the man, but none had noticed him.

For a small moment he almost believed he'd imagined him. But he knew he hadn't. He' been real, he'd been here.

• • •

After ten minutes he gave up. It was hopeless. The man had vanished. He walked around once more, but there was nothing. With a long sigh he moved down the alley and out into the market square.

Trading had begun and he shuffled along the rows, hemmed in by the crowds. There were more varieties of fish than he'd ever seen in his life, bolts of cloth lovingly stacked and skilfully displayed to show off their bright colours, barrels of apples plucked fresh from the tree, pots made from tin and iron, sacks of wool, bundles of sweet-smelling rushes and piles of tanned hides ready to be worked. Even in York he'd never seen a market this large. At the far side of the square men paraded horses for sale, huge animals that seemed too big for any man to sit upon. Elsewhere one man sold nothing but nails, and John cast a practiced eye on them, some good, some already afflicted with rust.

After a few minutes of walking around he felt overwhelmed by everything, all the sights and sounds, and his hunger was rising again. The baker had his shutters wide, the smell of fresh-baked bread filling the air. He bought gingerbread so thick with honey, saffron and cinnamon that it seemed to melt in his mouth as he bit into it. A cup of ale washed it down readily; refreshed, he returned to the market, watching a man cleverly turning wood on a small lathe he powered with his feet. John watched, assessing the construction of the tool and wondering whether to build one himself. It would take less than a day, once he had use of his arm again.

'You're lost in thought, my friend.' The words made him start, pulled from his reverie. He turned to see Brother Robert looking abashed. 'I'm sorry. I didn't mean to disturb you.'

'I'm only dreaming,' John told him wistfully. 'Is it always as busy as this?'

The monk nodded. 'It'll be worse in a few weeks when the harvest is in and men bring their corn to sell.'

'It's a wonder.'

'It is,' the monk agreed. 'One of man's wonders, anyway,' he added wryly.

'Where's your master?'

'He went back to his bed after we returned from Newbold.' Robert tried to keep hide his amusement, but his face was too open to conceal anything. 'He ended up drinking deep in the wine last night and now he says his guts are churning and his head hurts. He fears he might have caught some rheum.'

'I daresay it'll pass soon.'

'Aye, no doubt,' the monk laughed.

'I saw a man with red hair a few minutes ago,' John said. 'He disappeared into one of those small streets off the Shambles.'

'There are plenty of other men with hair that colour in Chesterfield,' Robert reminded him.

'I know.' He'd considered that after losing sight of the man. There'd been no reason he could give name to, no cause, but the man with the red hair had seemed like a person with something to hide.

'If you spot him again come to us immediately.'

'I will. So tell me, what brings you to the market Brother?'

'Nothing more than idle curiosity,' Robert admitted with a soft laugh. 'I'd go to the church, but there's no peace with all the workmen around. So here's as good as anywhere. I can be amazed by all the things man thinks he needs. What is that, anyway?' He nodded at the lathe. 'It looks like magic.'

John explained how it worked, taking pleasure in the monk's easy company and his astonishment at the way the tool had been fashioned and the things it could do. They began to walk between the trestles, pointing things out to each other as even more people arrived to browse and buy.

He spotted Martha, fingering a length of linen and talking with the seller, haggling down the price, and as they talked he gently guided the monk towards her.

'Dame Martha,' he cried, feigning surprise, when they were close enough for her to hear. She turned at the sound of her name, smiling to see them and letting the linen fall to the trestle.

'Good day, John,' she said. 'And Brother, a pleasure to see you. God keeps you well, I hope?'

'He does, Dame, praise Him for that.' Robert bowed graciously but looked tongue-tied, his eyes darting around as if he was seeking an escape.

'Your master's treating you well?'

'As ever.'

'He's not here today?'

'He's unwell.' The monk glanced at John, his eyes giving a warning to say nothing.

Martha laughed brightly. 'He supped too much last night, you mean? I remember him when he was a young man, he loved his wine then, too.'

Robert said nothing, his eyes on the ground.

'You didn't want the linen?' John asked.

She waved it away dismissively.

'I have linen, I have coverlets; I have everything I need until I die.' She grinned. 'There's more fun in the chase and the capture, anyway.' She stopped to run her hand over a bolt of fine wool dyed a deep green. 'Although I might buy something if it takes my fancy enough.' She glanced at Robert. 'What do you think of it, Brother? Would it suit me, do you think?'

'I'm sure it would, Dame Martha,' he replied, then said, 'I should return and see if my master's any better. I bid you both God's good grace today.' He moved through the crowd as quickly as his legs could carry him.

'He's scared of you,' John observed.

She chuckled. 'Back when we were young, before the church called him, we were sweethearts for a time.' Her eyes twinkled at the memory. 'We swore our love, everyone thought we'd marry. Then God found him, and I met my husband. Perhaps we've both had better lives because of it.' She shook her head. 'That's why he avoids me, for all the feelings about the past I stir in him. It makes him uncomfortable.'

'I didn't know,' John apologised. 'Forgive me.'

'There's nothing to forgive. If he has regrets, that's his business. My life's been happy enough.' She took the basket from her arm and placed it in his good hand. 'Since you're here, you can accompany me and carry everything home.'

'You said you weren't going to buy anything,' he reminded her.

'John,' she said, shaking her head and giving a small, chiming laugh. 'What a woman says and what she does are two different things. If you haven't learned that yet, perhaps it's time you did.'

He strolled with her, keeping alert, his eyes watching, looking for another glimpse of the red-headed man. They wandered for an hour, Martha loving his delight at the variety of goods, treating him to a pastry that tasted like roses when he bit into it, and buying a few small items before they ambled home.

'Perhaps there's some good from that arm, after all,' she said. 'You'd have been working otherwise and not seen the market.'

'Aye,' he said doubtfully. He'd enjoyed all the marvels but he'd have rather been at his trade. It hadn't even been a full day yet and already he missed it sorely.

In the afternoon he rested while Martha brewed a fresh batch of ale, the heat of the day lulling him into sleep. It was a luxury he'd never had the chance to enjoy before, and he stretched out under the sheet. He woke as the shadows lengthened, stretching slowly and feeling oddly content.

For all he'd said before, he thought to spend the evening in an alehouse. There was one on Soutergate where he'd been told the carpenters gathered after work; a few hours in their company might refresh him.

By the time he passed the churchyard most of the men had already collected their wages and gone. He joined the line for his money, what little there was of it, the coins jingling merrily into his purse, before he made his way along the path.

The master carpenter stood in the corner, his hand resting on one of eight long, thick tree trunks that lay on the ground. He was deep in conversation with the two men John had seen the other day. They were richly dressed folk, one in hose of deep burgundy that fitted close to his legs, the other in a black cote and a thin yellow surcote. He couldn't hear what they were saying but their faces were filled with anger, and Joseph nodded his head obediently as they spoke.

John didn't envy him. He had no taste for the responsibilities of that job, the need to please so many, to keep everyone in line. He was much happier using his hands, doing what he loved.

It was the end of the working week and the place was busy, with no room to sit on any of the benches. He ordered his drink, sipping as he looked around for familiar faces. A voice from the corner caught his ear, and he joined Stephen and James, the fellow with the scar who'd told him more about red-headed Geoffrey. Their eyes shone and they gulped down the ale as if making up for lost time.

'How's the arm?' Stephen asked.

John shrugged. 'A nuisance.'

'The master took on someone new today to replace you. He has his tools, but I swear he hasn't the faintest idea how to use them.'

'Who's up in the tower room now?'

'I am,' James replied. 'It's hot work up there.'

'Better keep your wits about you or you'll end up like me,' John warned him with a grimace.

'If I don't die from the engineer trying to work me so hard. He doesn't seem to understand a good joint takes time.'

'Just go at your own pace. He'll shut up after a while.'

They talked and complained, laughed and drank. He didn't even try to keep pace with them, although they hardly seemed to notice. Others came and went but the three of them remained, Stephen and James keeping the serving girl busy, trying to slide a hand down her bodice or up her skirt each time she passed. She played their game, slapping them away, but there was a promise in her eyes for one of them later.

Finally he'd had enough, ready to stop before the muzziness filled his mind. He used the jakes out in the back and returned to finish the mug. Before he left, he asked James, 'That Geoffrey, was his hair wild?'

'I doubt he ever owned a comb.' The man laughed at his own wit, his voice thick with drink, his eyes glazed and unfocused.

'Was he short with rounded shoulders?'

'Aye, that sounds like him,' James said, suddenly curious. 'Why?'

'I thought I saw him, today, near the Shambles.'

'Were you drunk?'

John shook his head. 'I tried to follow him but he vanished.'

'Happen you imagined it, same as I did.'

'He was real enough. No matter, anyway.' He shrugged. 'I'm off to my bed.'

'There was someone he knew in town,' James recalled slowly. 'I remember him boasting about her. I didn't believe it, he lied so much.' He raised his eyebrows. 'Maybe he was telling the truth for once.'

'Did she have a name?'

'He probably said it, but if you'd ever listened to him you'd have learned to ignore most things that came out of his mouth, too. She worked in an alehouse. That's something I didn't forget.' He laughed, showing the few teeth he had left.

It wasn't much, but it was a start he thought, as he strolled along the empty street. Maybe he'd find the man yet. He kept his hand on the knife hilt, ears pricked for sounds, but all he heard were the distant howls of cats preparing to fight. As he lay down he could taste the drink in his mouth and the slight giddiness of pleasure in his head.

• • •

Sunday came bright and sweet, with the first faint tang of autumn in the air. He brushed the dust and the dirt from his hose and his cote as thoroughly as he could, understanding how much he'd taken two good arms for granted, then rubbed a faint shine on to his boots.

He escorted Martha to church, once again leaving her with the widows and goodwives before joining the men in the back corner. Towards the front he could see de Harville, standing tall and proud in his best clothes next to a small, dark-haired woman.

Walter gave him a small wave and Katherine smiled before the service commenced. The priest droned through the mass in a low voice, his words vanishing before they reached John's ears.

He waited outside, standing away from the gentle folk of the town who greeted each other on the porch. The coroner noticed him and gave a small nod of recognition as he passed, then Walter was there, eager and excited, his sister at his side.

'Are you ready, John?'

'I'm yours to command for the day,' he said with a bow.

'Come back to our house first,' Katherine told him. 'I have something for you.' He discovered she'd packed bread and cheese in a sack for them. As they left, he turned and saw her watching them with pleasure in her eyes.

Walter led him along tracks and through woods, walking as if the landscape was imprinted on his heart. He stopped at the bottom of a gulley where trees grew on both sides to make an arch.

'Some people think that's a road to where the fey folk live,' he said, repeating it like an everyday fact.

'Do you believe them?' John asked and the boy shook his head in disappointment.

'I walked up it once and all it did was take me to the top of the hill.'

They ate their dinner in a wood close to Whittington, looking down over the quilt of strips in the fields, some ripe with grain, others dark brown where the crops had already been harvested, a few covered and fallow with the green of grass.

'Have you ever killed a man, John?' Walter asked. The question came from nowhere and took him by surprise.

'Me?' He shook his head. 'I'm not a soldier, I'm a carpenter.'

'But the other night …' the boy frowned, struggling to frame his thought. 'You looked like you could have killed him.'

John lay back and stared up at the clear blue sky.

'I didn't want to hurt him,' he explained. 'There's no pleasure in that. It doesn't make you a man; it doesn't make you any stronger.'

'Soldiers kill,' Walter insisted.

'When you're in a battle you don't have any choice,' John pointed out. 'Either you kill or someone else kills you. There are better things to do with your life.'

'Folk say you can come home rich from war.'

'And the ones who say that are the ones who want you to fight for them. You're more likely to die or come back wounded and useless. The only ones who return rich are the ones who had money when they left. There's no glory in dying.' He saw the lad's face fall a little. 'Why, had you thought of being a solider?'

'Maybe. I don't know.'

'You're better off in Chesterfield, believe me.'

They roamed through the afternoon. The boy seemed to take joy in his company, although he couldn't understand why. They walked an hour or more without words, stopping to sit and rest where they would, Walter sometimes pointing out one feature or another, the flat top of Higger Tor in the distance or the steep cliff of Curbar Edge.

Evening was close by the time they reached town, and Katherine was quick to answer the door when her brother knocked. She ushered the boy in and John hung back, not sure of an invitation. She turned to him, cocking her head, and said, 'Won't you come on in? There's ale, and there's supper too, if you've a mind to share it with us.'

He followed her into the small hall where two girls of about ten played in the corner and a woman sat silent in a high-backed chair, not even sparing him a glance. A spinning wheel and distaff had been pushed against the wall.

'Sit there John,' Katherine told him, clearing room on a bench and passing him a mug of ale. He drank gratefully, his throat dry from the long day. She sat on a joint stool, gathered her skirts primly around her ankles and looked up at him. 'I hope Walter wasn't too much trouble for you.'

'I enjoyed myself,' he said honestly. 'He showed me a great deal.' He glanced over at the boy who was leaning against the wall, a look of contentment on his face.

'I'm grateful to you,' she said, her voice carefully formal. 'You're welcome here at any time. Would you care for some supper?'

'Not tonight,' John said. 'I should go home.' That was a strange word, he thought – home. A word he'd hardly used since he was young, but today, at least, it felt right. He stood. 'Thank you for your hospitality.'

Katherine accompanied him beyond the screens to the door.

'Thank you,' she said gratefully. 'It meant a lot to him.'

'I like your brother. I'd be happy to do it again.'

'You're a good man.'

He raised the sling. 'I'm a broken man for now.'

She smiled. 'Joke if you like, but I can tell a man with a kind heart.' She rose up on her toes and kissed him lightly on the cheek. 'God's peace be with you.'

He returned to the house on Knifesmithgate bemused at her audacity, still feeling the softness of her lips against his skin. Happy, he unlatched the door and entered the hall to find Martha pacing restlessly.

'John!' she said breathlessly.

'What is it? What's wrong?'

'What have you done?' Her small hand reached for him, clutching his fingers.

'What do you mean?' He look confused. 'I haven't done anything.'

'The coroner sent a message over an hour ago. He wants you to go to his house.'

John frowned. 'Why? Did he say?'

She shook her head. 'Just that he wants you there immediately.'

CHAPTER EIGHT

Small splinters of light showed through the shutters at the coroner's house. He rapped on the door, and heard the sound of the servant's shoes on the floor. The girl held up a rushlight, peering cautiously at this stranger who arrived after dark.

'The coroner wanted to see me,' he explained, and after a moment's hesitation she let him in, guiding him through to a hall where de Harville was seated at the table, finishing a supper of sliced meat, his knife poised between plate and mouth. At the other end was the woman John had seen in church, staring at him with disdain as her long, pale fingers tore at a piece of bread.

'John the carpenter. It took you long enough to arrive.'

'I'm sorry, Master. I was out walking; I've only just returned.'

The coroner glanced meaningfully at his wife. She stood, saying, 'I'll leave you to your business, husband,' before leaving. A moment later Brother Robert entered with his desk, wiping the remains of a meal from his mouth as he unpacked his vellum, ink and quill.

John watched the pair curiously, wondering why they needed him here now, what it was that couldn't wait until morning.

'Where were you last night?' the coroner asked.

'I was in the alehouse on Soutergate,' he replied. 'Why?'

De Harville held up his hand to stop John's questions. 'Did anyone see you there?'

'I was drinking with two of the workmen from the church. And the serving girl would have seen me. I was there a few hours.'

'And after?'

'I went back to my lodgings.'

'Who did you see on the way there?'

'No one. What's this about, Master?' He could feel the fear slowly creeping up his spine. The coroner ignored his question.

'What have you done today?'

'I went to service then I was out walking with the boy, Walter.'

De Harville raised his eyebrows slightly. 'Is that the same one who was beaten by Mark a few years ago?'

'Aye, that's him,' John said.

'And Mark came for you after we'd talked to him about the murder at the church?'

'I told you that he had.'

'The men you were drinking with, was one of them in a fight with Mark at the church last week?'

'Yes.'

De Harville fixed him with his gaze. 'Late this afternoon Mark's body was found in the reeds by the river by the fulling mill. His throat had been cut.'

John didn't know what to say. He felt as if all the air had been taken from his body, that he couldn't breathe. He looked at de Harville, then at the monk who was scribbling the questions.

'I didn't kill him, if that's what you're wondering.' He held up the broken arm in its sling. 'I couldn't do much with this.'

'Someone killed him,' the coroner said coldly. 'You've been with two people who had reason to do that. You had good cause yourself.'

'Maybe,' John agreed warily, 'but I've done nothing.' He unsheathed his dagger and placed it on the table. 'You won't see any blood on that.'

'Blood wipes away easily enough,' Brother Robert pointed out.

'There's been none of Mark's on there.'

'Perhaps, perhaps not,' de Harville said. 'The facts speak for themselves, carpenter.'

He had no option but to nod. Taken together, things built up a case against him. At least he had witnesses who'd swear for his whereabouts.

'I could arrest you,' the coroner continued. He speared a piece of meat on his plate and began to chew it slowly. 'But I saw your eyes when I told you Mark had been murdered. You looked truly shocked.'

'I was.'

'I've seen people dissemble well before. Still, I don't believe you killed him.'

'Thank you, Master,' John said gratefully.

De Harville sat back in his chair. 'I'm going to place some conditions on your freedom. You can't leave Chesterfield. If you do I'll raise a posse to bring you back here and I'll charge you with Mark's murder. Do you understand that?'

'Yes, Master.'

'Be glad you have an open face. If I'd seen any guilt in you, I'd have called for the bailiff to take you away.' He nodded at a chair. 'Sit yourself down, pour some wine.' John did as he was told, letting the drink ease the dryness in his mouth. 'But all this begs a question. If you didn't kill him, who did?'

'I don't know,' he said. 'From what I've heard about him, there are plenty here who hated Mark.'

'Few will miss him, God save his soul,' the monk agreed sadly.

'If he'd just vanished, no one would care,' the coroner admitted. 'Truth to tell, we'll all breathe easier without him around.' He toyed with the goblet of wine. 'But the body was found and the hue and cry raised so I have to seek out his killer.' He sighed. 'Two murdered here in a week. That's a bad business.'

'Who discovered the body?' John asked.

'Upstanding people,' the coroner answered with a smile. 'In case you were going to suggest anything.'

'How long had he been there? Do you have any idea?'

'The birds and the animals had been at him,' Robert said. 'There were some signs of bloat.'

'Was he stiff?'

'He was.'

John ran his good hand through his hair. 'You said his throat had been cut. Was there blood around the corpse?'

'Was he killed there, do you mean?' the coroner asked.

'Yes.'

'There was little blood, and ample sign of the reeds trampled,' the monk told him.

'What are you thinking, carpenter?'

'It sounds like someone killed him elsewhere and took him there. Who'd do that in daylight?'

De Harville rested his elbows on the table and steepled his hands under his chin. 'That makes sense,' he admitted. 'Easier to move a body under the cover of darkness.'

'Have you looked in Mark's house?'

'In the morning. Come with us,' the coroner offered. 'You seem to have a good mind for this.'

'Thank you, Master.'

'What do you think, Robert?' de Harville asked.

'I believe there's more to Master John than he's shown us yet,' the monk replied quietly.

'Tomorrow, then, first light. And you can have your knife; I believe you didn't kill him.'

• • •

Martha was waiting, trying to sew, but he saw the needle stuck in the fabric, the anxiety plain on her face as he entered the house.

'What did they want?' she asked.

'Someone murdered Mark.' He let out a long sigh. 'The coroner thought it might have been me.'

She crossed herself silently, her lips moving in a prayer for the dead, then sighed.

'I won't wish something like that on any man, no matter who he is.' She looked at him closely. 'You didn't do it, did you?'

'No,' he told her nd her eyes softened.

'I didn't think you could. De Harville believed you?'

'He did, although he worried me at first. But he still ordered me to stay in Chesterfield.'

'Is that such a hardship?'

'No,' he admitted. 'I've nowhere else to go at the moment, anyway. Not with this arm.'

'Your arm will heal, and the coroner will get his man.'

'I pray you're right.'

'Besides,' she told him with a playful expression, 'I like having you here. There are very few I let lodge, you know. I don't need the money, but I do enjoy the company. You'll be welcome to stay as long as you wish – if you choose to remain in town when this is all done.'

He smiled at her. 'I'll have to see if there's work here when the casts comes off.'

'Of course,' she said. 'How was the day with Walter?'

'I enjoyed it,' he answered. 'He showed me the area. I told him we'd do it again.'

'Did Katherine ask you to supper?'

'Yes,' he said. 'Why?'

'I told you, she has her eye on you,' Martha told him with a sly smile. 'You could do a lot worse than her, too. She more or less looks after everyone in that house.'

'What about her mother? I saw her there.'

Martha shook her head and pursed her lips.

'Jane had a bad palsy a year or two back. She worked hard for the family before that, after her man died.'

'And now?'

'On a good day she can spin a little and sew a little. Mostly she just sits there. She can't speak much, and when she does it's hard to make out what she's saying. Has a temper on her these days, too. Look into her eyes sometime and you'll see it. So everything rests with Katherine and Walter, and for all he's a lovely lad, you can't call him responsible.'

'It must be hard for Katherine.'

'She bears it with good grace for someone so young,' Martha said with admiration. 'Every time you see her she has a smile on her face and time for hello.'

'I'm surprised she can even think about a man.'

'She's a girl, what else is she going to think about?' she asked, as if it was the most obvious thing in the world. 'But she's never had much time for the ones around here. I can't blame her, either, they're a feckless lot.'

'She won't do any better with me.'

'Perhaps she thinks she will. She's a determined young lass.'

'I'm not looking for a wife,' he said.

'You are,' Martha corrected him. 'She understands that you just haven't realised it yet.' She pushed herself up with her hands and slowly straightened her back. 'I'm going to sleep now. I've been up too late fussing and worry about you, John Carpenter.'

'God give you good rest.'

'But only a few hours of it, I pray. I'm not ready for eternity yet.'

• • •

Grey clouds and a light, misting drizzle arrived with the morning. He pulled up the hood on his cote as he stepped out of the door, careful to avoid the night soil tossed out of windows into the road as he walked to the High Street.

De Harville was dressed for the weather in a hat of deep blue and a long cape lined with rabbit fur, with high boots to keep the mud away from his legs. Brother Robert stood behind; the cowl of his black robe pulled back just enough to show a face that wore its aches and pains openly.

'At least you keep good time, carpenter,' the coroner said with a grin. 'I'd still be in my bed if the monk hadn't roused me.'

'I'm a working man, Master. We start early and finish late.'

'Then let's see how well you work for me today.'

He led the way across the market square, so empty and quiet today that Saturday's bustle might have been a dream, and out along West Bar to the cottage. The coroner lifted the latch and they entered.

John threw back the shutters to bring in some light and clear the smell from the place.

'God's blood, how did he live?' de Harville asked, covering his mouth with his hand. There was one small room, the floor just packed earth, and the bed in the corner no more than a filthy sheet thrown over old straw. Mould was growing on food left in a bowl, dust and filth gathered in the corners and along the wall. The only seat in the house was an old joint stool that lay on its side.

John looked around carefully, holding his breath as long as he could before having to gulp in the foetid air. It was a hovel, kept without care or hope. But there was nothing useful to see in it, no indication of why Mark might have died.

He waited until they were all outside before speaking.

'There's no sign of dried blood on the floor or the bed. He wasn't killed there, that's for certain.' John strode around the back of the house, where the small garden was overgrown, filled with weeds and tall grass. He made his way down a path, casting glances to each side. The land sloped sharply down to the River Hipper at the bottom of the valley.

Something caught his eye and he picked his way gently to the back corner before squatting and scratching at the ground

'Over here,' he shouted. 'You can see the blood here,' he showed the others when they joined him, 'and look at the way everything's been trampled. You said he was found by the fulling mill?'

The coroner nodded. 'That's almost straight down the hill.' He stood and pointed.

'What made you look back here?' de Harville asked, his expression a mix of admiration and suspicion.

John shrugged. 'He wasn't murdered inside. It had to happen somewhere.'

They followed the path down to the river, where the small fulling mill resounded with the noise of cloth being beaten over and over to tighten the weave, the heavy smell of urine coming through the open shutters. Downstream, where the river bent, smoke rose from the dyeworks and the tannery next to it.

'It was just over there,' Brother Robert said, 'down in the rushes.'

The imprint of the body remained on the ground, the reed stalks crushed flat. A little blood had soaked into the damp earth, leaving it a darker shade of brown.

'It's not so far to bring him,' the monk observed. 'There was a good moon Saturday night. Whoever did it would have been able to see where he was going.'

The coroner nodded his agreement.

'He'll have blood on his clothes, though,' John pointed out. 'That's something to look for. But if everything they say about Mark is true, it could be anyone.'

'He made enough enemies,' de Harville conceded. 'Keep your eyes open,' he told Robert. They walked along the riverbank to the Lord's Mill, with its waterwheel turning slow and steady, the rasp of the stones grinding corn, then on to Soutergate where a stone bridge crossed the flow, heading down towards Derby. John and the coroner climbed the hill leading to the church, Brother Robert falling behind and breathing hard on the slope.

'I have a little more on the red-headed man,' John told de Harville.

'Oh?'

'I'm told he had a woman in one of the places off the Shambles.'

'It's a warren back there,' de Harville said. 'There's little respect for the law. And they look askance at strangers, too, if you're thinking of going there.'

'It's somewhere to begin.'

'If this Geoffrey's even here,' the coroner said.

'I told the Brother, I thought I saw him on Saturday.'

'You thought, another man in his cups imagined.' De Harville shook his head dismissively. 'None of that helps much. Did you even see his face?'

'No,' John admitted.

'If you find out it's the same man and where he is, then I'll do something,' he said.

They parted at the churchyard, the coroner waiting for the monk before heading back into the town. John lingered by the wall, watching the work and wishing himself back up in the tower room. Beyond the east end of the building, two men were beginning to saw long oak tree trunks, sweating as they moved, the sawdust flying with each stroke.

The wood the men were cutting would have cost a pretty penny; good oak didn't come cheap. But even after cutting it would still need three years to dry and season before it could be used. He glanced around, eyes searching for piles of usable wood but seeing nothing. Slowly he made his way around the outside of the yard, but he still couldn't spot anything.

Finally he gave up. Perhaps there were carts on their way, late as usual, all packed with timber. It wouldn't matter to him, anyway, not until he was back and working – if he ever returned to the site.

• • •

'You were out with the lark,' Martha said as he sat by the table. She'd dished up a bowl of pottage for him as he walked in, the steam still rising from it, pieces of bacon mixed with the beans.

He ladled up a spoonful, blowing on the liquid to cool it.

'I was with the coroner and Brother Robert.'

'He invited you?'

'To look at Mark's house.'

'So you've moved from suspect to coroner's man overnight.' She looked at him and laughed in disbelief. 'That's quite a feat, John. And did you find anything?' she asked after a moment, her manner curiously eager.

'He was killed in the plot at the back then taken down to the river and left there.'

'Jesu.' Martha crossed herself, a shocked exclamation on her face.

'With luck they'll find his killer,' he said.

'What about the master carpenter?'

He told her about the red-headed man and the few things he'd managed to learn.

'If he's hiding away back behind the Shambles you might never find him,' she warned. 'They don't like the law in there.'

'I'd like to see if he's there.'

'Ask Walter,' Martha said. 'He goes back in the Shambles all the time, delivering messages and running errands for people. They won't even look twice at him.'

He considered it for a moment. 'No,' he said, 'I don't want to involve him in murder. That's too dangerous. It's not right.'

'Talk to him,' she suggested. 'Let him make his own choice.'

John shook his head. 'He'd do it just to please me.'

She gathered the empty bowls.

'Let the lad make his own choice,' she repeated. 'He's old enough to do that.'

'Katherine wouldn't want me to put him in the middle of this.'

'I thought you weren't interested in her,' Martha said sharply.

'I'm not, but even so…' he fumbled for a reason. 'He's her brother.'

'You said he's your friend.'

'He is.'

'Would you ask another friend to help?'

He bowed his head, knowing he was beaten.

'I know he's young, but don't treat him like a child, John. Ask him. Believe in him. Walter will take more pride in that than anything else. He might surprise you, too. He sees things and remembers them. And folk don't even notice him.'

He sat by himself for a minute after she left the room, then strode over to the alehouse on Low Pavement. He took the long away around, down Packer's Row, peering down the small streets into the Shambles, hoping in vain for a glimpse of red-headed Geoffrey.

The place was almost empty, most folk away at their work. The alewife had spread some thyme among the rushes and the scent rose as he walked across the room. Two old men were settled in a corner, ekeing out their mugs of ale, sitting in companionable silence, their heads bald and their mouths toothless.

The solitude gave him time to think. He was loath to bring Walter into this business. The boy still seemed so innocent. But perhaps if he just looked out for the man, if he didn't ask any questions or do anything that might bring attention to him, then it would be safe.

He finished the drink and found his feet taking him to the house on Saltergate. One of the young girls answered the door, her eyes wide and her face expectant when he asked for Katherine.

'Come in, John,' Katherine said, wiping wet hands on a piece of linen, her face flushed from cooking, the smells of food filling the small home. She guided him through to the kitchen garden, away from the heat and the noise of the family. 'I hadn't expected to see you again so soon.'

'I hadn't expected to be here,' he admitted, his face serious. 'But I wanted to talk to you before I speak to Walter.'

'Oh?' She cocked her head in curiosity. 'What about?'

'There's a service he could do for me.'

'I don't understand. You know he'll be glad to if he can.'

He nodded. 'That's why I'm hesitant.' He explained what he wanted her brother to do and she listened thoughtfully.

'Most men would have simply gone ahead and asked him,' she observed when he had finished.

'I don't want to take advantage of him.'

She reached across and took hold of his good hand. 'I think you've just proved you're a good friend, John. You care about Walter, not just what he can do for you.'

'Would it be fair to ask him, do you think? Just to walk around with his eyes wide when he's back in there.'

'You're sure he'd be in no danger?'

'As long as he doesn't start asking questions, he'll be fine,' he assured her. 'Dame Martha says he's often around there.'

'At times, yes.' She pushed a strand of hair back from her face. 'I don't understand why you're involving yourself in all this, though.'

'I'd like to see poor Will find some justice.' He held up the arm in its sling. 'And it's not as if I can do much else at the moment.'

She eyed him coolly, looking into his face before slowly smiling again.

'I was right about you. You're a good man. You didn't just come to ask my advice, did you?'

'I'd hoped for your blessing too,' he agreed.

'For whatever it's worth, I can give you that.' He started to speak but she raised a finger. 'The only thing I ask if that if Walter seems reluctant, you won't try to persuade him.'

'I wouldn't do that.'

'No, I don't believe you would,' she said, 'but best to have it in the open.'

He nodded. 'Do you know where he might be?'

She shook her head. 'He leaves in the morning and comes home with the evening with a few coins. Where he goes and what he does is up to him. He helps provide, and that's all I ask.'

'It looks as if you have enough to keep you busy here.'

'I don't mind it.' She raised her head and he could see the sadness in her eyes. 'I love my mother and my sisters.'

'You're a good woman, Katherine.' He mimicked her tone and watched her face brighten.

'Don't tease me.'

'You are,' he insisted.

'We're matched then, sir, wouldn't you agree?' she said boldly, her voice light. 'A good man and a good woman.'

'Perhaps.' He grinned.

'Thank you for coming to ask me.'

'I had to,' he told her. 'I value our friendship.'

'So do I,' she said sincerely. She kissed him on the cheek and once again he felt the smoothness of her lips. He raised his arm to draw her close but she pulled away with a small smile. 'I'll see you out.'

He walked around the town, keeping alert for Walter. But his mind kept drawing him back to the girl. She had a sound head on her shoulders, a pretty one, too, with her long, dark hair and lively face. He respected her and the way she looked after her kin, but he wasn't seeking a wife. He didn't even know what he would be doing when this cast came off, or where he'd be after that.

He finally found the boy by the churchyard, leaning on the wall and watching the men at work.

'Hello, Walter,' he said cheerily, settling beside him. The lad beamed to see him.

'What's he doing John? What's he making?'

'He's a woodcarver. He's making some of the decorations for inside the church.'

'Can you carve wood?' Walter asked.

'Not as well as that,' he laughed. 'That's why I'm just a carpenter.'

The boy pointed at the men working with the saw. 'What will they do with that wood?'

'Set it aside for a long time,' John explained. 'The wood in a tree is very wet. It needs to dry out before you can use it. It's called seasoning.'

The lad look confused. 'Why does it need to dry?'

He hesitated, wondering how to explain it. 'When the wood's dry it keeps its shape. If you work it before it's been seasoned, then it'll twist and warp as it dries. So if you've fitted the wood close it could become loose or change its shape.' He watched Walter nod his understanding. 'Tell me, would you be willing to do something for me?'

'Of course John,' the boy answered eagerly. 'What do you want me to do?'

He laid it all out, going over it three times. 'Just watch and tell me if you see anyone like the man I've described in there. That's all you have to do.'

'Do you want me to see where he lives?' Walter surprised him with the question.

'Only if you can do it without anyone noticing you,' he warned. 'I don't want you taking any chances.'

'I won't,' the boy promised. 'I can go over there now if you want.'

'There's no need to rush,' John told him.

'But he might be there now,' Walter insisted. The boy loped excitedly away.

He made his way home, not convinced he'd done the right thing but knowing he didn't have any other choice. As Martha had said, the people back in those streets would be wary of any stranger. He'd never manage to find Geoffrey himself.

'Well,' Martha said as he poured ale in the buttery, 'did you ask him?'

'Yes.'

'And did you talk to Katherine first?' she asked and he nodded. 'You like that lass, don't you?' she said with a grin. 'Don't bother to deny it; I can see it in your eyes.'

He grinned. 'Am I that open?'

'All men are.'

'Not all of us,' he protested.

'When it comes to the heart, all of them,' she corrected him. 'My husband realised that early on, God rest his soul.'

'Was he a better man for it?'

'Much,' she told him with a beatific smile. 'You men might think you have the charge of things, but if you look closer you'll see that it's a woman behind it all.'

He chuckled and shook his head. 'If you know so much, what do you see for me and Katherine?'

She stood and thought for a moment. 'That girl has plenty of sense. She won't try to rush things.' She eyed him carefully. 'But she won't let you get too far away either. By Christmas you could be wed and living on Saltergate, if that's what she wants.'

'Don't I have a say?'

She sighed. 'That's what I'm trying to tell you,' she spoke slowly, as if he was a child. 'It's up to the woman. It has been the whole length of creation and it always will be.'

'I might surprise you yet,' he laughed.

'You might,' she agreed, raising her eyebrows, 'but you won't.'

CHAPTER NINE

Walter didn't return that day, or the next. The hours passed with desperate slowness, as if they were reluctant to leave. With nothing to do, John chafed and roiled, moving around the house and garden like a restless ghost. His arm itched devilishly as the bone began to knit together, but he couldn't reach to scratch it. He remained acutely aware of the injunction the coroner had placed upon him not to leave Chesterfield. The man hadn't lifted that and he wasn't about to take any risks.

He became familiar with the streets, walking them so much he felt he could find his way around with his eyes closed. He saw the coroner and Brother Robert walking out along the Newbold road, and for a moment he was tempted to run and join them. But if de Harville had needed him he would have sent word.

He felt useless, without purpose in the world. He emptied the tools from the bag and cleaned them with the oiled rag, balancing each one awkwardly in his left hand, even the slight weight making him wince, then rubbed slowly with his right, relishing the feel of the metal and wood on his fingers and wishing the time away until he would be whole again.

Finally, in the late afternoon of the third day, there was a knock on the door. He was sitting in the hall, thinking of nothing in particular. He lifted the latch and the boy was there, breathless from running, his hair wild and his eyes glittering.

'I've seen him John!' he said excitedly. 'He's there!'

'Come in, come in.' He poured Walter a mug of ale and sat him on the bench. 'Tell me what you saw.'

'I had to deliver a message to someone in the inn above the butcher's shop,' he began, the words rushing out quickly. 'I did that then I started to go around, up and down Middle Shambles. He came out from one of the yards and walked right past me!'

John smiled. 'What did you do?'

'Well,' Walter grinned, proud of himself, 'I followed him.'

'Are you sure he didn't see you?'

'No,' the boy answered with certainty. 'He went into a tenement. I waited but he didn't come out again and then I ran over here.'

'You've done very well,' John told him. 'Now, did you see his face?'

The lad nodded.

'Can you remember what he looked like?'

'Of course. He was a little taller than me.'

'How tall?'

Walter thought and held a hand a few inches above the top of his head. 'Like that,' he said.

'What about his face?' He tried to keep the urgency out of his voice.

'His nose was flat.' Walter tried to squash his own to show what he meant.

'Go on.'

'I saw him smile at a girl and most of his teeth were missing.' He laughed. 'She looked away from him.'

'What about his hair?'

'It was red, just like you said.' Walter ran a hand through his own until it stood out from his skull. 'Like that.'

'Thank you,' John said with relief. 'That sounds like the man I'm looking for.'

The boy smiled at the praise. 'Do you want me to follow him again?'

'No,' he answered after some reflection. 'Best not. We don't want anything that might make him suspect you. You've done enough.' He clapped his hand on Walter's shoulder. 'You've helped me a great deal.' He stood, ready to go and find the coroner, then said, 'Come with me.'

At the house on the High Street they found de Harville and Brother Robert in the parlour. The coroner was dictating a report to the monk, the scratch of the quill on vellum loud in the room. Robert kept a short, stubby knife in his left hand, sharpening the quill after each line.

The serving girl showed them in and de Harville held up his hand to silence them until he'd finished speaking his thoughts. Walter gazed in amazement around the room, taken by the rich furniture and especially the bright, colourful tapestry that hung on the wall, a lifelike hunting scene with a man galloping on a horse.

'Put that in the rolls,' the coroner ordered finally, then turned. 'Now, John Carpenter, what brings you here?'

'You said to come and see you if I found Geoffrey. We've found him.' He put a hand on the boy's shoulder. 'Walter saw him a little while ago in the Shambles.'

De Harville looked at the boy. 'You're the Walter that Mark beat badly?' he asked.

'Yes, sir.' He bobbed his head nervously.

'What made you look for Geoffrey?'

'Master John asked me, sir.'

'Did he now?' the coroner asked quietly, turning to the carpenter. 'And why did you do that?'

'Walter goes in there to deliver messages. I thought no one would notice him.'

The coroner nodded slowly. 'You saw the man?'

The lad explained hesitantly, overawed by the authority and the splendour of the surroundings. De Harville paced as he listened while Brother Robert sat quietly at the table.

'You're convinced it's the same man?' the coroner asked when Walter finished.

'From all I've been told, it must be,' John answered.

'I'm reluctant to send men in there to apprehend this Geoffrey,' de Harville said, after long thought. 'If we find him and try to take him, there could be violence and a riot. If we miss him he'll be gone before we know it. What do you think, Robert?'

'I agree, Master,' he said, then added, 'Or I could go in there and observe. A monk would be as unnoticed as a boy.'

'They'll know you're my man,' the coroner objected. 'I'll have the bailiffs look for him. If they spot him outside that area I'll have them arrest him.'

John said nothing. He'd hoped for more, some decisive action, a willingness to find Geoffrey and question him about Will's murder.

'You look disappointed, carpenter.'

'I am, Master,' he admitted. 'You said you'd do something if I found him.'

'I am doing something. I'll give the bailiffs their orders.'

'They can't be watching for him all the time. If they find him it'll be pure chance.'

'It's not for you to tell me my job,' de Harville told him coldly. 'I've more things to consider than you can imagine.'

He knew this was a battle he could never win. The coroner had power and he was no one. He was less than that, a stranger here, without status of any kind in the town. He bowed his head and nodded, then asked, 'What about Mark's murderer? Have you had any joy there?'

'Not yet,' the coroner admitted with irritation.

'Two dead and no killers.'

For a moment de Harville's pale face flared into anger. Then it vanished and he gave a deep, heartfelt sigh, raising his hands.

'You've made your point, carpenter. You can help me.' His look took in both John and Walter. 'I won't send the bailiffs in for your Geoffrey, but you can find Mark's killer for me. You know what to do.'

'And if we find him?'

'Arrest him,' the coroner answered flatly. 'I'll give you my authority for that, the pair of you. What do you say, boy?'

'I'd like that, sir,' Walter answered, the words close to a stammer as he spoke.

'There's not much I can do with one arm,' John said.

'Work together, then. You wanted me to do something, and I have. The brother will prepare something that shows you're working for me.' He nodded at the monk and left the room.

'I'll send the paper to Dame Martha's,' Robert said sympathetically. 'You goaded him, John, and he outfoxed you.'

'So it seems,' he replied ruefully.

The monk lowered his voice. 'He has plenty on his mind besides murder. He and his brother are in the courts over their father's will. They were always an argumentative family.' He shook his head sadly. 'All that'll happen is that they'll make the lawyers rich.'

'Then we'll do our best to ease his load,' John said, 'won't we, Walter?'

'Yes, sir,' the lad said eagerly.

Outside, the sun was shining, the air clear. He breathed deep.

'Are we really going to catch Mark's killer?' Walter asked.

'Maybe,' he said cautiously. 'We're going to look for him, at least.'

'How will we know who he is?'

He explained about the blood that would be on the man's cote as the boy listened, his eyes growing wider. Walter was abuzz with excitement and the sense of responsibility. 'We just look,' John emphasised carefully. 'Don't do anything without me, you understand?'

'Yes.'

'I mean it,' he said and the boy nodded. 'There's little we can do today. It'll soon be evening and people will be tucked in their beds. We'll start tomorrow. Tell your sister I'll keep you out of danger.'

'I'm not scared John,' the lad said firmly, his gaze steady and sincere.

'I know you're not,' he told him with a smile. 'But there's no shame in a little fear. Remember that.'

'I will. Do you want me to work with you?'

'Of course I do,' he assured the boy. 'You've already helped me.'

He was rewarded with a grin before he sent Walter off home. It wasn't the outcome he'd wished, but the monk was right; the coroner had outwitted him and put him in a position where he couldn't refuse. He walked back along the High Street, then cut through Glumangate towards the house on Knifesmithgate. De Harville had presented the challenge, certain he would fail; if it was possible, he would prove the man wrong.

• • •

'So you work for the coroner now?' Martha asked as they sat with their ale and a supper of bread a cheese. The monk had sent the warrants, words John couldn't read written on parchment. It lay next to him on the table.

'Walter too.'

'He'll love that,' she said, 'although his sister might not be as happy. You'd better make sure you look after him.'

'I will.'

'Still,' she chuckled, 'it's something for you to do while you're a bird with one wing.'

• • •

He'd barely finished washing and dressing in the morning before there was a knock at the door. He looked at Martha, who was sweeping the rushes in the hall. She shrugged silently. Walter stood there, and beside him Katherine. The boy's eyes gleamed, impatient to be about his task, but the girl's face was closed and cautious, her eyes hooded and wary.

'Master, Mistress,' he said. 'Welcome. Come in.'

Martha put up her besom. 'I'll fetch you some ale,' she offered, and disappeared back into the buttery.

'Are you ready John?' Walter asked.

'Soon enough,' he answered with a gentle smile.

'It's true, then?' Katherine asked. 'The coroner's given you both a commission?' Her tone was sharp and disapproving.

'Yes,' he admitted. 'I didn't ask for it,' he told her, 'and I don't want it. But I couldn't refuse it.'

'Out of pride?' she wondered caustically.

'Out of justice,' he answered, and her head dipped slightly.

'What about my brother? Why do you have to involve him in this too?'

He spread the fingers of his good hand on the table, gazing down at them.

'It wasn't my choice. The coroner gave the order to both of us.'

'You shouldn't have taken Walter there.'

He'd thought about that during the night, in the long stretches when sleep wouldn't come. He'd wanted to convince de Harville that Geoffrey was still in Chesterfield, and he'd believed that the lad's testimony would tip the balance. He'd never foreseen anything like this, and he felt the guilt, the weight of it, strongly.

'No,' he agreed slowly, his head bowed. 'You're right.'

'But I want to do this,' Walter said.

'What if you find the man?' Katherine continued as if her brother hadn't spoken. 'How will you arrest him?' She looked pointedly at John's arm in its sling.

'We'll find a bailiff to do that,' he assured her. 'I'll make sure

Walter's safe.' John glanced at the boy; he had his fists clenched, a look of frustration on his face.

'You promise that?' she asked, her face softening, allowing the beginnings of a small smile onto her face.

'On my life,' he replied.

'Thank you.'

Walter took his sister's hand and turned her to face him.

'I've told you I want to do this,' he said. His eyes were glistening with tears. 'I've told you and told you.'

'I know,' she said, stroking his cheek to soothe him. 'I know you do. But you're my little brother and I can't help worrying about you.'

Martha bustled back in with the ale. John was sure she had heard it all and waited for the right time before returning, making all the tension evaporate from the air.

'It's a fresh brew,' she said, looking around the faces and smiling. 'It's turned out well.'

John drank and nodded his satisfaction, glancing over at the girl. She looked back for a moment and gave him a smile, but it was tinged with sadness and he knew he'd disappointed her. He wanted to take her aside, to convince her that it wasn't his doing, but this was neither the time or the place.

'When can we start John?' Walter asked eagerly.

'After the ale,' he said. 'But all we do is observe and see if we can spot the man. Nothing more than that.'

'Yes, John,' he said, the corners of his mouth turning down.

'I mean it,' he said. 'I don't care what the coroner said, we're not going to try and arrest anyone. That's not our job.' He was saying it for Katherine's benefit as much as Walter's, but repeating the warning would do no harm. Finally he put the mug on the table. 'We should make a start.' The lad jumped up, ready to leave. 'Could you wait for me outside for a minute? I just have to do something.'

Once he had gone, the door closing loudly, John turned to Katherine.

'I really didn't ask for this, you know.'

'I know,' she said with a small sigh. 'Just look after him, please.'

'I will.' He reached out and closed his hand lightly around hers. 'I'll make sure nothing happens to him.'

'I've never seen him so excited about anything.' She shook her head in wonder. 'He could barely settle down to sleep. It's the first time anyone's treated him like a man.'

'He's old enough to be a man,' John reminded her.

'I know. But there's still so much of the child in him. Ever since…' She didn't need to voice the thought. 'He follows his heart too much. Watch him for me.'

'I will.' He smiled. 'I'll guard him with my life.'

'I should go back, the girls will be getting restless.'

'And your brother and I have a killer to find.'

They left together. He glanced over his shoulder and saw Martha grinning her approval.

• • •

'What are we looking for?' Walter asked as they made their way towards the church.

'Someone with blood on his cote. He'd have that from what he did and from carrying the body.'

'How will we know its blood?'

He considered his answer. 'It'll be dark red and dried.' He decided to make a start at the weekday market in the area north of the church. There'd be a crowd in the small marketplace, plenty of folk for them to watch. It was close to the workers, too. He wanted to look at them, too; it could just as easily be a labourer who was guilty.

'What if he's got rid of the cote?'

John shook his head. If that had happened there was nothing they could do. But clothes were expensive; men kept them and mended them, and wore them until they fell apart, beyond any use. He was wagering that the murderer would take the risk of keeping the cote and hoping luck would keep him safe. 'We'll hope he hasn't.'

Walter pointed out every stain, wondering if it was blood, but he learned quickly enough, becoming more discerning. After an hour John had to admit the killer wasn't there. He strolled over to the wall of the churchyard, leaning lazily against it and casting his eye over the men. Most of them were stripped to their shirts or bare-chested, skin gleaming with sweat.

'We'll need to come back later if we're going to check them,' he said. He noticed that no shipment of seasoned wood had arrived yet. They'd need it soon if they were going to make any progress with the spire.

The pair of them walked to Low Pavement, eyes assessing every man who passed. But there was none with a large enough stain. He'd have more luck in the evening, once most folk had finished with their work. He'd go to the alehouses then, mixing and mingling, and he'd go alone, too, saying nothing to Walter.

The sun broke through the clouds, the heat sultry. For their dinner he treated the lad to a meat pie from a cookshop, squatting against a wall to eat it, watching as Walter gobbled the food down. He remembered those years when he was growing so fast and always so hungry that one goodwife he lodged with joked that he had hollow legs.

'Here,' he said, pressing a coin into the lad's hand. 'Go and buy us a pastry and some ale.'

He threw his head back as he waited, relishing the feel of warm sun on his face. He opened his eyes when he heard footsteps stop close to him.

'Not doing your work, carpenter?' the coroner asked.

'We've been looking all morning.'

'Anything?'

John shook his head, watching the monk shuffle up slowly,

favouring his left leg, the desk hanging by its strap from his shoulder.

'Not so far. But we're not giving up. Have your bailiffs spotted Geoffrey?'

'No.' Walter returned, his hands full. De Harville turned to him. 'Are you enjoying working for me, boy?'

'Yes, sir,' he answered brightly. 'We'll find him for you.'

The coroner graced him with a smile before moving away.

'Master.' John stood. 'You told me not to go out of Chesterfield. Does that rule still stand?'

'Go where you want,' de Harville replied. 'Just make sure you come back here each night.'

He nodded his acknowledgement. As the monk passed, he said, 'You're limping, Brother. Is something wrong with the strap?'

'Nothing like that.' Robert told him with a wry grin. 'That's just age, and no one can fix that. But God bless you for asking.'

• • •

'What now?' Walter asked, after they'd finished the food and drunk the ale.

'Nothing more today,' John announced.

'Why not?' The disappointment was evident on the boy's face.

'We've looked for now and done what we can. You have money to earn, don't you?'

The lad nodded.

'A man has to work. He has to earn his bread.'

'Can we look for him again tomorrow?'

'Yes,' he replied. 'In the morning.'

He watched the boy leave, wondering what to do with himself for the remainder of the day. He could keep walking and searching for Mark's killer, but that would be a fool's errand before evening. He could go home and rest, but he wasn't weary.

Better, perhaps, to enjoy these last days of summer, especially now the coroner had granted him some freedom. He walked down Soutergate, then followed the riverbank by the Hipper, going west past the Lord's Mill and the stench of the dyeworks, the tanners and the fulling mill. Soon the town, with its noise and bustle, was behind him and he was surrounded by the sounds of the country. The river burbled lazily and somewhere over the hill he could hear cows lowing.

After a mile he stopped, taking off his boots to dangle his feet in the water and let its coolness take the sting of heat out of the day. He lay back, closing his eyes, letting his thoughts drift. They might never find Mark's killer. He knew Walter was eager and so proud to be part of the hunt, but he needed to learn that failure was always there, too, brooding at a man's shoulder. Even if it angered him, he also understood the coroner's reticence over sending the bailiffs in to roust Geoffrey from the streets behind the Shambles. A riot was hard to contain, and the damage costly to repair. He'd incur the anger of those running the town and of its good citizens, and all just to find someone who'd issued a threat long before, words he had probably forgotten after a day, once the fire of his temper had passed. In de Harville's place he would have done exactly the same thing.

Slowly he roused himself, drying his feet on the grass then dressing. He meandered; there was no rush to anything – he'd go wherever his feet took him and relish the peace all around.

He stopped in Brampton, climbing the short hill up from the river and seeing a cottage with a branch nailed above the door, the leaves beginning to wilt, but the sign of the alehouse obvious. The floor inside was clean, lavender and thyme among the rushes to scent the air. He bought a mug of ale, the goodwife presenting it and taking his coin without a word, cautious around a strange face. He stood in the doorway to drink, tasting the malt and the wheat, the drink sliding down easily, then a second one to follow it and take away his thirst.

The village street was empty. The men would be at work in the fields, some at their own crops, some for their Lord, the women at their business in the cottages. It made him think of Leeds. The town was larger than this, but he could recall the same summer stillness about the place, as if the world was holding its breath for what might come next.

But what had arrived in Leeds had been the darkness, the sores and buboes that brought death, so that the silence in places all over the land was because no one remained. It was a time when no one could escape the cloying stink of decay, when the miasma hung low over the country.

He drained the mug, his mood soured, and started the walk back to Chesterfield. It was a poor road into town, unpaved, the ruts from the cart wheels dried into awkward peaks and valleys that made walking difficult.

In the distance he could see the tower of the church standing tall on the hill. Once the spire was built the building would become the landmark for travellers; it would draw people from all around as it pushed up into the heavens. He tried to imagine it, but he couldn't. But with God's good grace he would be a part of it, putting the timbers together and helping them climb in the sky.

The thoughts and hopes swirled in his mind. The work would last months, certainly through to the next year, and he began to see a little security in his life again.

Then he was falling. His boot caught on the edge of a rut and he was tumbling down. He put out his good hand, wincing as the impact jolted through his bones, but he was unable to stop his left arm crashing down on the ground. He screamed as the pain tore through him.

CHAPTER TEN

He lay in the road, taking short, shallow breaths. His right hand was bleeding where a stone had dug through the flesh. He could feel his heart pounding in his chest and the sharp agony in his left arm. Very slowly he pulled himself upright, his legs shaking so badly that he almost fell again.

Upright, he stood still, gaining his balance, cold sweat on his face and down his back. The pain from the arm was intense and he knew he'd broken it again. Every slight movement jarred and burned through him so he had to bite down on his lip to keep from crying out.

Very carefully he took a few small paces, holding the arm to keep it still. Blood was seeping bright red through the cast. He breathed in and took another step, his sole slipping for a fearful moment on some gravel.

One more step, one more breath, then a second and a third before he halted. He looked up towards Chesterfield and suddenly it seemed so distant, like a place he might only reach in a dream. The sweat was dripping into his eyes, stinging them and making him blink; he stopped to wipe it away with his sleeve before moving on again, swallowing hard.

Each time his foot touched the ground a spike of pain shot up his arm and through his chest. Every few yards he had to stop and rest before carrying on again. There was no traffic on the road, no one to stop and help him, no one to even offer him a drink. He set his face grimly and walked, halted, then walked again.

The shadows were long by the time he reached the town, the linen around the cast a deep crimson. All he needed was to go a little further, stumble the final few steps to where the bone-setter lived at the end of the High Street. He waited until his breathing had steadied, tasting blood in his mouth where he had bitten through the skin. Finally he knocked on the door.

An old servant answered, a stinking tallow candle in her hand, crossing herself as she saw him, eyes widening at his bloody arm before gathering herself and showing him in.

• • •

He drank the ale gratefully, his throat parched, averting his eyes as the bone-setter worked carefully with his sharp scissors, cutting through the bandage and easing it away from his flesh. He winced as the old man removed the splint, all the blood that had pooled inside it spilling onto the floor. Then he drew his breath in sharply as he saw the white end of bone protruding through his flesh.

The bone-setter poured cold water over the arm before examining it with a light, confident touch, his fingertips cool. He finished and sat back on his stool, frowning.

'How did this happen?'

'I was walking and I fell.' John held up his other hand. 'I tried to stop myself.'

The man stood and stroked his chin thoughtfully.

'You've broken it again, but at least it's in the same place as the first break,' he said slowly. 'That's something.'

'Can you set it?'

'Yes,' the bone-setter answered, 'but I'll tell you the truth: I can't say how well it will heal, how strong it will be.'

'I need two arms to work properly,' John protested.

'Once I put the bone back in place, it's with God,' the man said quietly. 'Prayer will help. Are you ready?'

He brought fresh linen, torn into strips, more of the mixture to harden the cast, and a clean splint, thicker and sturdier than the first. Finally he produced a piece of hard leather.

'Put this in your mouth,' he ordered, 'and turn your head away. It's going to hurt.'

John did as he was told, biting down hard as the man swiftly manipulated the bone. His eyes teared and then the nauseous wave of pain receded. He watched as the bone-setter gently wrapped the wound in linen, tending it like a baby, working methodically and skilfully until everything was in place, the arm in a clean sling on his chest.

John paid, for once glad to part with his money.

'Take this,' the man said, giving him a small bottle of liquid.

'What is it?'

'Just some poppy juice.' He gave a smile. 'Put a little in some wine tonight, it'll help you sleep well. Keep the rest for when you need it.'

'Thank you.'

The arm throbbed as he walked to the house on Knifesmithgate. His heart was weary and all he wanted to do was sleep.

Martha stirred, putting aside her sewing as she entered. Her expression was bright, eyes dancing until she was his face.

'Sweet Jesu,' she said. 'What happened to you John? You look like death.' He told her, watching her blanch and cross herself. Once he'd finished, she asked, 'Will it heal well?'

'He doesn't know. With God's good grace, maybe.' It was something he didn't want to think about, what it might mean, what he could do if the worst happened. 'Do you have any wine? The bone-setter gave me something to help me rest.'

'I'll bring you a cup. Sit down.' In the moments it took her, he was lost in bleak thoughts, wondering if he would ever use his father's satchels of tools again. The worry would haunt him until the weeks passed and he knew the answer. But it was in God's hands now, far beyond his control. 'Here,' Martha said gently, placing the cup beside him.

He poured in some of the poppy juice, sparingly at first, then a little more, stirring the mixture with his finger. It tasted foul and he grimaced, then forced himself to down the rest in a single swallow.

'You go and lie down,' Martha advised. 'You'll sleep well tonight.'

'I need it,' he said. His body ached and his head was pounding from the worries and the pain rattling inside.

• • •

When he woke it was full day. Through the shutters he could hear the carefree music of the birds calling to each other. Slowly he sat up, looking down at the damaged arm. It still hurt a little, but it was a pain he could live with; the bone-setter had told him it would ache for a few days.

He'd never slept this late in his life. He was a creature of daybreak. As far back as he could recall that had been his hour, accompanying his father to one job or another or heading off to his own work. Lying abed was for those who had the luxuries of money and time, not for folk like him.

He washed and dressed as best he could, using water to try and remove the stains of yesterday's dried blood from his cote. Mark's killer might have done this, he thought. The colour would never go entirely, but already it was less, the water in the bowl the colour of rusted metal. They'd been looking for something obvious, and they might have been mistaken.

Walter was waiting in the hall, bouncing to his feet when John entered.

'I was worried about you,' he said. 'Dame Martha said you needed to sleep so I just sat here.'

'Did she tell you what happened?'

The boy nodded, his face in a frown. 'Did it hurt?'

'Yes. I wish you'd been there to help me,' he said honestly then shook his head. 'But that's yesterday. We have work to do, don't we?'

'Do you think we'll find him today?'

'I don't know.' He poured himself ale, washing the tastes of the night from his mouth. 'I've had a few thoughts.' He explained what he'd discovered. 'We'll walk around now. Then we'll go out again later, near dusk, when men are going home.'

The streets brought them no joy. There were few men around, most of them richly dressed, bustling about their business, or older folk seeking a way to pass the lingering hours. It was a small frustration. After an hour they returned to the boy's house on Saltergate, the worry obvious in Walter's eyes.

'Don't worry, lad,' John assured him. 'It's early days yet.'

'But the coroner might be angry.'

'There's nothing we can do about that. We'll succeed or we won't. He knows that, whatever he might say.'

'Is that you, John?' Katherine's voice came from beyond the screens. 'Come in, please.' She was sitting at the spinning wheel, her hands working the wool deftly. Her mother sat on the other side of the small room, staring into space, while the two girls played quietly in the corner. She stood and flexed her fingers. 'Would you care for some ale?'

'Thank you,' he replied.

'Walter,' she said, 'can you look after everyone? I'll sit in the garden with John.'

It was a neat, ordered plot. Most things had been harvested and the earth hoed. A pair of apple trees hung heavy with fruit, almost ripe for the picking.

'I saw Martha at the baker's this morning,' she began slowly, glancing up into his face. 'She told me about your arm. How bad is it?'

'I won't know until the cast comes off.' He took a sip from the mug, looking into the liquid and gently swirling it around.

'Does it scare you?' Katherine asked softly.

'Yes,' he admitted slowly. 'I work with my hands. It's what I've always done. It's the only thing I can do.'

'Then I'll pray it heals well.' She put a hand on his good arm. 'But the world won't end if it doesn't.'

He sighed. 'It might as well, there'll be nothing in it for me.'

'God has His plans for us all, you know, even if we can't see them.'

'It's hard for me to believe that just now.' The bitterness in his voice surprised him.

'He's testing you, John. And there are folk here who care about you. Martha, Walter, me – we know you're a good man.'

'Thank you,' he told her and smiled.

'You'll always be welcome here.'

He grinned and offered her a small bow. 'My thanks, Mistress.'

'Walter would do anything you asked, you know.'

'I'll never put him in any danger, I told you that.'

'He likes working for the coroner,' Katherine said. 'It's the first time he's ever felt important.'

He raised his face to the sky, waiting a while before replying. 'There's nothing special about it. It's just words.'

'But it makes him happy and that's important to me.' She paused. 'I know there's no real place for him in the world. He's not quite like other people.'

'He doesn't have to be. He's fine as he is. Anyone would be proud of him.'

'I am,' she assured him. 'He's very loving, he's wonderful with the girls. He looks after our mother, hard as that can be at times.'

'And you care for everyone.'

'I try.' Her smile was small and tight. 'Sometimes I feel like I'm carrying everyone's cares on my shoulders.'

'That's too much weight for a girl.'

She shrugged. 'It's nothing more than other people do. Things are what they are, there's nothing I can do to change it.'

'Are you trying to teach me a lesson?' he asked quietly.

'No.' She drew the word out. 'I'm sorry, I've spoken too much and taken your time.'

'I don't mind.'

'Good,' she said firmly. 'So do I. There aren't many I can talk to.'

'I'm honoured to be one of them.'

She began to blush, suddenly flustered. 'We should go back in.'

He followed her and took his leave, with instructions to Walter to meet in the evening. He rested through the afternoon, surprising himself by sleeping more. But at least he woke refreshed, the pain in his arm dulled.

• • •

The boy was waiting in the market place, his eyes moving intently from person to person as they passed him. He waved as he spotted John.

'Have you seen anyone?' Walter shook his head. 'Come on, let's walk.' They set off towards the church, the shadows growing. 'We'll stroll until it is dark and then we'll look in some of the alehouses,' he explained. 'Maybe we'll have more luck there.'

It was a curious procession of faces, he thought: the careworn and the hopeful, the hungry and the content, the weary and the excited, but no one with a ruddy stain on his cote, neither dark nor washed out.

They watched the workers parading out of the churchyard, and he exchanged nods with a few, waiting until the place was empty. Then they drifted along Knifesmithgate, past Martha's house where a light shone through gaps in the closed shutters. His thoughts were wandering when Walter said, 'What about him, John?'

He followed the boy's gaze. It was impossible to be certain from a distance, but there was certainly something. He didn't recognise the man, tall and raw boned with a furtive face. He wore an old cote, heavily frayed at the cuffs, ripped here and there with a large patch of discolouration across the chest.

'It could be,' he admitted. 'Do you know him?'

'That's Roger,' Walter told him. 'He used to work for the smith but he doesn't anymore.'

They waited as the man passed. He paid them no attention, his eye drawn by a girl in the distance. The stain could well be blood, John decided.

'Do you know where he lives?'

'Near the bottom of Soutergate, just up from the bridge,' the lad answered. 'He lodges there.'

'We'd better go and see the coroner.'

'Now?' Walter seemed surprised. 'But it's almost dark.'

'He wanted an answer, we'll give him one.'

CHAPTER ELEVEN

De Harville was in the parlour, his coffer open on the floor, piles of coins stacked on the table. A long-bladed knife lay close by, the blade glittering in the candlelight. Brother Robert was faithfully copying figures onto the account roll.

The coroner looked up lazily. 'Have you found our man, carpenter?' He was wearing a robe with a dark fur collar that made his hair look even more pale than usual.

'Maybe.' He nudged Walter, whose eyes were fixed on the money. 'We saw someone you should talk to.'

'You had my authority to arrest him,' he said testily.

'I doubt he'd pay much attention to us.'

'Who is it?'

'A man called Roger.' He looked at the boy, urging him to speak.

'The man who used to work for the smith.' Walter stumbled nervously over the words.

'I know him,' de Harville said with a curt nod. 'He's spent almost as much time in the stocks as Mark did. What makes you think it's him?'

'There's a large strain on the front of his cote that could be blood. Walter spotted it.'

'Did he?' The coroner raised his eyebrows. 'You've done well there, boy. I'll have the bailiffs bring him in tomorrow and question him. I heard about your mishap,' he told John.

'Word travels quickly here.'

'Gossip flies on the wind,' the monk said quietly, 'the same way it does everywhere. You'll have my prayers.'

'Thank you.' He turned to de Harville. 'I'd like to be with you when you talk to this Roger.'

'Oh?' the coroner said with curiosity. 'What can you do that I can't, carpenter?'

'For a short while you believed I'd killed Mark,' he reminded the man. 'Then you charged us with finding whoever did it. I'd like to know if he's guilty.'

'I can tell you that after I've seen him.'

'True enough, Master; but I did find where he'd been killed.'

'Go on then,' de Harville said wearily with a shake of his head. 'God's blood, you're a thorn in my side. Be here early; I'll have them roust him at dawn.'

'Yes, Master.'

• • •

'Why do you want to be there John?' Walter wondered as they walked home. 'Can I come, too?'

'Not this time,' he explained kindly. 'You've done well finding him – the coroner told you that.' Walter beamed with pride. 'There are just a few things I want to ask him, that's all. And you'll be able to earn more money if we're not hunting all over the place.'

'But I like doing things with you.'

'We'll do things where we're not looking for murderers. On Sunday again, if you like.'

'Yes, I would, please.' The lad smiled.

'Now you go on home. I need to sleep if my mind's going to be sharp tomorrow.'

'Good night John. God be with you.'

'And with you Walter. He was right, you know, you did a good job on this.' He waited until the boy's running steps had faded round the corner then let himself into the house on Knifesmithgate.

'You look happier,' Martha told him.

'We found someone who might have killed Mark. The coroner's arresting him tomorrow.'

'Who is it?'

'Roger. Walter says he used to work for the smith.'

She sighed. 'That's no surprise. He's as bad as Mark was, God rest his soul. All drinking and fighting.' She cocked her head. 'The pair of them were close once, if I remember it right.'

'Oh?'

'It was a long time ago now,' she said, as if the history was of no weight. 'He had a girl for a while. I saw them together at church with a little baby; don't know what happened to her. Must be two or three years ago. So he's the murderer, is he?'

'He might be,' John told her with a shrug. 'We'll know more tomorrow.'

'We?' she asked sharply, narrowing her eyes.

'I asked if I could be there for the questioning.'

'What makes you so interested in all this?'

He wasn't even sure himself why he wanted to be there. The answers he had given before were true enough, but they weren't the whole tale. Above all he wanted to try to understand why one man could kill another. There was already so much death and destruction in the world. If Roger was guilty, he wanted to hear him say why he had done it to try to make sense of it.

'I don't know,' he answered finally.

'What about your arm? Is it giving you much pain?'

'Not today, God be praised.'

'When I told Katherine what had happened, I thought the poor girl was going to faint.' She gazed at him shrewdly. 'I told you, she has her eye on you.'

He smiled. 'I'm away to my bed.'

• • •

He was outside the coroner's house before dawn came. The stars were clear in the sky and the air was chilly. Before long the autumn gusts would begin and the leaves would change and tumble. He pulled his cote closer around him and drew his head deeper into the hood.

A full half hour passed before he heard the bailiffs. They were on either side of the man he had seen the evening before, one holding each of his arms as he cursed and swore at them.

John stood back while they knocked on the door, then followed them into the parlour. The coroner, dressed and groomed, sat in his chair, the monk next to him, ready with his quill and his vellum. He leaned against the wall where he could watch Roger's face.

'Open the shutters,' de Harville said. The glass of the windows was thick and uneven, small panes set into lead. The light in the room was milky and pale, but enough to see Roger's face with its mix of arrogance and fear. He stood tall, his chest puffed out, but his eyes betrayed him, his gaze shifting rapidly around the room. The stink of last night's ale seeped from his skin.

The stain on his cote stood out clearly, splashed dark across his chest. The bailiff had taken Roger's knife, but John glanced down at the man's boots to see if he had another weapon there; it was a trick he'd seen men use before.

'Your name is Roger?' the coroner began.

'It is.' He had a voice that seemed to build in his chest, deep and dark.

'You'll call me sir or Master when you address me.' De Harville spoke quietly, but there were generations of authority in his words. 'Did you know a man named Mark, who was killed in the town?'

'I did … sir.'

'How did you know him?' the corner asked, sitting back and resting a hand on his chin.

'When we were young. We did our drinking together, and our whoring, too. Sir.' He grimaced as if there was bile in his mouth.

'Did you remain friends?'

'No.' He shrugged. 'I met a girl. She had a baby and I settled down for a while.' He let the sentence hang for a moment. 'Sir.'

'What about Mark?'

'He didn't want to change, Master.'

'When did you see him last?'

'Maybe two nights before he was killed. I was in the alehouse with some friends and he was there too, sir.'

'Did you talk to him?'

'Just hello and God speed.' One of the bailiffs prodded him sharply in the back. 'Sir.'

De Harville picked up a mug of ale and drank slowly, keeping his eyes on Roger.

'That stain on your cote – what is it?'

'I killed a pig last week, sir.'

The coroner raised his eyebrows in astonishment. 'Did you now? You live in lodgings but you kept a pig?'

'It was in the garden behind the house, sir.' John watched the man shift his balance slightly from foot to foot.

'And if there's blood on your knife I suppose it came from the slaughter?'

'Yes, sir.'

'So you didn't kill Mark?'

'No, sir.' Roger gave an emphatic shake of his head.

'Do you know who did?'

'No, sir, only that it wasn't me.'

'This girl you had a baby with, what happened to her?' John said.

Roger turned to face him, his eyes wide at the question. 'She went back to her mam and dad. Said I beat her.'

'Did you?'

Roger straightened his back. 'A man has the right to discipline his woman. Everyone knows that.'

John nodded slowly, as if acknowledging the point. 'What did you do with the pig after you killed it?'

'I sold it to one of the butchers in the Shambles.'

'He paid you well?'

'Well enough.'

'Most people would have had the butcher do the killing.'

Roger shrugged again and said nothing.

'Do you remember which butcher?'

'The first one I saw who offered me money.' There was sweat on his forehead, and he flexed his fingers into fists before straightening them out again.

'A pig brings good money,' the coroner said. 'You must have some left.'

'I drank it all away, sir.'

De Harville sat quietly for a minute, then ran a hand through his blonde hair and ordered, 'Take him to the goal. He can go down to Derby to stand trial for murder.'

'But I didn't do it!' the man shouted.

The bailiffs took him by the arms and bundled him away.

The coroner turned in his chair. 'You agree with me, carpenter?'

John nodded. 'I'm sure of it. I'd just like to know why he did it.'

De Harville shook his head. 'I don't understand you, carpenter. Isn't the fact that he did it enough for you?'

'No,' he answered plainly.

The coroner snorted. 'Then go and see him at the gaol if it interests you so much. He'll be there for a while yet.'

'I will, with your permission, Master.'

'You have it. What do you think, Robert? Is the man guilty?'

'As like as not,' the monk said. He turned his eyes to John. 'That was a good question about his wife and baby. Where did you hear about that?'

'Dame Martha.'

'God's blood,' the coroner complained. 'We might as well have all Chesterfield add what they know. But the brother's right, you have a strange mind for a man who works with his hands.'

'A man can have a skill and a mind.'

De Harville nodded. 'Tell that Walter he has a keen eye.'

'I will, Master. He'll be glad of the praise.'

'Don't think I've forgotten about the other murder. There's a fine line to tread and I need to walk it carefully.'

John bowed, seeing Robert wink slyly at him, then left.

CHAPTER TWELVE

The sun was full raised, burning the thin haze from the ground. Looking down into the river valley he could see a ribbon of mist clinging stubbornly to the cold water; it too would be gone soon enough.

And now he had little to fill his days. He'd visit Roger and learn what he could. But first he'd give the man some time in the gaol, a chance to ponder his own brief future among the rats and the dirt; that might make him more eager to talk.

Without even thinking, he found himself at the church. The men were clustered in small groups in the yard, some of them drinking, others talking quietly, their faces dark and serious. He saw Stephen at the ale barrel and walked across to him.

'Good day to you.'

'Not such a good one here,' the man replied.

'What happened?'

'One of the labourers fell from the church roof.'

John looked at the building, assessing the height; fifty feet, perhaps a little more, he guessed. 'Is he dead?'

Stephen shook his head.

'No, by God's blessing. But he hasn't stirred or come to yet. They've sent for the apothecary.' He spat on the ground. 'I'm beginning to think there might be a curse on this place – first Will, then you, now this.'

'There are always injuries, you know that.' He glanced at the man's arm, where the knife wound was now no more than a pale line against the sunburned skin. 'They found the man who killed Mark.'

Stephen grunted. 'Did they pay him for a public service?'

'He'll go to trial in Derby and then he'll hang.'

'Pity.'

'Did you receive a delivery of wood yet?' John asked.

'Wood?' The man looked confused. 'There's a pile of it over the other side of the church.'

The carts must have finally arrived, he thought. Not before time, too, if they were going to keep the men working.

'Are they ready to start on the spire yet?'

'Soon enough. The cross-bracing's done. They're just setting up the windlass in the tower room so they can haul up the material.'

The knowledge made him wistful. The first time he'd seen a windlass used had been in York and he'd admired the ingenuity. Two men marched endlessly inside a large wooden wheel, going nowhere but achieving a great deal. Their steps turned the axle, winding a thick rope around the wood. The rope was tied around the material and as the men walked it rose up the outside of the building. It was a simple enough device but a beautiful idea, one that made work faster and easier.

'Will you be working on the spire?'

Stephen shrugged. 'The master carpenter hasn't said yet. I hope I'm not,' he confessed. 'There'll be more men hurt and dying up there, you can lay a wager on that.'

'Maybe.' It would be dangerous, he knew that, putting up the spire piece by piece. The men would be up high, out in the air with nothing to hold them in place.

'The new master doesn't say much at all, really,' Stephen continued. 'Spends all his time with the rich folk who come around. About the only time he talks to any of us is to complain about what we do.' He turned his head and spat. 'But he does that often enough, mind.' He nodded over at the path. 'Looks like the apothecary's arrived.'

John turned to see a self-important man with a long, dark robe over his cote striding over the flags. A servant followed, carrying a large bag of the man's potions and unguents.

'You'll be back at work soon enough.'

'Better be,' Stephen grumbled. 'You know how it goes; they'll cut our wages for the time lost. When I started here this was a good place to be. We all laughed. Look at them now.'

'It's always like that when someone's hurt,' John reminded him. 'You know that.'

'Aye,' the man admitted with a sigh, 'but there's little joy here now. You're better away from it.'

'I just hope I can return.' He explained what had happened with the new fall, seeing the man wince at his description.

'God's help with your healing,' Stephen said finally. 'I'm going to the jakes and get rid of some of this ale.' He walked away, already tugging at the rope that held up his hose.

• • •

John returned to the house and lay down on his bed. He wanted to rest, but sleep was no friend to him today. He struggled to find a position that left his arm comfortable and closed his eyes. Yet his thoughts wouldn't slow down, turning around and around, pictures and ideas that spun through his mind.

Finally he rose again, put his left arm back in its sling and went back outside. The goodwives and the servants were out at their shopping, tongues clacking in conversation and gossip. He considered going to the alehouse on Low Pavement but dismissed it; all he would be doing there would be passing another hour.

He heard someone whistle and glanced up. Katherine was approaching, a young man behind her leering and saying something that made her walk faster, trying hard to leave him behind, her face close to tears. But this one was persistent, refusing to be shrugged off so easily.

John stepped into her path. 'Good day, Mistress,' he said.

At first her eyes were panicked, then relieved, swallowing hard to try and appear calm. 'Good day, Master John.'

The man hung back a few yards, suddenly less sure, his glance flickering between the pair.

'Is he bothering you?'

'Not as much as he'd like to,' she answered, regaining her courage, the colour coming back to her face.

He stared at the man. There were still youthful spots on his cheeks, angry little boils that stood out vividly on his skin. He was thin, his clothes an ill fit, old and badly worn. The youth seemed unsure what to do, whether to challenge or run, balanced on the balls of his feet.

'Are those your manners?' John asked him loudly. 'To insult a girl on the streets?'

'What business is it of yours?' He could hear a tremor of fear under the lad's bravado. 'I was just talking to her.'

'It didn't look as if she wanted to talk to you.' He took a threatening pace towards the youth.

'John,' Katherine began, steel in her voice. 'Escort me home, please.'

'She needs someone with more than one arm,' the lad said in parting.

He took the basket she was carrying and held it in his good hand.

'I'd have been fine,' she chided him. 'If you ignore them they give up.'

He had expected her gratitude, not her anger. 'I'm sorry,' he told her.

'I know you meant well.' She smiled briefly but there was still fire behind her eyes. 'And I thank you for that. But leave it be, please.'

'I will,' he promised.

'They're all harmless unless they've got ale in them. Pay them no mind.' She shook her head as if to clear it. 'Walter said they arrested a man for Mark's murder.'

'He's guilty. He'll be going to Derby to hang. It's thanks to your brother, too.'

'He told me what he saw.' She stopped at the corner of Saltergate and looked up at him. 'I know you were doing the right thing, John,' she said kindly, 'but incidents like that happen often, and there's not always a good man there. Women have to learn to look after themselves. I should go before the gossips faint with excitement.' She took the basket from him, bobbing a small curtsey. 'Come and visit again soon, Master.'

He walked away slowly, unsure how badly she had reprimanded him. She had been curt and then honeyed; frowns and then smiles. He didn't understand her any more than he'd been able to make sense of any woman he had ever met. Perhaps he should have gone to the alehouse instead.

• • •

The days passed quietly. On Saturday he wandered the market place with Martha, stopping at each stall to examine the merchandise – the softly worked leather of the glover, a taste of cheese fresh from the farm. He enjoyed the wonders of the place, its vastness, with everything under the sun on sale.

His arm ached at times, but he prayed each morning and evening that it might heal well. He passed the Shambles every day, hearing the frenzied lowing of beasts on Packer's Row as the knife took their lives, and looking into the streets for a glimpse of Geoffrey. To his knowledge the bailiffs hadn't taken him.

Sunday he paraded to the church with Martha. The first timbers of the spire protruded above the walls of the tower, rising like spindly fingers towards the heavens.

'It'll look beautiful when it's finished,' she said, awe in her voice. 'A present to the Lord.'

She was right, he knew that, but he saw it differently. In his mind's eye he saw it rising, foot by foot and heard the sounds of hammers and the curses of the men as they worked. He still found it almost impossible to believe that just the weight of the spire could keep it firmly in place, that God would keep it safe from the strong breath of the wind. Above all, he wished to be up there, working on it himself.

After the service he stood outside, with his head craned back to stare at the tower. It would progress slowly, that was obvious, but there was a beginning and that was the talk of the congregation, men pointing it out to the goodwives and children, telling them how splendid it would look, as if it would be completed in a week.

'Do you like it John?' Walter asked. He hadn't seen the boy in a few days, too wrapped in his own thoughts to seek him out.

'Good day,' he said. 'What do you think of it?'

'I don't know.' The lad frowned. 'How tall will it be?'

'More than two hundred feet to the top. You'll be able to see it for miles.'

The boy smiled. 'Would you like to walk today?'

'Yes,' he agreed suddenly. 'I'd like that.' He raised the sling. 'But I'd better be careful.' After a while he said, 'The coroner praised you for your sharp eye in spotting Roger.'

'Did he?' Walter smiled and stood a little taller.

From the corner of his eye he saw Katherine part from a group of young women and come over to join them. 'Mistress,' he said, bowing his head.

'Master John. Are you admiring it?'

'John says people will be able to see the spire from all over,' Walter told her.

She looked at him.

'It's true,' he said. 'From everywhere in this part of the county.'

'When will it be done, do you think?' she wondered.

'Maybe a full year,' he answered after some thought. 'There's not much more they can do this year or winter will destroy all their work.'

'Will you walk with us?' she asked.

'Gladly,' he agreed.

'Walter, will you see to mother and the girls, please?' Katherine asked. 'Just bring them along slowly.'

The boy dashed off.

'I was short with you the other day,' she apologised as they fell into step. He gave a nod to the coroner and Brother Robert as they passed, de Harville turning to watch the girl. 'I didn't mean to be.'

'Please, don't think anything about it,' he said, trying to keep his voice light. He had come back to the incident often in his thoughts, wondering what else he could have done.

'I was upset,' she explained. 'People forget how words can hurt; I've seen it so often with Walter. I'm the one who hears him crying in the night after people have insulted him. They think he doesn't notice, but he takes everything to heart.'

'I'll go walking with him this afternoon.'

'Would you?' She brightened, her eyes dancing. 'He was hoping so, but he hadn't seen you. He was scared you didn't like him anymore.' She shook her head at the memory. 'I told him you had a loyal heart.'

CHAPTER THIRTEEN

They took the dusty road out towards Newbold. He kept a slow, even pace, although he knew that Walter was eager to go faster. But the memory of his fall was too fresh, the consequences too awful, to risk anything else.

The sun was beginning to take on the lemon paleness of autumn, and there was a delicious freshness in the breeze. Soon enough there'd be rain, the roads muddy and heavy, and days like this would be few and far between.

'John?' Walter said, dragging him from his thoughts. 'What will happen when the spire's finished?'

'What do you mean?' he asked.

'What will you do?'

He understood now. It would be easy to give a reassuring answer, but the lad deserved the truth. 'I'll go where there's work. That's what carpenters do. It's what any craftsman does. There's always work somewhere if you're good at your trade.'

'So I won't see you anymore?'

'No.' He gave a gentle smile. 'Other people will come. New friends.'

'But I like you.'

'You're forgetting something,' he pointed out. 'Until the bone-setter takes off the cast I won't know if I can still be a carpenter. I might have damaged my arm too much.'

'Would you stay here then?' Walter asked hopefully.

John kicked at a stone and sent it skittering off into the grass. 'I don't know yet,' he said finally.

'We like you here. Me, Katherine, Martha – even the coroner likes you.'

'I think he finds me useful when he needs me,' he said with a laugh. 'Anyway, what would I do if I stayed and couldn't work with wood?'

'I don't know,' the boy admitted.

'I'm not sure if I can explain it to you, but wood talks to me.'

'Talks?' Walter turned his head sharply. 'You mean like we're doing now?'

'No, not quite.' He smiled and tried to find words the lad might understand. 'I can run my hands over it and I know where to cut it, how to shape it to what I need. The wood tells me what's right, the things I can do and the things I can't.'

'How?' he asked quizzically.

'I can't tell you. I just feel it.' He glanced over at Walter. 'Does that make sense?' The lad shook his head slowly. 'I'm sorry, but that's the only way I can say it.'

They continued out to Newbold, another of the tiny villages that dotted the countryside where a small stone chapel stood at the roadside.

'We can go further if you like,' the boy said.

'Not today,' John answered. 'I'd as soon go back and sit.'

'Would you like that?'

'Yes. Thank you.' He wasn't weary, but he was surprised at the feeling that being on these roads gave him. His body was tense and he was fearful in case he should fall again. He had never been like this before. Distance, the city, the town, the country; he'd never given it a thought, it was all one. Now he felt safer with people around. As they strolled back, he kept his eyes on the ground, planting his feet carefully, glancing up from time to time and smiling to himself to see the church tower growing closer.

At the house he was ready to leave Walter, but Katherine would have none of it.

'It's dry as bone out, you'll need some ale,' she insisted. 'I brewed fresh a few days ago. Come in and have a mug, please.'

From sitting in the hall, where Walter entertained the girls in some childish game and their mother slept, Katherine led him outside to sit on the ground in the shade of an apple tree.

He leaned back against the trunk and let his eyes close.

It was a pleasurable silence. He could hear her breathing close by, and then she leaned her head against his good arm, the feel of her pleasantly warm.

'I could stay like this for hours,' she said dreamily.

He said nothing, but there was a smile on his lips. He had ale to refresh him, good weather, and a pretty girl with a spark about her at his side. For the moment, at least, he was content.

• • •

Monday brought rain, and cooler weather swooping out of the west. The clouds hung low and threatening on the horizon. He kept the shutters closed, hearing the water against them and pitied those who had to work. Today, at least, he could feel grateful for his injury.

Martha fed him dinner, asking for his tales and he gave her stories of York, of the size of the Lady Chapel the archbishop hoped to create and the view from the top of the tower when the whole city spread out below him, covering such ground as seemed impossible.

Her eyes were entranced by his words and the pictures they put in her mind.

'I don't understand why you left it,' she told him, then her eyes narrowed shrewdly. 'It was a woman, wasn't it?'

He smiled guiltily and shrugged.

'I should have guessed,' she said, smoothing down the apron over her skirts as she stood. The green veil that covered her hair shimmered in the light. 'Running away from your responsibilities, were you?'

'There was more to it than that.'

'There always is, when a man's telling it,' Martha said acidly. 'I thought you had more about you than that.' She gathered the bowls.

'Wait,' he said. 'Please.' He wanted her to understand why he had done it, to regain her respect. He liked the woman, enjoyed being here in her house, and he didn't want their relations to be soured.

'Go on, then,' she answered, sitting again and putting her hands primly in her lap, her face set hard.

'I was courting a girl there. Her father was a mason at the Minster.'

'Did you love her?'

'Of course I did,' he replied, stung by the question.

'You'd lain together and she was having a child? It's an old story, John,' Martha told him wearily and began to rise again.

'I wasn't the only one she had lain with.'

She raised an eyebrow. 'How can you be so sure? Or did you listen to gossip?'

'There was talk,' he admitted. 'But I asked the ones who had been named and they said it was true.'

'How many of them?'

'Five.' At first he had been certain it was all lies, dark rumours to blacken her reputation, and he had gone to the first man in a fury. But he admitted it readily, laughing about it, and all John could feel was his own shame. By the third his humiliation was complete, knowing he had just been one of many. 'But her father insisted I should marry her.'

'Did he know the truth?'

He raised his eyes. 'I didn't say anything. How do you tell a man his daughter will sleep with anyone? Who would want to believe that?'

'So you came here.'

'Her father was becoming more insistent. She was more and more demanding, not the girl I'd met and wanted. Most of the time we were together I felt the sharp edge of her tongue and none of the kindness.' She reached out and placed her hand over his, her fingertips rough against his skin. 'I didn't want to end up as one of those men you see in the alehouse, cowed and cuckolded. I didn't want to have to spend the rest of my life admitting my shame every day.' He looked at her, sighed and shook his head. 'So I left York, and I didn't tell anyone I was going.'

'That's the truth?'

'Every word.'

She gave a small, sad smile. 'Then I owe you an apology. At my age I should know there's always more beneath the surface. I was too quick to judge you.' He didn't say anything. He'd brought the memory out again and it tumbled in his head. For a while at least, he had loved the girl and believed he could have been happy with her. 'There are lasses like that,' she told him. 'You're not the first to be played for a fool. But remember, men are just as bad.'

'I know.'

'Worse, from what I've seen. But don't let it sour you on all women. There are plenty of good ones out there.'

'Like Katherine?' John asked wryly.

'I told you, you could do a lot worse than her.'

'If I was looking,' he countered.

'You're looking. If you're not wed, you're looking.' She chuckled. 'And half of them that are married are looking too, come to that.'

'I've noticed that. A few years of marriage and they're looking at everything.'

'Not all of them. My husband didn't. Most of them are all talk, anyway. They'd run a mile if a girl offered herself to them.'

'Probably,' he agreed with a laugh.

'I've known Katherine since she was born. She's had a few things thrown at her in her life and she's carried on.'

'She's courted, you said?'

'You see, I knew you were interested in her.' She patted his hand lightly. 'She needs someone steady, does that girl.'

'Like a carpenter who can't even work at the moment and might not again?'

'I never claimed there was reason in love. God didn't make it that way.' She stood once more. 'Don't run from your heart, John. That's all I can tell you. But you'll do what you do, no matter what I say.'

• • •

He tried to rest in his room, but he felt as if the walls were contracting around him, closing him in. His throat felt tight, and he was restless, pacing the floor, a few steps one way, a few back. Finally he let himself out of the house quietly, pulling his hood up against the rain and holding his cote tight against his chest.

The gaol was up Holywell Street, close to the church and the cross that stood by the weekday market. It was a small stone building, one room with the cells down in the ground, the only light through a small barred window just above the ground.

The gaoler was dozing in his chair, his head snapping up quickly as the door opened.

'The coroner said I could talk to Roger.'

The man shrugged, standing and stretching lazily as he selected one of the keys from the ring on his belt. He unlocked one door and led the way down the stone steps into the darkness.

The smell was rank, harsh and cloying, a mix of urine, faeces and the stench of all the bodies who had spent time here over the years. He began to cough, feeling the bile rise in his throat.

'You'll get used to it after a while,' the gaoler laughed. 'Especially if you're here a few weeks.' He turned a key in the cell door and winked. 'Shout when you're done. If you're lucky, I might hear you.'

Roger was seated on the floor, his back against a wall where moisture ran down the stone, glistening in the half-light. He had a manacle around one ankle, connected by a chain to an iron staple in the floor.

A few days here had changed him. He was dirty, his face empty of hope, the hair matted against his head.

John stood, waiting until the man looked up and met his gaze.

'Happy to see me here?' Roger asked.

'You killed Mark. Do you think you deserve better?'

'I did the town a favour when I got rid of him.' He narrowed his eyes. 'Who are you, anyway? You're not a local man.'

'I'm the one the coroner first thought had murdered him.'

The man gave a short laugh. 'You should have. Sooner you here than me. All that's left is a journey to Derby and a rope.'

'Pray for forgiveness.'

'You pray for me.' Roger turned his head and spat. 'You helped put me here, it's the least you can do.'

'Why did you kill him?'

'Why?' Roger shook his head in surprise. 'He owed me money and he wouldn't pay.'

'That's it?'

'When you've got nothing, it's enough.'

'How much was it?'

'Sixpence,' the man said wearily. Sixpence: a day and a half's wages for a skilled man – little enough to die for.

'Don't you feel any sorrow for what you did?' John wondered.

'I'm sorry I'm here, if that means aught. If you want to do me a good turn, give the gaoler a couple of coins to buy me ale. You'd better watch him, though, he's a thief.'

'I'll do that.' A little ale for a dying man; it was charity, nothing more.

'There's something else. You'd better get your coroner over here. I want to approve someone.'

CHAPTER FOURTEEN

'Approve? Who?'

'That's for me and the coroner,' Roger said with a smug grin. 'I'll see what he offers first.'

He knew of approving, of course, a man accusing others of crimes in return for some favour; from all he'd heard it happened often.

'I'll tell him,' John said. 'But what he does then is up to him.'

'He'll be here, right enough,' the man said confidently. 'It's about a murder.'

'Whose?'

The man closed his mouth and tapped the side of his noise with a finger.

He left. There was nothing to be gained from staying. Roger wasn't about to say more to a man who had no power; he'd save his words to make a bargain. John gave the gaoler a pair of coins to purchase ale for his prisoner, watching the man's eyes gleam at the money.

The rain was still heavy, soaking him as he walked to the High Street. It was a fruitless journey; de Harville was out, the servant said, Brother Robert with him, and they weren't expected until late. He left word and made his way home.

He stripped off slowly and awkwardly, careful of his arm, and towelled his body with the scrap of linen, hanging his cote and hose to dry, dressed just in shirt and braies. Could Roger know who'd killed Will? That was the only other murder he knew of in Chesterfield. Or was it something older?

Never mind, it was the coroner's business. He would be interested, John was certain of that, but he doubted he'd soil his fine clothes at the gaol; he'd have Roger brought to him in chains and see him in the yard behind the house, where the smell wouldn't contaminate the rooms.

Roger had been right about one thing, he thought. For a man with nothing, sixpence was a fortune. It could buy him a cheap room for a week, feed him and buy him ale. He would have readily believed him, too, if the man hadn't stunk of drink when they'd questioned him. He wondered how much Roger had carried in his purse when he was arrested and whether there was anything in his room.

He lay on the bed, hearing the rain still heavy on the shutters, knowing that he would have spent the day cursing the weather if he'd been working. They'd have done precious little on the spire, but then, there'd be little they dare attempt before spring. In truth, he was surprised they'd started it at all with winter a few short months away.

He lay down and pulled a blanket up to his neck, the wool rough against his skin. Sleep came, but it was a troubled rest, peopled by folk with gargoyle faces, and bringing him back to wakefulness breathing hard, the pictures still vivid in his mind.

He sipped at some ale, letting the dream fade like mist, sitting until his heart beat more slowly. His clothes were still wet but he dressed anyway; they'd dry on his body.

Martha had set up a brazier in the hall, the warmth spreading around the room, and rushlights burning in the sconces. She sat on the bench working on her embroidery, stopping to hold the frame away from her to examine the stitches.

'Time was when I could see up close without any problem and do this all day without my eyes growing tired,' she told him. 'Eyes get old, too, John, but inside I'm the same age as

Katherine.' She gave him a bright smile. 'Remember that when the years have passed you by.' She glanced at his damp clothes that were beginning to steam in the heat. 'Where did you go?'

He told her, and she stuck the needle in the fabric, setting it aside to listen to him, asking questions about the gaol, saddened to learn of the reason behind the killing. In her eyes, though, in spite of the sympathy, he saw she couldn't understand anyone killing for so small a sum. But she'd never wanted for anything, never had to choose between somewhere to sleep and something to eat. She had a large, kind heart, but some things she would never have to comprehend.

They'd eaten supper and he was finishing the last of his ale when there was banging on the door. Brother Robert stood there, a sad, drenched figure, his habit soaked, the cowl pulled over his head.

'You left word for the coroner.'

'Come in,' John said. 'I thought he'd wait until morning, not send you out in this.'

'We've been out in it all day,' the monk answered, settling close to the heat and accepting a drink. 'What do you want?'

'I visited Roger today.'

'Did he tell you what you wanted to know?'

'In a manner of speaking,' he said slowly, 'but he also said he wants to approve.'

'Who? What?'

'He wouldn't tell me. He says he'll only talk to the coroner and see if he can have some better treatment.'

'The master will listen, but I wouldn't wager on him making things more comfortable for Roger.'

'He said it was about a murder,' John told him and Robert frowned.

'Aye, he'll definitely hear him out then.'

'How many unsolved murders do you have?'

'Four. Five, with your master carpenter.' He thought for a moment, idly chewing on his lip. 'I'll have him brought over in the morning. I suppose you'd like to be there.'

'Will your master allow it?'

'He'll complain for a while and then he'll accede,' Robert said with a chuckle. 'For some reason, he likes you. He respects you.'

'His trust flatters me,' John said as the monk stood to leave. 'Roger said he killed Mark because of a debt of sixpence. I wonder how much money Roger had in his purse when the bailiffs took him.'

'I'll ask them,' the monk said thoughtfully. 'However little it was, it'll be in their pockets now. Come in the morning, an hour after dawn.' He bowed his head slightly. 'God grant you good rest, carpenter.'

'And the same to you Brother.'

• • •

The rain passed in the night, leaving a brisk, warm wind behind. The ground was sodden, mud clinging fast to his boots as he walked along the street, the dust of the weeks before just a memory.

The servant directed him through to the cobbled yard. De Harville and the monk were in the stables. The coroner was sweetly stroking the nose of a roan, greeting it with soft words, while a stallion whinnied and snorted in another stall, eager for attention. Hay was stacked high in the loft.

'Good day Brother,' John said to the monk, and the coroner turned.

'In good time, carpenter, they haven't brought the prisoner yet. You say he wants to approve?'

'That's what he told me.'

'If he says enough we can give him more food and the promise of a quick end when the noose goes around his neck.'

He reached into his robe, took out an apple and gave it to the stallion. 'How does that sound for a bargain?'

'It's not mine to make, Master,' he answered.

'After a few more days in that place he'll probably agree to anything. Robert, go and see where they are.'

The monk limped out. When he was beyond earshot, the coroner said, 'You're a clever man, carpenter.'

'Thank you, Master.'

'But I don't know what to do with you.' John looked at him with curiosity but said nothing. 'You possess a subtle mind and you seem to learn things about people, but I don't understand you and that troubles me.'

'I'm just a man who works with wood.'

De Harville snorted and shook his head. 'If that were true you wouldn't be standing here now.'

'Would you like me to leave, Master?'

'No. You can stay. You might as well hear what Roger has to tell me.'

The monk's sandals slapped across the yard. 'They're bringing him now,' Robert announced.

In the daylight the man wasn't a pretty sight. Rats had bitten the flesh of his arms, his clothes were covered in filth, and the rusted chains and shackles weighed him down so he could only move slowly and painfully.

The coroner regarded him as he approached. 'You want to approve?' he asked.

'Maybe,' Roger said, looking around the faces.

'What crime?'

'Murder.'

'Whose?'

'The master carpenter at the church.'

John stood straighter, suddenly attentive.

'Who killed him?' de Harville said.

'What's it worth to you?' The man gave a smirk.

'If you tell me the truth, food and a clean, quick hanging.'

'And ale. He –' Roger nodded at John '– paid for some but the gaoler's watered it down.'

The coroner gave a short nod. 'If your information's good, I'll see you have all that.'

'Why should I trust you?' the man asked suspiciously.

'He gave his word.' Brother Robert spoke quietly. 'That should be enough for you.'

'Who killed the master carpenter?' de Harville asked again.

'A red-headed man named Geoffrey, lives by the Shambles.'

'Why?'

'Because he was paid to.'

The coroner glanced at John, his expression blank. The stable was silent except for the snuffling of the roan in its stall.

'Who'd pay him to do something like that?' de Harville asked finally.

'I don't know,' Roger admitted with a shake of his head.

'How do you know all this?' John wondered. He pushed himself away from the wall to stand in front of the man.

'I heard him boasting about it in an alehouse.'

'How did you know his name?'

'One of the men he was with called him Geoffrey.' Roger looked over at the coroner in desperation. 'I'm telling you the truth.'

'Had you ever seen him before?' John continued.

'No.'

'What about the people he was talking to?'

'No. I thought they were all workers on the church.' His gaze shifted around the room, uncomfortable with the onslaught of questions.

'When was this? Before or after the murder?'

'Before. About a week or so.'

John rubbed the stubble on his chin with his good hand.

'And you didn't know Geoffrey at all?'

'That's right.' There was a thin sheen of sweat on the man's face.

'Yet you know he lives in the Shambles.'

'I've seen him back in there. I watched him. People there seemed to know him.'

'Why should I believe you?' the coroner interjected, exasperation in his voice.

'I've no reason to lie.'

'You've every reason to lie if it gets you what you want,' de Harville said dismissively.

'Why do you want to approve this man?' John said.

'For what I can get,' Roger answered. 'And so I'll be prepared before God.' He gave a sly smile. 'I can see from your faces that you know who I'm talking about. Do we have a bargain … Master?'

'Take him away,' the coroner ordered the bailiffs. 'Give him food and see that the gaoler doesn't water his ale.' He paced angrily around the stable then stopped in front of John, his face red, fury in his eyes. 'It seems you were right about this red-head Geoffrey. That should make you happy.'

'It doesn't,' he said simply. Too many things remained unexplained.

De Harville began to pace again, hands clasped behind his back. 'What do you think of what he said?'

'I don't understand it,' John admitted. 'I don't see why anyone would pay Geoffrey to kill Will.'

'An angry husband perhaps?' Robert offered.

'No,' de Harville said. 'Do you believe him?' he asked John.

'He had no reason to lie, he was right in that,' he said after a moment then paused. 'But he had no reason to tell all the truth, either.'

'God's blood!' The coroner's face was red. 'You weigh one side, then the other and you come down right in the middle. Was he telling the truth or not?'

'I think he was,' John said. He looked at the monk, and Robert nodded his agreement.

De Harville blew out a long breath. 'So now I need to send men into the Shambles to arrest this damned Geoffrey. This spire had better be one of the wonders of God's creation for all the trouble it's causing.' He turned to Brother Robert. 'You'd better give the bailiffs their orders. Tell them not to be afraid to break heads if they need. I want them back here with this man, and to do it without causing a riot.'

They watched the monk leave. The coroner shook his head. 'So you've no idea why anyone would want your friend Will dead?'

'No. Geoffrey had threatened to kill him, but that was back in the spring.' He shrugged. He didn't have an answer, he couldn't think of anyone, or any reason.

'We'll have to make sure he tells us then,' de Harville continued. 'I'll send word when they have him.'

CHAPTER FIFTEEN

John walked along, hearing the bright prattle-prattle of the goodwives as they darted from shop to shop, their baskets heavy with breads and cheeses. The more he tried to think about the murder, the less sense it all made.

He prayed that the bailiffs would take Geoffrey easily and that he'd tell them the truth. Right now it all stood before him like a maze. He stopped at a cookshop to buy a pie and took it to the alehouse on Low Pavement. Four men sat in one corner, their heads low, conversing quietly. He paid them no mind, eating and drinking, lost in his thoughts.

Shouts roused him, the sound of yelling and blows from over in the Shambles. The bailiffs had entered. The other men drained their mugs and left, curious at the violence. The noise grew louder, and he watched through the window as people gathered in the street, keeping a safe distance; the women fearful and the men just relieved not to be part of it.

It lasted a few minutes and then gradually quiet returned. Slowly he finished the ale, brushed crumbs from his cote and stood.

'Another, Master?' the alewife asked hopefully, her face falling as he shook his head and left.

For once, Packer's Row was empty, the shutters closed tight on the shops for all that it was the middle of the day.

At the house, Martha was asking questions even before he had closed the door.

'What's going on? I was out in the garden and I could hear people shouting. I thought war had come here.'

'The bailiffs went into the Shambles to arrest someone,' he told her.

'Did they find him?'

'I don't know. It ended soon enough so perhaps they did.'

'Who were they after?'

He explained it all to her, fetching ale and sitting beside her on the bench.

'It's a bad business,' Martha said when he had finished.

'If they've caught Geoffrey, we may know the truth soon,' he offered.

'Maybe.' She sounded doubtful.

'If he confesses then that's an end to things,' John said.

'Is it?' She glanced at him sharply. 'You don't look like you think so.'

'No,' he admitted with a sigh. 'I don't. Not if someone really did pay him to kill.'

'Do you believe that?'

'I do,' he answered after a while. 'It seems such an unlikely thing that I can't imagine Roger putting it in unless it was true.'

'Who'd gain from a murder like that?'

He shook his head in frustration. 'That's it. There's no one that I can see.'

'I wish you weren't involved in all this,' she said.

'I am, though.' He gave her a tight smile.

'I worry something will happen to you. I've come to like having you here, John Carpenter.'

'No one's interested in me,' he assured her.

'I pray God that's true.'

'It is.'

Before she could say more, someone banged at the door and he was grateful for the distraction. He had come to feel like he could have a home here, a dangerous sentiment for a man who might leave in a few weeks.

'The coroner wants you to come,' Brother Robert said.

'They caught him?'

'Just come now, Master.'

He kept slow pace with the monk down Knifesmithgate, seeing the pain on the man's face with every step.

'Have you asked the apothecary to give you anything?'

'There's no cure for old age.' Robert forced a smile. 'It's worse when the seasons turn. I talked to the bailiffs. They swore Roger's purse was empty when they took him.'

John nodded.

De Harville was in his parlour, fingers drumming impatiently on the table.

'You wanted me, Master?' John asked. The monk took his seat quietly.

'I sent in four bailiffs. One has a broken head, one was stabbed in the arm and Geoffrey got clean away.' His voice was tense. 'What do you think of that?'

'Have you sent men after him?'

'Of course I have,' the coroner shouted, his anger boiling over. 'But I want to know what it all means. You tell me that.'

'I wish I knew.'

'Then find out,' he ordered. 'Use that lad with the sharp eyes and bring me some answers.'

'I'll try, but –'

De Harville slapped his hand down hard on the wood, the crack of sound filling the room for a moment.

'I don't want excuses,' he shouted. 'If someone paid the man for murder, I want to know who it was and why.'

'Yes, Master.'

'My men will find Geoffrey. You bring me the reason.' He sighed as the fire in his eyes burned out and he drank deep from a cup of wine. 'This whole affair is vexing me. I want it over and done.' He looked up. 'Well, carpenter, you have your task.'

• • •

How, he wondered. How could he discover what the coroner needed? How did he even begin when he had no idea what to search for? All they had for proof was an overheard conversation in an alehouse.

De Harville wanted him to use Walter, but he didn't want the lad involved. If there really was money, then there was danger and the boy was better away from that. He was too trusting, too open.

John made his way to the gaol. Holywell Street was quiet; a cart passed carrying stone for the church, the ox weary in its traces, the driver frustrated as he used the whip. The gaoler let him in reluctantly, escorting him to the cell in silence. John held his breath against the stink for as long as he could.

Roger was as he been before, slumped against the wall, but this time he had a mug of ale at his side and an empty bowl pushed away on the dirt floor.

'I thought someone would come,' he said with a sly smile.

'The coroner kept his promises.'

'Aye, he did,' the prisoner acknowledged. 'I'll grant him that.'

'Which alehouse were you in when you saw Geoffrey?'

'The one down on Soutergate,' Roger answered. 'Why?'

'How did you come to overheard him?'

Roger shrugged. 'The place was busy and I was standing close by.'

'What about the other men with him?'

'I told you before, I didn't know them.'

'How many were there?'

He thought for a while. 'Three, perhaps; I was listening to his words, not giving them any mind.'

'If you didn't know Geoffrey, how did you learn his name?'

'One of the others used it. I told you that.' He grinned, showing brown, broken teeth. 'You don't believe me, do you?'

'Should I?'

'I'm telling you the truth.'

'What else did Geoffrey say?'

'Just that he was going to kill the master carpenter and someone was giving him good coin to do it.'

'Did he mention any names?'

'No,' Roger replied firmly.

'What else can you tell me?'

'There's nothing more to tell,' the man said. 'Just a few snatched words, that's all. Do you work for the coroner?' He nodded at the broken arm. 'Can't be easy with that.'

'It's not.' He yelled for the gaoler. 'You'd best make your peace with God.'

'Him or the devil, it'll be one of them.' He shrugged. 'As long as I go to the gallows drunk, I don't really care.'

Back outside the gaol, he breathed the sweet air deeply. He knew nothing more than he had before, but at least he was convinced that the man was telling the truth. It rang all through his story. A liar would have added more to make an elaborate construct. This lacked detail and that made it real.

But it still offered him nowhere to start, no thread he might unravel. Come evening he could go to the church and seek out James, the one who'd believed he had seen Geoffrey back in town. He might have something. It was a slender chance, but the only one he had for the moment.

But that was still hours away. He looked up at the sky, willing the time to pass quickly.

'What are you looking at, John?'

He shook his head and smiled. 'Nothing, Walter. I'm just idle today.'

'I saw you come out of the gaol. Did you go to see Roger?'

'Yes. I had some questions for him. It wasn't anything important.'

'What's it like in there?'

'It's dank and it's dirty, and maybe Hell itself smells like that,' he said, the sadness strong in his voice. 'It's not a place where anyone would choose to spend their time.'

The boy frowned. 'Did you hear what happened earlier?' he asked.

'In the Shambles?'

Walter nodded. 'They said the coroner sent in the bailiffs to find Geoffrey but he escaped.'

'He did.'

'Are you looking for him?'

John laughed. 'That's not my job, praise God. He's sent men out to do that.'

'I liked working for him.'

'It would be better if he paid you a wage for it, though. Not that he would think of that.'

'Do you think they'll catch Geoffrey?'

'If they can find out which way he went, they'll probably be dragging him back here tomorrow. Anyway, don't you have work to do?'

'I just wanted to stop and talk to you,' Walter said, hurt in his voice and his eyes.

'I'm glad you did,' John told him and saw the boy brighten again, his expression changing as quickly as summer weather.

'Do you think he'll want our help again?'

'He might. Just don't sell yourself short if he does,' he advised. 'Tell him you want paying for it next time.'

'I will.' With a wave he ran off down the hill towards Beetwell Street.

For a moment he regretted not saying anything to the lad about the task he had been given. Walter would have loved the importance and the adventure. He knew what Martha would have advised, to ask the lad himself if he wanted to be involved. And Walter would have agreed without a second thought. For now, though, there was nothing he could do, nothing anyone could do.

His arm itched under the cast and he cursed it. If he hadn't been so clumsy he wouldn't be standing here now, having to ask himself these questions. He could be working like an honest man.

• • •

He waited until the shadows were lengthening before going to the churchyard. The first of the workers were coming out of the building, some with their shoulders hunched against the end of the day, other stretching tall at their freedom. He spotted Stephen already at the ale barrel, draining one mug, then a second as he walked over to join him.

'Thirsty?'

'Drink where it's free,' the man laughed and winked. 'Saves money later.'

'That's true enough.' He nodded at the tower. 'Are they staying busy up there?'

Stephen shook his head. 'Too windy today. Did you hear the engineer's gone?'

'No. What happened?'

He shrugged. 'No idea. He was here one day, didn't show up the next. The master carpenter's in charge up there now.'

'Do you know where James is?'

'James? He's gone too.' He finished a third mug of ale. 'You're better off away from here. I think six have left since you broke your arm, and the replacements don't know anything; these local lads can barely hammer in a nail.'

'Why did he leave?'

'All I know is that he and the master carpenter ended up in a row that would have woken the devil. I thought they were going to come to blows. Then James took his pay, picked up his tools and went.'

'Do you know where?'

'No.' He shook his head. 'Somewhere he'll find good money, if he has any sense.'

The night was drawing closer. Half the men had gone from the churchyard, the remainder talking in small groups, their bags of tools slung over their shoulders.

'Who else might remember Geoffrey, do you know?'

Stephen thought for a moment, chewing the skin at the side of his thumbnail. 'No one really. He left back in the spring, didn't he?'

'That's right.'

'There are only a few of us still here from that time. Did you talk to Thomas?'

'I tried,' John said wryly.

'Aye, he doesn't have much to say, does he?' he laughed. 'I don't think there's anyone else who knew him. I heard he's been accused of Will's murder.'

'He was living in the Shambles, but ran when the bailiffs went in for him. They're after him now.'

Stephen raised his eyebrows. 'He might as well have said he's guilty.'

'Can you think of anyone who'd pay to have Will killed?'

'Pay?' He gave a low whistle of astonishment. 'Why would anyone do that?'

'I don't know,' John said. 'It's just something I'd been told.'

'I wouldn't believe it. Even the ones who didn't like him here respected him.'

'Except Geoffrey.'

'Aye, well, I'd forget it if I were you,' Stephen said. 'How's the arm? When are you coming back? We need someone with real skills.'

'I keep praying it heals properly.'

'God's blessing on that.' He put down the mug. 'May He go with you, too. If I don't leave now I'll still be here in the morning.'

John stood there long after Stephen had left, until he could no longer make out the base of the spire jutting above the tower, and then turned for home.

• • •

In the morning, he walked out along Holywell Road, passing the well where the town ended and the countryside really began. It was no more than ten minutes' walk to the dwelling that sat alone at the edge of the road.

It was a tumbledown cottage, but Will had done some work on it, putting up new shutters and a fresh door, cleaning up the thatch and the stonework. It was a place to live, though, not a home, and he could sense the sorrow that lay all around as he knocked on the door.

'Mistress,' he said, and bowed his head as she answered. 'We met at your husband's funeral.'

'I remember,' she said guardedly, keeping a tight hold on the door. She was a drab woman, her hair gathered close under an old wimple, her eyes washed-out and her cheeks pale.

'I'd like to ask you a few questions about your husband if I might?'

'Why? I thought they were already after the man who killed him.'

'The coroner sent out men, but he asked me to look into things, too.'

'You? Why?' She looked confused. 'I thought you said you were a carpenter. Now you're telling me you work for the coroner?'

He held up the arm in its sling.

'I can't do much carpentry with this, Mistress.'

'What do you have to do with the coroner?' Her mouth was a thin line, her voice suspicious and wary.

'He's ordered me to help.' It was the simplest explanation he could offer.

'Come in,' she said finally.

The room was spotlessly clean, a bed standing in one corner with a small chest at the foot, the rushes fresh on the floor. A table sat by the wall, two chairs pushed against it.

'Sit down,' she told him. 'I'll bring you some ale.'

He waited until she was seated, then said, 'I wouldn't ask you these things if I didn't have to. I don't want to bring you more pain.'

'The pain's there every morning when I wake up without him and it's still there when I go to sleep,' she said, her voice dull and empty. 'How can you bring me more than that?'

'He was a good man.'

'Aye, he was,' she agreed, her eyes beginning to glisten with tears.

'I feel guilty, Mistress. I've come to ask you questions and I don't know your name.'

'Alice,' she replied softly.

'Had he had any arguments with people at work? Did he say anything?'

'Will never said much about what happened there. There's man's work and there's family. I didn't ask.'

'Nothing at all?'

She shook her head. 'It wasn't his way; never had been as long as I knew him. I respected that. We were happy together, he earned a good wage.'

'Did he have friends in the town?'

'A few to say "God speed" to when we went to church on Sunday,' she said after some thought, 'maybe some he drank with on a Saturday night, I don't know.'

'How was he in the days before he died?'

'What do you mean?' Her eyes looked down and her hands were locked together so tightly that her knuckles were white.

'Did he seem worried about anything?'

'Will never carried his cares lightly,' Alice told him. 'There was always something pressing on him, no matter where he worked.' She paused. 'But maybe a little more before he died.'

'And he said nothing to you about it?'

She shook her head again quickly, her mouth tight.

'Mistress, I'm just trying to uncover the truth about what happened to your husband.' He kept his voice low and gentle, wanting her trust. 'He never confided in you at all?'

'No. He said it would be wrong to burden me, that it would only make me unhappy.' Her eyes widened. 'But he talked in his sleep sometimes.'

'What did he say?'

'Just little words, mostly.' She began kneading her fingers against each other. 'Mostly I couldn't even make them out.'

'But there was something you heard?'

She nodded sadly. 'About a week before ...' She paused, not wanting to say the words and invoke the memory. He let the silence lie until she cleared her throat. 'He sat up in the middle of the night and said, "I can't do what they want", as clear as you speaking to me. Then he lay down again. I asked him in the morning and he didn't remember it. He said the nightmare must have come calling.'

'And nothing else?'

'No.' The word was just a whisper.

'Thank you, Mistress,' he said. 'What will you do now?'

She sighed. 'I have a sister in Lincoln. I'll go to her; she's a widow too. The carter is coming for all this next Monday.'

'God speed you on your journey.'

'It's one I'd sooner not have to make.' Her voice was bleak and her eyes distant. 'But there's nothing for me here.'

He stood. She'd told him the little he knew. The memories of her husband might torment her now, but soon her mind would polish them into comforts for the long evenings.

'Your arm,' she said, 'will it heal enough for you to return to work?'

'If God's willing.'

'I'll offer my prayers,' Alice told him. 'You're like Will, I can tell, you like to work with wood.'

He gave a small bow of thanks. 'It's what I was born to do.'

'It's a pity you never had chance to know him. I think you'd have made good friends. I hope you find the man who took him from me, Master. I hope that with all my heart.'

• • •

I can't do what they want. He gnawed at the words as he walked back into town, trying to find some reason in them, to unlock them. But they could be anyone, and he had no idea what they might have wanted of Will.

It might have been exactly what he claimed, a nightmare that visited and claimed him for a while. By the time he reached the market square his mind felt frustrated and tangled. He bought a pie at the cookshop, eating it slowly as he tried to find something to follow in his thoughts.

But there was no path to take, no landmark he could see. He was dragged away from his thoughts by a hubbub of voices, a group of men walking down the High Street, one of them leading a pack horse with a corpse slung over his back, a gaggle of men and women in their wake. He stuffed the rest of the pie in his mouth and hurried off to the coroner's house.

They were gathered outside, the questions and rumours flying through the air. John pushed his way through the small crowd and caught Brother Robert's eye. The monk gestured and he went into the yard.

The men were dirty, their hose stained and boots sodden. One held a dog on a rope, the animal contentedly working at a bone, the meat still red and raw where it clung. Another man was sawing through the bonds that had held the body to the horse before pushing it off to land heavily on the cobbles.

The red hair was wild, matted with small twigs, and the eyes stared sightlessly towards heaven.

'Who found him?' de Harville asked, his voice raised to make himself heard. The man with the dog came forward, dragging the hound behind him.

'I did, sir.' He sketched a small bow. 'This one did, anyway.'

'Who killed him? I wanted him brought back alive.'

'He was already dead, sir.'

CHAPTER SIXTEEN

The men started to all talk at once, a welter of words that wound around each other. Finally, the coroner raised his hand for silence.

'You,' he said, pointing to the man with the dog. 'Tell me what happened.'

The man looked at the others, nodding at one, then at a second face.

'He had a good start on us, sir. It wasn't until last evening someone said they'd spotted him on the road to Bolsover. A couple of us went to the village, but they hadn't had any sign of him there, and we thought he might be in all those woods over that way.' He glanced at de Harville, who nodded for him to continue. 'When it was light we could start looking properly.' He jerked on the rope to bring the dog to heel. 'It was this 'un who found him. Smelled the body. Then we brought him back here. Killed himself rather than be taken.' He smiled proudly.

John glanced at the coroner. The man was frowning, chewing on his lower lip.

'How did he die?'

The man pushed at Geoffrey's head with the toe of his boot. 'Cut his own throat.'

The gash was wide and deep, most of the blood drained away from it.

'Where was the knife?' John asked, and the men turned to him in surprise.

'I see this drew you, carpenter,' de Harville said with a nod. 'You can answer him,' he told the man.

'Right by him. Jacob brought it.'

Another man, taller and thinner than the rest, dressed in the old style with a knee-length patched tunic, took a dagger from the horse's pack and held it up. The blood had dried on the blade, a deep, rusted red that coated the steel. He placed it next to the body.

John opened his mouth to speak, but de Harville quieted him with a sharp look.

'You've done your duty well, men,' the coroner said. 'I thank you all. Go to your beds and rest.' He waited until they'd dispersed and the yard was empty. Brother Robert closed the gates and joined them, making the sign of the cross over Geoffrey and mouthing a prayer. 'You don't need to say it, carpenter, but he's dead. Let that be the end of it.'

'He's dead right enough, but he wasn't the one who did it. You know that as well as I do. Men don't cut their own throats.'

De Harville shook his head and paced. 'Does it matter? Maybe one of the men killed him and they're saying nothing.' He nodded at the corpse. 'There's Will's murderer and justice has been done.' John knelt by the body, picked up the knife by the handle and tried to fit it in the empty sheath. It was too long and too thin, not the one that belonged there. 'What of it?' the coroner asked in frustration when John looked up. 'Does anyone care if he was murdered? Call it retribution. What do you say, Brother?'

The monk kept his head low, his lips moving silently. John stayed on his knees, the fingers of his good hand tracing Geoffrey's flesh.

'From the feel of him, he's been dead quite a few hours,' he said. 'Do you think they would have waited until now to bring him in if they'd killed him yesterday evening? They could have been home in their beds and not missing another day of work.'

'Leave it, carpenter. We have our man.' He began to walk towards the house.

'I thought you wanted me to find out the reason. We still don't know who paid him to kill Will.'

'If anyone ever did,' the coroner answered over his shoulder. 'You told me yourself that they had an old grievance. The only person saying your corpse was paid to kill is a murderer himself. I know what I said before, carpenter, but it's time to leave this be.' He closed the door behind him.

Jesu, John thought, the man was as changeable as the weather. 'What do you think, Brother?'

Robert looked down at the body pityingly, then lowered himself slowly and painfully to close the man's eyes. 'Have you found any reason someone would pay to have your master carpenter killed?'

'No,' he admitted. 'Not yet.'

'Maybe the master's right.' He pushed himself up with his arms, wincing as he straightened. 'All you have is Roger's word that someone was paying Geoffrey. We've found our murderers, justice has been done.'

John shook his head. 'There's more here. I can feel it.'

'God sees the truth of everything,' the monk told him. 'He doesn't always reveal it to us. I need to see to this man's burial.'

Alone, he looked at Geoffrey one last time. Whatever secrets he kept had gone with him. He closed the gate behind him.

• • •

The men had gathered in the alehouse on Low Pavement. John guessed that they'd celebrate before resting, washing down the dust of the hunt. He paid for a flagon of ale and took it over to the bench.

'Thank you, Master,' said the man with the dog. The animal was lying among the rushes, still concentrating on its bone.

'I'd just like to know, and please tell me the truth,' John asked them, 'was he truly dead when you found him or did you kill him? The coroner doesn't care either way, he's just glad it's done.'

The men look at each other with no guile in their eyes.

'It's exactly the way Alan said,' another told him. 'He was there with his throat slashed and the knife at his side.'

'I believe you,' he said with a nod. 'Can you tell me where you found him?'

Between them they gave him directions. It had been about two miles short of Bolsover, off along a charcoal burner's track into the woods. He asked enough questions to ensure he would find the right spot, before he thanked them, leaving the ale behind for them to share.

The coroner and the monk seemed content to leave it with Geoffrey's death, but John wasn't ready to stop worrying at it yet. There were too many questions without answers – the knife that didn't fit the sheath, the way Geoffrey had died … the man had run, but someone had known where to find him. This murder could well have been to prevent the man ever saying who'd paid him to do his killing.

He wanted to walk out there, to look at the place himself, but he didn't want to go alone. The memory of falling and breaking his arm was too fresh, too painful, for him to choose to be out that far by himself. It was no more than a few miles, but the thought brought a chill to his spine. He needed a companion.

At the house on Saltergate, Katherine answered the door, smiling to him and quickly pushing the long hair back over her shoulders and smoothing down her skirts.

'This is a pleasant surprise, John.' A flush rose on her neck and into her cheeks.

'The pleasure of seeing you is all mine,' he said with a gallant flourish, watching her colour deepen. 'I'm looking for your brother today, though.'

'He's off delivering messages. I doubt he'll be home before dark. He'll be somewhere in town if you want to find him.'

'It can wait. Could you ask him to come in the morning? I'd like his help, if he's free.'

'You know he'll make time for you,' she told him merrily. 'Please, come in and have some ale.' In the hall the young girls were carding and combing well, concentrating on their tasks as the woman in the chair stared blankly ahead, the wimple tight around her empty face. Katherine led him through to the garden. 'They'll be fine without me for a few minutes. Now,' she said eagerly, 'tell me the news. I heard they brought a body into town this morning.'

He gave her the truth of it, better than all the tittle-tattle she had hear from the goodwives, explaining why he wanted Walter to go with him.

'What do you think you can learn by going out there?' she asked.

'Probably nothing,' he answered with a bemused laugh. 'But all I have right now is time.'

'John,' she began tentatively, 'what will you do if you can't continue as a carpenter?'

He sat still, toying with the ale she had given him. However much he tried to banish the question it returned every time his arm itched or ached under the cast. And he didn't have an answer.

'I don't know.'

She reached out and took his good hand, watching under her lashes to see if he pulled away. He curled his fingers lightly around hers.

'I pray for you, John.'

'Thank you.'

The girlish voices inside erupted into loud argument and Katherine marched into the house. Just her presence quieted her sisters.

'I should go,' he said. The brief magic had gone. She looked up at him, sadness in her eyes. 'Can you ask Walter to come after first light?'

'I will.'

She showed him to the door. Beyond the screens, where no one else could see, he kissed her gently on the forehead and the cheek. He bent his mouth to her ear. 'Thank you once more, Mistress.'

• • •

The day felt like bright autumn. Light clouds skittered across the sky and the sun shone pale. Walter had arrived with the dawn, staying for ale before they took the road east, down into the valley, over the ford and up the hill beyond.

He found a stout branch and gripped it between his legs before smoothing it into a staff with his knife while the boy watched every movement of his hand.

'How do you do that, John?'

'Do what?'

'Work the wood like that.'

'It's like I told you, it talks to me.'

'I didn't hear it.' Walter laughed loud at his own joke, pleased with his wit, and they strolled on.

The path was exactly where the men had said, a thin snake of bare earth that wound between two fields to the woods at the top of the hill. In the distance he could hear the rhythmic chopping of a pair of axes.

'Up there,' he said, letting the boy lead the way. He lost his bearings between the trees, casting around for anything to help him. Eventually he could see where the grass had been trampled down and followed it through to a clearing

'Here.' There was a stain in the earth that still felt sticky to his fingers. When he brought them to his nose he could smell the iron tang of blood. He walked around the area slowly, but too many had been here for it to tell him anything useful.

'Move around and keep your eyes open for a knife,' he instructed the boy, but after ten minutes they'd found nothing. Finally he had to admit that the journey had been wasted.

'Do you want to go back, John?' Walter asked.

'Not just yet.' The sound of the axes returned. 'Let's go over and ask them if they saw anything.'

The two men had a flagon of ale, working for five hard minutes, then taking a short break to drink, leaving their axes embedded in the thick trunk of the oak.

'God's blessing on you,' John cried from a distance, making sure not to startle them, watching as they nodded their wary greeting to him. 'Were you out here yesterday?'

'Aye.' One of them glanced over his shoulder at the tree lying on the ground. 'Takes a good day to fell one of them. More for some of 'em. Why?'

'Did you see the men out here?'

The man took a drink and passed the bottle to his companion. Small chips of wood were scattered across his chest and in his hair. He had stripped off his hose, standing in just his braies and boots, sweat running freely down his face.

'Heard them,' he answered. 'Not our business. Sounded like they found who they wanted anyway.'

'Had you seen him? A short man, with red hair?'

The man pursed his lips, looked at the other man and they both shook their heads.

'Was there anyone else around?'

'Just us. And the steward, evening afore last. He come up to check we was working hard. Daft bugger. What does he think, these fall over by themselves?'

'What's the wood for?'

The man shook his head. 'Don't know. They never tell us. We just chop it down and get some beasts up here to haul it away. It's Sir Henry's wood, he arranges the sale. It's just folk like us who do the work. I'll tell you something though, it's the best oak in the manor up here.' He reached out and patted the tree affectionately. 'Brings in good money: you know wood?' he asked.

'John's a carpenter,' Walter said proudly.

'Oh aye?' the man said. 'Not much use like that, though, are you? Accident?'

'Yes,' he replied without explanation, and stroked the tree trunk lightly, feeling the roughness of the bark against his fingertips, the grain and the life in the wood. 'You're right, it's good oak.'

'I'd offer you a drink afore you go, but there's only enough for the pair of us,' the man apologised. 'Don't expect to see strangers up here.'

'We'll be fine,' he smiled. 'It's not far back. Thank you. God give you good day.'

'Aye, I hope you find what you need.' He rubbed his hands and pulled his axe out of the wood as easily as plucking a flower. The constant, even rhythm of the blades accompanied them through the woods and down the track.

'What are you thinking, John?' Walter asked as they reached the road.

He shook his head and gave a short bark of a laugh. 'That I'm a fool to my own ideas. I thought I'd find something out here to show how clever I was.'

'But there wasn't anything to see,' Walter said, confused.

'I know. Perhaps the coroner's right.'

'What do you mean?'

'Roger's going to hang for killing Mark and Geoffrey's already dead. Maybe I'm just seeing confusion where there's really none.' He leant on the staff as the rocky path wound downhill, taking each step cautiously and carefully. Dear God, was he going to be like this for the rest of his life, afraid to stride out? He was like an old man, creeping along, scared of everything life might bring. If he left Chesterfield it would takes him weeks to reach anywhere else at this pace.

• • •

In his room he put the bag of tools on the bed, taking each one out and hefting it in his good hand. Working slowly, he rubbed the metal with the oiled cloth, the smell familiar and welcoming and he worried whether he'd ever use them again. The thought of his father came unbidden into his mind and he wondered if he would ever have a son of his own, someone to teach and pass the tools on to. They were his legacy and his livelihood, more than most men had. God had given him this gift with wood. He had used it well, he believed, and prayed that He wouldn't take it from him.

He packed the tools away again, feeling the arm itch under the cast, a torment he could do nothing to ease. The bone-setter had warned him that it might become worse, but that it was a good sign; it meant the bone was knitting together well. With the Lord's good grace, in a few weeks he'd be back at his trade.

He hefted the satchel before returning it to the chest in the corner, the weight comfortable and natural. In the buttery he poured himself an ale and wandered through to the hall. Martha was sitting on the bench, a cushion plumped at her back, her wimple crisp and white over her hair. She had fabric stretched over a hoop, her needle moving deftly, a frown of concentration on her face.

Finally, after finishing a row of stitches, she looked up.

'You have a strange face on you,' she said.

'I've just been thinking.' He sat on the joint stool.

'I can see that.' She set the embroidery aside. 'Not good thoughts, by the look of you.'

'Not all of them, no. Sad.'

'Thinking about the future?' she asked sympathetically.

'If there is one.'

'There's a reason God doesn't let us see what's ahead of us, John,' she told him quietly.

'I just want to know what to expect when this comes off.' He held up the sling.

'You have time to plan. He's given you that blessing.' She flexed her fingers and he saw the small pain in her eyes.

'It hurts?'

'Just age.' She held out her hand. 'You see the brown spots on there?' He nodded. 'Age,' she told him. 'Do you see the way the knuckles have grown big and the fingers change their shape. That's age, too.'

'It'll happen to me?'

'It might, if God spares you that long,' she told him. 'Live this long and you don't worry about what might happen weeks and months in the future. You give thanks each day you wake.'

'You make it sound like you might die tomorrow.'

'I might,' she said, an edge to her voice. 'I know that full well, believe me. Any of us could. You know that, too.' He nodded his agreement sadly. 'Be grateful for what God has given you, John. Look at you, you have your strength, you have your health. You have a good mind – even the coroner can see that. If God takes one thing from you, He'll give you another.'

'He'd be taking the thing I love.'

She let out a slow breath. 'You can love more than one thing in your life. You'll see that.'

'Maybe,' he said doubtfully.

'You listen to me,' she told him firmly. 'I've been on this earth a lot longer than you and I've learned some things. I'm telling you the truth.' She leant forward and patted him on the knee.

'The black times happen, but give God your trust and they'll pass.'

'I don't have much choice, do I?' He gave a small, wan smile.

'No,' she agreed, 'you don't. You need to remember that. Whatever happens, there's plenty for you here. You have a home in this house, friends, a girl who has her eye on you; that's a good start. There's always work for those who look for it.'

'You're likely right.'

'Of course I'm right,' she laughed gently. 'You've hardly been here two minutes and you already have more than some people manage in a lifetime. Think about that.'

'I will,' he promised.

'Did you find anything today?'

'No.'

'Leave it be,' she advised. 'None of this was ever your problem, John Carpenter. No one will think any less of you. Robert de Harville has what he wanted and he might never have done it without you. Some tales have an ending, you know.'

'I know.' He drained the mug and stood. 'I think I'll walk a while.'

'You do that. But think about what I said. God has his plan for you.'

• • •

He ended up at the church. Although it was still just afternoon, the men were standing around, drinking ale and talking. Another accident, he thought. This place was having too many of them lately.

'What happened?' he asked one of the workers who was passing, a face he had never seen before – young and fresh and pale now.

'Someone fell from the tower.' The hand holding the mug was shaking slightly. 'Landed on the path over there.'

'Dead?'

The man nodded, his eyes haunted.

He glanced upward at the low wall around the top of the tower. They'd have added a ceiling to the tower room before starting the spire. It would be all too easy for a man to take a tumble over that, with the ground more than a hundred feet below.

'Do you know who it was?' he asked.

'Someone said his name was Stephen.' The young man shrugged. 'I don't know, I've only been here a few days.'

John crossed himself. Another good man gone. 'Go with God,' he said and walked away. Maybe it was best that he wasn't working here, after all. It could have been him toppling and giving the long scream that would end so quickly. The church was being built on blood.

He saw Walter in the market place and waved, but he was in no mood for talk. The boy seemed to sense that, smiling back but keeping his distance. John went to the alehouse on Low Pavement and ordered a quart of ale, looking around the other faces in the small room. Most of them showed vanished hope, souls who survived one day and then another.

He drank deep, giving a silent toast to Stephen and wishing him a short time in purgatory. More would die, too, before the spire was raised. The taller it grew, the greater the danger for anyone working on it. At least it would be impossible to do much more on it before spring, when the weather warmed and the frost and ice passed, and the cruel winter winds had ended.

Before he knew it he'd finished the drink and called for another. He sipped more slowly, wary of losing himself in the ale. He'd find out when they were burying Stephen and go. It was all he could do for him now. They'd talked several times but he knew nothing about the man, not where he was born, what kin he had, if he even had a woman and children.

'Deep in thought?' The quiet words pulled him out of his head as Brother Robert sat down on the other side of the bench. 'You've heard what happened?'

'Yes. You've been there?'

'The coroner has to examine all deaths.' He shook his head. 'At least it was quick, God rest his soul. Did you know him?'

'A little,' John answered. 'Not enough.'

'It's never enough, is it?' The monk smiled kindly.

'I didn't think your order would let you in places like this.'

The brother grinned. 'They don't deny us all life's pleasures. The most tempting don't interest me anymore, anyway. Have you given up on looking into the murders?'

'I went out to where they found Geoffrey.'

'Did you see anything?'

'There was nothing worthwhile to see. Just two men out cutting trees and they didn't know anything.'

'That's Henry's land. For now, anyway. He's made good money out of that timber.'

'Henry?'

'The master's brother,' Robert explained. 'He inherited the manor there, or so he claims. It's in the law courts now. The master insists that their father had promised him that manor and that Henry changed the will.'

'That's a serious charge.'

'Aye,' the brother agreed with a nod, 'if he can prove it. Henry has powerful friends and money. It's his wood they use for the church and he's arranged a hefty price for it, from what I've heard.'

'The coroner has money, too.'

'Not like that. He has a manor south of here and another by Unstone. That one hardly brings in any rents, though. Most of the people died in the pestilence. He's not likely to win the suit. Henry will string it out until the master can't afford it any longer.'

'How long has it been going on?'

'A year now.' He sighed. 'Every month the master sends his money to his lawyer and nothing more happens. It's cost him dearly. He and the mistress keep arguing about it.'

'Maybe he'd be better off like us and not married.'

'You'd never hear him admit it,' the monk said slyly. 'He wants an heir.'

'You never wanted marriage? Dame Martha told me that the two of you were close once.'

'When we were very young.' Robert sipped the ale, his eyes distant. 'That was a lifetime ago, now. Then the church called me and her father arranged the marriage with Gilbert the cutler.'

'Is that the man she married? She never told me his name.'

'He was ten years older than her, and he had a reputation as a rogue with girls. Promise them, bed them and leave them. But Martha decided she wanted him.' He smiled at the memory. 'You know what she's like. Once she sets her mind to something, that's it. Wrapped him around her finger in weeks. I left before they married.'

'She loved him very deeply.'

'I daresay he was a good husband to her, too.'

'You should visit her, Brother.'

He shook his head. 'It's better to leave the past where it belongs. We don't have anything to share besides memories.'

'Friendship.'

'No, too much time has passed for that. Her life's gone a very different way to mine.' He finished the drink. 'I should go back. The master might need me.'

'He works you hard.'

'There's always something to be done, that's why my abbot sent me here.'

'So this is God's work.'

'For me it is,' the monk said with a nod. 'I serve as I'm instructed. But soon, perhaps, he'll let me return. I'm growing too old to hare around all over the county. What about you? When will you be back at work?'

'A few weeks yet, if it heals well.'

'God's blessing for that.'

'Thank you.'

After Robert had left he sat a little while longer, sipping at the ale, then pushed it aside and left, going back to the house on Knifesmithgate.

CHAPTER SEVENTEEN

By the time the sun rose on Saturday he felt as if he hadn't slept at all during the night. He had tried often enough, turning awkwardly under the blanket, trying to will rest onto himself, but it wouldn't come. Instead the night hours had stretched out like torment. He had risen twice, drunk ale, but nothing had worked. His eyes seemed filled with grit, his body ached and his mind was slow. He almost fell as he dressed, reaching out with his good hand to steady himself then breathing deeply, feeling his heart racing.

There was a chill in the air. It felt as if autumn was arriving already, a fresh scent, crisp and clear. He rested his arm in its sling, the linen dirty now, the only whiteness where his cast was covered by the cloth, and cut a heel of bread from a loaf.

Outside, men walked with their hoods raised. A few had jerkins made of rough leather, buttoned tight against their chests. He walked down to the square, relishing the sounds and the smells of market day, the crush of people filling the aisles between the stalls. His breath clouded in front of his mouth as he moved artfully through the crowd. He saw Martha, absorbed in haggling over a length of silk, and then de Harville, the fur collar of a long velvet robe close around his neck, standing by a stall selling spices.

'Good day, Master. God be with you.'

The coroner turned. 'Carpenter,' he said with a smile. 'You've saved me sending for you.' John cocked his head. On the other side of the trestle the man began to speak but de Harville waved him away. 'Come with me.'

They walked out along West Bar, past the house where Mark had lived, to the very edge of the town.

'What do you know about me, carpenter?' the coroner asked.

'Not much, Master.'

'Brother Robert's told you a few things. He confessed that to me last night.'

'He has.'

'He also suggested something to me.' John waited, with no idea what to expect. 'He said your arm might not heal well.'

'Pray God it will.'

'Of course,' the coroner said with a sharp nod. 'But if it doesn't, what will you do?'

'I don't know, Master.'

'You have a quick mind, carpenter.'

'Thank you, Master.'

'Did the brother tell you about my manors?' John nodded. 'Then you know the one near Unstone is in bad repair. It needs tenants and it needs work if it's going to make me any money.' John stayed silent, concentrating on the coroner's face. 'Are you a loyal man, carpenter?'

'Loyal?' The question made no sense to him. None of this did.

'Loyal,' he repeated. 'When you work, do you work hard? Do you follow the instructions you've been given?'

'Of course.'

De Harville nodded slowly. 'Brother Robert made a suggestion last night. If your arm doesn't heal properly I'd like you to be steward at my Unstone manor.'

John stood silent. The teeming sounds of the market seemed a world away. He stared at the coroner, watching his face to see if this was a joke, but his expression was serious.

'Me?'

'You. You can think and that's more than I can say for most men.'

'But I don't know anything about the land or farming,' he objected.

'The steward at my other manor will help you.' De Harville ran a hand across his chin. 'It's not charity. You'll work hard. The barns have been falling apart. You'll work with wood, with animals and with the tenants. I've seen you with that boy. He trusts you. And you'll have to do work on my other manor, too. I'll pay you fairly and you'll have a house. What do you say, carpenter?'

Thoughts flooded through his mind, roaring like a river. He knew nothing of the job or whether he could even do it. But if he could no longer be a carpenter, what else would he do? Travel the roads and do what he could? No one had made him an offer like this, and no one would again. Perhaps what Martha had said was true: if God was taking away the chance to use his skill, He was giving something in its stead. He took a deep breath.

'Aye, Master, if I can't be a carpenter, I'll gladly be your steward.' He extended his good hand and de Harville took it to seal the bargain.

'I'll warn you now; I'll work you to the bone. I want a profit from that land.'

'I'll give you one.'

The coroner nodded. 'I believe you will. You'd better thank Robert for this when you see him; it was his idea.'

• • •

He'd expected to spend most of the morning at the market, but his mind flew away every moment, unsure whether the whole thing had been a dream and that he would wake with a start. Instead he returned to the house, where Martha had her fabric spread over the table, the blue of the silk rippling like water in the light from the window.

'What do you think?' she asked.

'Are you going to make yourself a new dress?'

'I am,' she said. 'It's a foolish thing at my age, but this was so beautiful I had to buy it. Am I stupid and vain?'

'No,' he told her. 'You deserve it.'

She smiled. 'I do,' she agreed. 'At least they can bury me in something pretty.'

'You won't die for many years yet.'

She raised her eyebrows. 'You're in a good mood for someone who hardly slept. I heard you moving around in the night.'

'The coroner's offered me a job if my arm doesn't heal properly.'

'De Harville?' she said in surprise. 'What kind of work can he give you?'

'He wants me to be the steward on one of his estates. By Unstone.'

'You?' She couldn't keep the astonishment from her voice, and then joy filled her face, her eyes bright and happy. 'I told you, John Carpenter. I told you. Faith can bring everything.' She took his good hand between hers, rubbing it gently. 'A steward? He must think highly of you,' she said with pride.

'It was Robert's idea,' John explained. 'He suggested it.'

'Did he now?' she wondered, then smiled again. 'Now you don't need to worry, whatever happens. And I know you were worrying, I could see it in your eyes,' Martha said. 'It's good land out by there.'

'He told that it's more or less gone to rack and ruin since the Death.'

She nodded.

'There's nothing new in that tale. It's the same everywhere, I expect. God's judgement on us was harsh.' She paused. 'But he spared some of us and we should give thanks for that. For your new chance, too. You could even have a wife out there,' she teased.

'I'll have plenty to do without that.'

'You'll manage it,' she told him with confidence. 'You're clever, you think; de Harville's an intelligent man, he wouldn't offer this to someone who couldn't do it.'

'Thank you.'

'Don't you sell yourself short, John Carpenter, it's not charity; he's spotted your value to him.'

He smiled, realising he felt happier than he had in months. Whatever happened, he had a future now, one that would keep him around here. He'd be able to come to the market and see Martha, Walter, and Katherine. He could watch the spire grow into its full glory. For the first time since his father's death he would have a real home.

'What are you thinking?' she asked.

'Nothing,' he answered, then shook his head. 'Everything, maybe. I don't know.' He gave her a bemused smile. 'I keep thinking I'll wake and realise none of this will be real.'

'It's real enough.' Martha grinned. 'I can pinch you if you like.'

Before he could reply there was an urgent banging at the door. He looked at her then strode to answer it.

'Walter,' he said. 'Come on in, lad. What's so important?' The boy's face was flushed, as if he had been running hard, and he was carrying something wrapped in a piece of dirty sacking. He led him through to the hall.

'Hello Walter,' Martha said. 'You look hot. I'll get you some ale.' She flashed John a curious glance and he returned a small shrug.

'What is it?' he asked. He waited until the boy had drunk and caught his breath.

'You looked so sad the other day John,' the lad said.

'Sad?' he asked, not understanding.

'When we were in the woods. You wanted to find something.'

He nodded. The joy of a future had pushed the deaths from his mind. 'I hoped we would, but there wasn't anything there. You saw that.'

'I wanted to try and make you happy, so I went back there this morning,' Walter announced with a smile. He held up the sacking. 'I found this.'

'Let me see.'

The boy unfolded it slowly to expose a knife. The handle was worn, plain wood, the blade short and lightly pitted with rust. John picked it up, running his thumb along the edge; it was still sharp.

'Where did you find it?' he asked.

'At the edge of that clearing where you were searching. Are you pleased, John?' he asked hopefully. 'Is it useful?'

'Aye,' he said thoughtfully. 'I think it might be very useful indeed.' He smiled broadly and clapped the lad on the shoulder. 'You've done very well indeed.'

'Thank you, John.' Walter looked over at Martha, the grin wide on his face. 'What is it? Do you know?'

'I think it might be Geoffrey's knife.' He wrapped the blade once more. 'Do you want to go and find out?'

'Yes.' His voice was eager.

'Come on then.'

The High Street was busy; a press of folk looking at the goods the shops were displaying, apprentices crying their Masters' wares. In the market place the traders were dismantling their trestles, some smiling at the profits they'd made, others surly and disappointed.

The servant answered the door and showed him in without question. The monk was in the parlour, copying a list from a scrap of vellum to a longer roll. His fingers were stained with ink, his face pinched in concentration as he read and wrote.

'Master Carpenter,' he said with a nod. 'Walter. The master's gone for the rest of the day if you're looking for him.'

'You can help me. And I owe you my thanks,' John said, but the monk waved the gratitude away as the boy looked on, confused.

'You'll do well there, and the master will have someone he can trust. But from the look of you, that's not why you're here.'

'Have you buried Geoffrey yet?'

'This morning. Why?'

'What about his goods?'

The brother nodded at a chest in the corner. 'Over there, for whatever little they're worth.'

'Does that include his knife?'

'Yes, that's in there, and his sheath. Why?'

John pulled back the sacking to show the knife. 'You remember I said that the knife we found with Geoffrey didn't fit his sheath?'

'I do.'

'This morning Walter went back to the clearing where Geoffrey died. He found this there.'

'And you think it's Geoffrey's?'

'I'd like to see if it fits.'

Robert thought for a moment then rose slowly and limped across the room, drawing a key from his belt to unlock the chest. He searched through two or three items before straightening, one hand against the small of his back. He dropped the sheath on the table, the knife so loose inside that it skittered out along the wood.

John nodded at Walter, watching the boy slide the knife into the leather.

'Well?'

'It's the right knife,' the monk accepted with a sigh. 'But we already agreed he was murdered. This doesn't make any difference to that.'

'It's proof.'

'Proof of something we already know.'

'But there's a duty to find out who killed him,' John insisted.

'The coroner's made his decision. That's an end to it.' He paused. 'You'd do well to heed it.' Robert's face softened. 'It's for the best in the long run.' He gave soft emphasis to the final words.

John stood silent for a moment, his eyes fierce. Then he nodded, turned on his heel and left, Walter rushing after.

'What is it, John?' the boy asked once they were outside.

'The coroner doesn't want to do anything. He knows Geoffrey was killed and he wants to ignore it.'

'But what else? There were other things he was saying. What did he mean?'

John took a deep breath to calm himself. 'I told you my arm might not heal properly.' Walter nodded. 'If that happens, the coroner offered me the job of steward at one of his manors.'

'But isn't that good?'

'Yes,' he answered. 'But Brother Robert just warned me, too.'

'Warned you how?'

'To let things drop and not cause any problems.'

They walked silently, dodging around the people, the boy frowning hard.

'What will you do?' he asked eventually.

'I don't know,' he answered, shaking his head in frustration. Would the coroner really withdraw his offer so easily? For a moment he wondered if he had only been given the stewardship to keep him from this, but that was foolish. Even now, with the knife, he knew no more than he had before. It gave him nothing new. All it had done was rekindle his desire to find whoever had killed Geoffrey.

He should leave it, be satisfied with the truth of the knife, and everyone would be happy. He could spend the weeks quietly until the cast came off, knowing that whatever happened he was safe.

'What are you thinking, John?'

'I'm just dancing with my demons,' he replied darkly, then gave a weak smile. 'Pay me no mind. You did an excellent job out there, and I'm very grateful. Come on, I'll walk home with you.'

Katherine was there, entertaining the girls with a game of nine men's morris, jumping up and smoothing down her skirts when they entered. The little ones complained, but she soothed them gently until they were laughing as she ruffled their hair.

'Good day to you, John,' she said, the hair hanging loose and wild. 'Forgive me, I wasn't expecting a visitor.'

'It's my fault,' he apologised. 'I'm intruding.'

'None of it,' she countered. 'Walter, can you fetch Master John some ale?'

'Your brother's done well,' he told, explaining what the lad had found.

'I told you, there's more to him than most people think,' she said proudly. 'But how does it change things?'

'It probably doesn't,' he admitted. He looked at her. 'I should tell you something. The coroner has offered me the stewardship of a manor if I can't be a carpenter any longer.'

'John that's wonderful!' Her eyes were wide and she bit her lower lip. 'A stewardship,' she said in amazement. 'Where's the manor?'

'Near Unstone.'

'That's close enough for you to come into town often.' She glanced over her shoulder. 'Come out into the garden.' He followed her, curious. Once they were away from other eyes, she hugged him, blushing crimson, and then lowered her eyes. 'I was afraid you'd leave and I'd never see you again.'

'With God's will I'll end up a carpenter here instead.'

'Of course,' she agreed quickly. 'I pray for it every day.' He believed her, the words so heartfelt. 'But even if you don't it means you'll stay around here.'

'I'll be in Chesterfield for the market every Saturday,' he promised with a grin. 'You won't be rid of me that easily.'

'Then you'd better find the time to visit us,' she cautioned teasingly. 'I'll be disappointed otherwise, although, you'll be a busy man.'

'I'll be a confused man,' he laughed. 'I don't know anything about running a manor.'

'I have faith in you.'

He sighed. 'So does the coroner, it seems, although, I don't know why.'

'He knows a good man when he sees one.'

'Thank you, but I doubt goodness has anything to do with his offer.' He bowed his head with a small, easy smile. 'You shouldn't compliment me so much, Mistress.'

She laughed and lightly tapped his good arm with her small fist. 'You'll tell me next you don't like it, Master.'

'The danger is that I might believe it,' he teased her.

'You're a man, John.' Her eyes twinkled. 'You'll believe whatever a girl tells you if her words are honeyed enough.'

He put back his head and roared. It was the first time in far too long that he had laughed loud.

'You should do that more often,' Katherine said. 'They say it's good for the blood.'

'There's been precious little to laugh about. So it seems I must thank you once more.' He bowed again, more deeply, hearing her giggle, and it sounded sweet in his ears. 'I'd better take my leave of you.'

'You can stay as long as you wish,' she told him, choosing her words carefully.

'Better I go for now.' He saw a flicker of sorrow in her eyes. 'But I'll be back, I promise you that.'

CHAPTER EIGHTEEN

There was light drizzle in the air on Monday, enough for him to pull up his hood as he walked to the church. Cloud hung low in the sky, the air misty with a damp that nestled in the chest.

Seven of the workers stood by the grave, Stephen's coffin already resting deep in the earth. He bared his head and joined them. The weather suited his mood – dank and dismal. How many had he known over the years who had died from accidents? Five in York alone over the space of two years; others elsewhere. Each one left him reflecting on just why God had spared him, his mood dark and sombre for days.

The priest intoned the words John had heard so often but didn't understand; at least it sounded holy. Then, like the others, he picked up a handful of dirt and dropped it onto the wood, hearing its quiet resonance. With that it was done, a life ended, soon to be forgotten. Some of the men would go out tonight and drink in Stephen's name, but then he would fade until he was nothing more than a blurred memory.

He walked around the yard, his hose damp against his legs, the grass and dirt slippery under his boots. Cut wood was piled against one of the walls, canvas thrown on top to protect it from the damp. By habit he started to feel the grain and examine the cut, seeing how each piece could best be used and worked. He'd expected to find the timber dry and seasoned, all the moisture gone from the heart of it. But he could feel the wetness there, still close to the surface. He tried another piece, then a third, but they were all the same. Frowning, he pushed back the canvas and began running his hand over all the pieces he could reach, bending to push his good arm into the gaps between boards. Everything was the same, all the timber unseasoned and green.

John stood back, thinking. There was a second pile of timber a few yards away; when he checked, his fingers on the roughness of the wood, he could feel the same wetness just below the surface.

'What do you think you're doing?'

He turned and saw Joseph, the master carpenter, a few yards away with a wooden mallet in his hand. The man narrowed his eyes, thinking. 'You're the one who was working in the tower room.'

'Aye, Master, that's me.'

Joseph relaxed and let the mallet hang, swinging from a thong around his wrist. 'How's the arm healing?'

'Well, God willing. A few more weeks and I'll be back.'

The man wiped the thick stubble on his chin with the back of his hand. 'I've everyone I need at the moment. They're not that good, but they're cheap. I'll be getting rid of most of them soon for winter, anyway.' He shook his head. 'Still, you're welcome to come back when you're whole and I'll see if I can do anything for you.'

'Thank you.' He indicated the timber under the canvas. 'Is this for the tower?'

'The framing and the braces,' Joseph said. 'Why do you ask?'

'It's not seasoned. You can't use it.'

The man spat. 'It'll be out here until spring. That's ample time to season it.'

'It needs two or three years,' John told him. 'You know that.'

'I know what folk say and I know what my experience has told me,' Joseph countered. 'All that talk of years, good oak doesn't need that. A few months and it'll work just fine.'

'It'll warp as it dries,' John said with certainty.

'You're wrong lad. Anyway, I have my orders, and they're to use that wood for the rest of the spire, the frame, the bracing and for the oak tiles that are going to face it.'

'Whoever gave those orders doesn't know what he's doing,' John said in disgust.

'They're the ones paying the wages and for all this. You'd do best to remember that if you want to work here again. I'll say nothing this time, but I won't tolerate any troublemakers.'

'It's the weight of the spire that's going to hold it in place.'

'I know that,' Joseph said before turning his head to spit.

'How's it going to do that if the wood warps?' he asked. 'You won't have any control over that.'

'I've said it once and I'll not repeat it. It'll be fine.' The master carpenter's jaw set hard. 'I think you've spent enough time here. I wish you well with your arm.' He took hold of the mallet again.

'God speed to you,' John said as he left.

'And to you, lad. And to you.'

• • •

He sat in the alehouse, lost in thought. After that conversation there'd be no job waiting for him at the church, even if God saw fit to make his arm whole again. But something was wrong there: any carpenter with worth who'd worked a few years knew that wood had to be properly seasoned, oak most of all because of its hardness and the way it lasted. The wood at the church was so new it was green. To build the spire from that was dangerous; as it dried and bent, it would twist; it could maybe even topple.

He drank slowly, trying to think it through, barely tasting the ale. Money. That was the only possible reason. Someone, somewhere, was making a profit from this. He sat upright with a start.

Someone had paid Geoffrey to murder Will. That had been Roger's testimony. Then someone had murdered Geoffrey, his body found close to where they were cutting wood to use in the church. Wood that would be used well before it was ready. He laid the pieces out like a chain in his mind, one leading to the next and the next.

Will had been a competent man, someone who knew his craft and valued it – an honest man. He recalled what the man's widow had told him, the words he had spoken in his sleep that had made no sense to her: 'I can't do what they want.' Put with everything else, the meaning became clear.

But in the end, who would care? No one would listen to his accusations, to what he had to say. He was a carpenter. The only wealth he had, he carried with him in a small purse. It was enough to last him a few more weeks and then he'd have nothing. Those with property and full coffers had louder voices, one that authority listened to. If the spire fell, or if it twisted and turned, the workmen would be blamed, not the people who'd made their crooked bargains and pushed everything through.

The only person with any authority he could tell was the coroner and he'd already washed his hands of it all. He would want no part of this, one man of privilege accusing others of murder, especially when the dead were nobodies with nothing to pass on.

He drank slowly, working his way gradually to the bottom of the mug. When it was done he slid it across the bench, then stood and walked out. He knew he should leave this whole business alone. He should be pleased that he would have any job waiting when the cast came off his arm, but this new knowledge was going to weigh too heavily for silence.

John walked across the empty market place to the coroner's house on the High Street, and knocked loudly on the door with his good hand.

'The master's out,' the servant told him. 'He's gone to his manor for the day.'

'Is Brother Robert here?' he asked.

'In the stables,' she said with a snort, inclining her head towards the yard. 'But don't ask me what the old fool's doing out there.'

The monk was stroking the head of the roan, talking to the horse in a soft, lulling voice. Robert had been newly tonsured, the hair clipped away so only a circle of it surrounded the shine of his scalp.

'God's peace to you Brother.'

The monk continued to stroke the horse, but turned his head, acknowledging the carpenter with a small nod and a smile. 'You'll need to learn to ride when you work out at Unstone.'

'Horses scare me.'

'Find a gentle one and you'll have no trouble.' He brought an apple from the leather scrip around his waist and held it out on the palm of his hand. The animal sniffed at it, then snickered before taking it contentedly into its mouth. Robert stroked it one more time then left the stall. 'You look troubled,' he said.

'I am.' Slowly he explained what he had learned, the monk listening intently, never interrupting, waiting until he had finished.

'Why does wood have to be seasoned?' the brother asked. 'I don't understand that.'

'When you fell a tree, there's moisture in it. It's wet inside. You need to give the wood time to dry, to take that moisture out. If you don't do that before you use it, then it'll come out later and whatever you've made with the wood will warp, it won't stay true the way the carpenter fashioned it.'

The monk nodded. 'But they're leaving the oak in the churchyard until spring.'

'Out in the weather, in the cold,' John pointed out. 'A few months isn't long enough to dry out oak, it's different, it takes two or three years.'

Robert raised his eyebrows. 'That long? Are you sure?'

'It's my craft.' He smiled gently.

'But the new master carpenter disagrees?'

'He does.'

'Maybe he's right,' the brother began, his voice low, raising a hand to stop John objecting. 'He's there because it's his craft, too. And he must know it well to have his position. Have you considered that you could be wrong?'

'I'm not,' he insisted. 'I've worked with wood as long as I can remember. I've seen master carpenters reject wood because it wasn't properly seasoned. They could still feel the dampness in it and they knew what would happen.'

Robert frowned. 'You truly feel this might be connected to the murders of the men Will and Geoffrey?'

'I do,' he answered with feeling.

'You feel the master should investigate this?'

John sighed. 'That's a decision he has to make. But if he doesn't, then justice won't be done, will it Brother?'

Robert paced around the stable, the horses in their stalls watching him. 'Do you know who owns the church?' John shook his head. 'It's the diocese of Lincoln, under the bishop. And you know where the wood comes from?'

'The manor the coroner's brother owns.'

'His own kin,' the monk said with a sigh.

'You told me there's a lawsuit.'

'There is, but that's something different. That's at the courts, it's far away. The master still sees his brother and the rest of his family.' John looked at him in confusion. How could a man fight with another, even his brother, and still treat him as a friend? 'I know,' the brother said with a bemused chuckle, 'It's the rich. Maybe it makes no sense to us, but it does to them. Do you see what you'd be doing if you ask him to do this?'

'So he won't?'

'Most likely not.' He paused. 'What do you know about Henry de Harville?'

'Only what you've told me.'

'That's precious little. Henry has manors all over the country. I doubt he visits the one near Bolsover more than once a year, if that. The steward looks after it for him.' He gave John a pointed glance. 'He was clever after the pestilence. Land was cheap, as many of those who owned property had died. Henry had money and a good eye. He found places that could turn a profit and bought them. He's a rich man now, far richer than the master will ever be.'

'And you can't fight money?' John asked wryly.

'Not if there's enough of it,' Robert replied honestly. 'But it's more than that. Henry has the ear of some very powerful people in the land, including the Bishop of Lincoln. Even King Edward himself, from what I've heard. What chance does anyone have against that?'

'So he won't even try?'

The monk shook his head. 'A sensible man learns to choose his battles carefully. There's no point in fighting if you know you can't win.'

John thought for a moment.

'You said the steward looks after the manor?'

'The same way you'll look after one for the master. A steward has a great deal of responsibility.'

'Do you think this could be his doing?'

'Without his master's knowledge?' Robert smiled. 'It's possible. Trying to prove it would be a different matter, though, can't you see that? I've met that steward. Hugo's arrogant enough to do it, but he looks after three manors for Henry.'

'I don't understand,' John said.

'Henry trusts him. He would be loath to lose a man like that.'

'Even if he's being cheated?'

'Hugo's not a fool. He'll see that Henry receives a good share of the profits in his coffers.'

'So there's nothing we can do?' he asked.

'No,' the monk answered sadly. 'Nothing that would make any difference, anyway. It's like I said, you need to choose your battles. I can talk to the master, but I know what he'll say.'

'It'll just go on?'

'You're a young man, there's still fire in your blood,' Robert sighed. 'There are things in this world that we can change and things we can't. Remember, though, God sees it all and there will be justice in the end.'

He could feel the anger building inside even though he understood the truth of what the monk had said. He kicked out at the pile of straw, sending stalks flying into the air to settle all over the floor.

'Go home,' Robert advised gently. 'You've told me, you spotted what might have been happening.'

'Might have been?'

'There's no proof, John. Even the wood is your word against the master carpenter's, and people will believe him. Take your time, let your arm heal and then do what you will. The coroner's offer for the manor will be there for you.'

'Thank you,' he said, although he felt precious little gratitude.

'Go with God.'

• • •

'I've seen that Hugo,' Martha said with contempt after he had told her. 'To look at him you'd think the manor was his. Wears a fur-lined robe and rides a rich man's horse. Always has airs around him. I'd not put cheating and murder past him.'

'Brother Robert made it clear that the coroner wouldn't pursue it.'

'Of course he won't,' she told him. 'They might never have seen eye-to-eye but he's not going to accuse his own brother of killing. Not when his brother would sue him for slander for it. The man's not a fool, John.'

'All that's missing is justice.'

She eyed him carefully. 'Do you really think there can be justice for an ordinary man? You should know better than that at your age. All those above us care about is that we pay our taxes.' He stayed silent, his eyes still blazing. 'Leave it,' she told him. 'You won't do any good. Not for yourself or anyone else. Stay away from trouble.'

It was what everyone was saying and he knew it was true. Nothing he could do would make any difference. He leaned back on the bench. 'You're right,' he admitted finally.

'Just live your own life. From what you've said they won't have you back at the church.'

'No,' he admitted, 'I don't think they will.' He had barely given that much thought, too outraged by what he had discovered. If God granted him full use of the arm there would be work elsewhere, other churches and castles where a carpenter could earn a decent wage. But winter was coming, the roads would be harsh, and little chance of employment before spring arrived.

'Soon enough you'll have tenants of your own to look after. If you want to fight for someone, do it for them, John Carpenter. That way you'll only have to go against the coroner.' She chuckled. 'You won't win, but at least you can feel as if you've tried.'

'All I have to do is fill my time until then.'

'There are still weeds in the garden if you've a mind to be useful.'

'I might well pull them up for you,' he said with a grin.

'Don't worry, I'm sure I can find more for you to do.'

He bowed his head. 'I'd be grateful to be of service.'

'If you really want to help, why not go and see what you can do for Katherine. I doubt there's been anything done on that house of theirs in years. Walter's a good lad but he can't do anything to help in that way.'

'I'll do that.' He rose from the bench. 'I'll go over there now.'

'It's a good excuse to spend time with Katherine, too,' Martha said slyly.

'It's just Christian charity.'

'If you say so John.'

In truth, it was more to be doing something, anything. He felt restless and useless. But when he saw the smile of pleasure on Katherine's face as she opened the door to him, there was perhaps a little more.

'I have time on my hands. I thought perhaps there were jobs a willing hand could do on your house.'

She brought him in. 'John,' she laughed, 'if you have enough time you can build me a new one.'

'You might need to wait for that.' He lifted the sling. 'But I'll do what I can for now.'

He followed her around the place as she listed the things that needed to be done. The building had been neglected, leaving it shabby and worn. Pieces of limewash crumbled in his hand as he touched it.

'I can do some of the things,' he told her. 'Others will have to wait until I have two hands.'

'I'll take whatever you can offer,' she said gratefully. 'Walter can help you. Or I can.'

'That would be very kind.'

'It seems to me that the kindness is yours, John. I can't pay you.'

'Just give me ale when I'm working and some company now and then,' he said with a smile.

'I'll willingly do that,' she agreed.

He glanced around the hall. 'There are some small things I can do today.'

She glanced around at her mother and the girls. 'If they won't get in your way.'

He smiled, hefting the leather satchel on his shoulder. It had seemed strange to carry it again, the weight so natural, the way it slapped against his side with each step. He worked for more than an hour, even the smallest job taking longer when he only had one hand.

The girls crowded around at first, asking their eager questions about what he was doing, what each tool was for. He had always kept his distance from children, wary and unsure of them, but Janette and Eleanor had something of their older sister about them, the same charm and easy manner.

Katherine shooed them away, only for them to return a few minutes later as he knelt to repair the hinge on a cupboard in the corner, standing so close he could feel their breath on the back of his neck, their eyes fixed on his hand at it moved.

He stopped as she lit the rushlights, the day almost gone. He'd been concentrating so hard that looking up to see the deep shadows in the room came as a surprise.

Katherine brought him a mug of ale and he drank gratefully, his throat dry and dusty.

'Thank you, John. You've done so much, I don't know what to say.'

'I've enjoyed myself,' he told her truthfully. 'It feels good to be doing honest work again.' He flexed his good hand. 'It's been too long.'

'You'll do plenty of this when you're a steward.'

'Then a little practice won't come amiss.' He winked and watched her giggle, then stop and blush furiously. Walter returned, full of life and the smell of fresh air, happy to see John, full of questions and talk to fill the hall to the rafters.

It was full dark when he left, tired and content. He'd be back the next day and the one after, every day until he had completed each task he could manage. He'd forgotten the satisfaction in finishing even the smallest job, in working with his hand and tools using the gift God had given him. He hoisted the satchel higher on his shoulder, his thumb in the strap. Tonight he'd sleep well.

For a moment he thought he heard footsteps behind him, and he turned quickly, reaching for his knife. But there was only the night and silence. He put the blade back in its sheath, his heart bumping hard and fast in his chest. It was the first time he'd sensed any danger since Mark had tried to attack him; that seemed so long ago now, another lifetime, back when he could use both his arms.

• • •

The next morning he arrived early at the house on Saltergate, smiling and ready to work. The morning was bright and he spent it outside, working slowly to remove areas of old limewash then mixing and spreading fresh. He ate dinner with the family, sharing their pottage, hungry from his labour, and gladly accepting when Katherine refilled his bowl. He heard her working inside, urging on the girls as they carded and spun wool, looking after the mother who sat trapped inside her silence. She managed to steal minutes here and there from her responsibilities, coming to bring him fresh ale and chat about nothing. He relished glancing up to see her standing there, the warmth of her smile and the sound of her voice. Then she had to leave and he had return to the job.

Walter returned early, helping as he worked outside. John showed him how to smooth out the limewash and the boy worked patiently, going over and over the surface until it was flat and even.

'Keep on like that and we'll make a labourer out of you,' he said and the lad beamed, lapping up the praise. 'Clean up now, it's getting too dark for any more today.' He straightened, feeling a pleasant ache in his back. He watched Walter clean the tools with the oiled rag, making certain he rubbed all the metal. Finally he packed everything away in the satchel and took his leave.

The evening was crisp and he could smell the fires burning in the houses, the sweet scent of woodsmoke that always meant autumn to him. He slipped the satchel onto his shoulder and left the house, walking briskly back towards Knifesmithgate. The sky was clear, the stars already shining. There'd be a chill by morning, he thought, but not cold enough yet for a frost. That was still a month or so away, God willing, or it would be an early winter.

CHAPTER NINETEEN

They came at a run, so fast they must have been waiting for him. He barely had time to draw his knife and turn. They were big men, faces he'd never seen before, with hoods pulled up close on their heads and murder in their eyes.

Both had their daggers drawn, holding them out, ready to stab. He moved from foot to foot, watching them carefully, just waiting for them to move apart. With one arm there wasn't much he could do, but he might be able to hurt them before they killed him.

'You need to learn to shut up,' one of the men said quietly. John watched the pair of them, his gaze steady. The other man took a small pace forward and John moved his knife in a slow arc. He couldn't turn and run; they'd be on him in a moment. He could feel a trickle of cold sweat down his back.

The man who'd spoken was smiling, showing dark, ugly teeth. 'You've upset the wrong people.' He poked forward with the knife, probing. John stood his ground, watching and waiting. Soon they'd be ready, done with words.

The satchel was still on his shoulder, weighing down against his side. When they came he wouldn't be able to move his good arm freely. If they wanted to kill him they'd manage it easily enough. His palm was wet, the knife handle slippery in his hand. He tightened his grip on it, still staring at the two of them, trying to keep his breathing slow and steady.

The talker edged forward, grinning. John watched the man's legs tense, ready to spring … and then the man gave a cry of pain, reaching for his shoulder. He heard a short sound and the other man bent forward, dropping the dagger and clutching the back of his head. Yet another sound, and the first man cried out, then took off at a run, his companion close behind.

He listened in confusion as the footsteps grew fainter, put the knife in its sheath and ran a hand slowly over his face.

'Did they hurt you, John?' Walter came out of the shadows, his hand down at his side, clutching a slingshot. 'I tried to stop them before they could do anything.'

'Your timing was perfect.' He began to laugh, a mix of relief and fear, carrying on until his body was shaking and his eyes close to tears.

'What's wrong, John?'

'Nothing,' he said finally, once he could catch his breath. 'You just saved my life, Walter.' He shook his head, as if the last few minutes had been a bad dream. 'Thank you.'

The boy reached into his scrip. 'You'd left your chisel. I was bringing it back in case you thought you'd lost it. I didn't want you to be angry.'

He shook his head in wonder. 'After that, I don't think I could ever be angry with you again. Where did you learn that?'

Walter shrugged. 'When I was little they paid me to keep the crows off the fields.'

'I'm glad they did. Without that I'd be lying there.' He nodded at the ground.

The boy looked around, frightened. 'Will they come back?'

'Not tonight,' he said. 'And those two probably won't ever return.' He laughed again. 'They must have thought devils were attacking them.'

'Were they going to kill you, John?' the lad asked seriously.

'Probably,' he answered. 'I'm in your debt: truly in your debt.'

'You're my friend.'

'I am,' John told him. 'I definitely am.' He extended his good arm. The shaking had stopped. 'I think I've had enough of tonight.'

• • •

He lay in the dark, reliving the scene again and again, his heart pounding each time he closed his eyes and the visions came. He'd upset the wrong people. He needed to learn to shut up. He knew what it meant. There could only be one thing.

He'd told Martha and Brother Robert. The monk might have told the coroner, but that wouldn't have brought men looking to kill him. But he'd also talked to the master carpenter. With that, it all began to make sense, one more piece of the chain falling into place. Joseph was willing to use unseasoned timber on the church, and even say it would make no difference, although he must have known the truth. Someone was paying him, the same people who'd paid Geoffrey to kill Will.

Wood. Two men had died so someone could make a profit from timber. He sat up awkwardly in his bed and reached to the floor for a mug of ale. He could have been the third one killed; he was certain that murder had been the order. He'd seen the anticipation in the talker's eyes, the way he licked his lips.

He had survived by sheer luck, nothing more than that. If Walter hadn't been so conscientious about a chisel and so good with a slingshot, he'd be dead now. How far would the coroner have investigated? Would he have simply called it a robbery, or would he have gone deeper into it? Would he have even cared?

He sighed and drank more of the ale. They were questions he couldn't answer. Those men had gone, but would others come to silence him? He needed to be alert every moment now. Until his arm healed he was going to be at a disadvantage in any fight.

At least he could be certain who'd sent the two men. Hugo, the steward. He was the only person who could have done that. He had made a powerful enemy. Would the man be satisfied now the warning had been delivered, or would he want silence?

He felt safer once dawn arrived. It was foolish, he knew that; a knife could end his life in daylight just as quickly as it could in the darkness. But with people around, voices on the streets, it seemed less likely.

'You look pale,' Martha told him as he cut part of a loaf to break his fast.

'It's nothing,' he said. 'Just a bad night.' That, at least, was true. He had no wish to worry her by telling everything. 'I'll be fine once I start working.'

• • •

He look a longer route to Saltergate, watching all the folk around him, his good hand resting lightly on the hilt of the knife, ears alert for any unusual noise, of boots straying too close. By the time he reached the house he was breathing hard, feeling a thin sheen of sweat on his face.

Katherine led him straight through to the garden, her face serious, mouth set hard. She closed the door behind them and said, 'Walter told me what happened last night.'

'Did he tell you he saved my life?'

She shook her head. 'He didn't say that. He was fearful for you.'

'Well, it's true. Without him I'd probably be dead,' he said honestly.

'Why were they after you?' Before he could respond, she added, 'And don't tell me they were trying to rob you, because I won't believe that. Walter was there long enough to hear what they said.'

He sighed. He didn't want to involve her in this. None of it concerned her; it shouldn't touch her.

'Are we friends?' she asked sharply.

'Of course,' he said.

'Then you'd better tell me the truth.' Her eyes were hard on him. 'If you value me you'll give me that.'

He explained it all, glancing across as he made each point to catch her listening intently.

'You're certain?' Katherine asked as he finished.

'I am,' he admitted sadly. 'It's the only way it makes sense. There's no other reason anyone would want to kill me.'

'Trees,' she said bleakly, shaking her head. 'The coroner won't do anything?'

'Brother Robert claims he won't.'

'Have you told them what happened last night?'

'No.'

'You should. At least tell the brother.'

'Do you think he'd do anything?'

'I don't know that, John.' She took his hand in hers. 'But if anything else happens, he'd know about this.' He nodded slowly and she added, 'I pray to God it doesn't.'

'So do I,' he said with a smile. 'I'm attached to my life.'

'Go and see him today.'

'I will,' he promised. 'Right now I have things to do, if you still want me here.'

'Of course I do,' she answered, slapping him lightly on the arm. 'And I expect a full day's work from you, too.'

'Yes, Mistress.'

'I'll bring you some ale.' Her voice became serious again. 'I mean it, John. Go and talk to Brother Robert. Let him know.'

He nodded and slipped the satchel off his shoulder. 'I'll start with the last of the limewash back here.'

He worked steadily until dinner, joining the family again at the table in the hall. It was the same pottage as the day before, with more beans, thickened with flour and a few small pieces of bacon for flavour. The girls were lively as bubbles in a stream, making him smile with their joy, defying all Katherine's attempts to calm them. The meal done, he stood and said, 'I'll be back soon.' She looked at him curiously. He nodded in reply and saw the brief smile on her lips.

• • •

Brother Robert was with the coroner in the parlour. The coffer was open, piles of silver coins lined up on the table as the monk scribbled on a piece of vellum, stopping only to sharpen his quill with the short knife in his left hand.

'Well, carpenter, what do you want?' de Harville asked.

'I was attacked last night, Master.'

'Oh?' The coroner sat up straight, suddenly interested. He glanced at Robert. 'Where was this?'

'Between Saltergate and Knifesmithgate.'

'How many men?'

'Two.'

'And you fought them off with one arm?' de Harville wondered. 'That's impressive, carpenter. I'd no idea you were a fighter, too.'

'Someone came along and they ran off.' It was close enough to the truth, and it kept Walter away from all this.

'Then nothing happened?' the brother asked.

'They weren't trying to rob me,' John told them. He turned to Robert. 'Did you tell him?' The monk nodded once. 'One of them said that I'd upset the wrong people and I needed to learn to shut up.' As he spoke the words he could hear the man's voice, the leer of violence on his lips.

The coroner steepled his hands under his chin. Light from the window caught the pale stubble on his cheeks. 'You think this has to do with the murders?'

'What else could it be?'

'I don't know. You tell me. And what do you expect me to do about it?' de Harville asked brusquely.

'Nothing,' he answered simply, watching the coroner glance at the monk once more. 'But if it happens again and I'm killed, at least you'll know the reason.'

'You place a high value on yourself, carpenter.'

'If I don't, no one else will.'

'Are you trying to prick my conscience?' de Harville picked up his knife, using the tip to carefully dig dirt from his fingernails.

'No,' John said. 'Your mind's made up. I just wanted you to know in case anything happens.'

'Robert said he advised you to leave it.'

John gave a short, harsh laugh. 'I'd decided to do what he suggested.'

'What made you do that?' the coroner asked.

'I can't do anything by myself. The brother told me to choose my battles. The thing to do was withdraw from this one.'

'Wise,' he said with a nod. 'But too late, it seems.' He sighed. 'I'll be honest with you, carpenter. This whole business disturbs me, and not just your part in it. You know who's buying the wood?'

'I do.'

'And who's selling it?'

'Yes.'

'He's a powerful man.'

'That's what I've been told.'

'You know I have a suit against him in the courts?'

John looked at the monk. 'Robert explained it.'

'It's bankrupting me.' He gestured at the money on the table. 'Every month some of this goes to pay a damned lawyer who speaks fine words and writes letters but never seems to do me any good.'

'I'm sorry, Master.'

'If I had absolute proof that my brother or his steward was defrauding the church, that might help my case, the King might not look too happily on it; they say Edward's a man of principle in these matters.'

'Yes, Master,' he replied, unsure what to say.

De Harville was silent for a long time, rubbing his chin thoughtfully. 'You really feel that these two murdered men deserve justice, don't you?'

'I do.'

'It's possible that your justice and my justice might end up helping each other, carpenter.'

'Yes, Master.'

Brother Robert was shaking his head.

'You don't approve, monk?' the coroner asked.

'No, Master, I don't. You want to use him.'

'Aye,' de Harville admitted with a dark smile. 'I do. You know as well as I do that Hugo's behind all this. He'll be the one who sent men after the carpenter last night. If we get proof against Hugo it'll sit awkwardly for Henry. He might even be willing to give up the manor rather than have it all come out.'

'But you won't do it officially,' the monk berated him.

'I can't,' de Harville agreed. 'I've already said the deaths are closed and that's how it must remain –' he glanced pointedly at John '– unless someone finds new evidence.'

'Is that what you want, sir, for me to go hunting and see what I can find?'

'The choice is yours,' de Harville said, guardedly, gazing out of the window. 'Perhaps you feel your friend Will deserves more from the law than he's had and you decide to look on your own. Perhaps you'll find something damning and have no choice but to come to me so I can do something about it. What do you think?'

'You're asking him to play a very dangerous game, Master,' Brother Robert warned, but the coroner held up a hand.

'You were willing enough before,' de Harville said. 'Or have you been scared away?'

John watched the man's face, seeing the calculating stare and mocking eyes. Then he thought of Will and his widow.

'I'm still willing,' he said finally. 'If that's what you want.'

The coroner waved away the words. 'It's nothing to do with what I want. I don't even know anything about it.' He paused. 'Do you understand that?'

'Yes, Master.'

Robert shook his head quietly. 'This is wrong,' he said, his voice grave.

'Well, carpenter?' de Harville asked.

'I told you,' John said. 'I'll do what I can.'

'People remember success, carpenter,' he warned. 'You came here today to report a common assault. You've done that, the brother will write it down. I don't think there's anything more, is there?'

'No, Master.'

'Then go with God, carpenter.'

Outside, he breathed deeply. At the alehouse on Low Pavement he ordered drink, sipping slowly and wondering exactly what he could do. The attack had scared him; with the broken arm he was vulnerable, he couldn't defend himself properly. The next time men came they'd take care to be certain he couldn't escape.

By the time the ale was gone he still had no idea what to do. The coroner had been happy to quietly change his mind again if he could benefit from it. John knew he was on his own, a pawn who could easily be knocked off the board. Before anything else, though, he needed to fulfil his promise to Katherine and work on her house.

'What did they say?' she asked as she answered the door and saw his grim face.

'Nothing of any use, of course,' he said, his heart heavy for not telling her the truth. 'Since I couldn't identify the men and no one was killed, the coroner wasn't interested.' She frowned, unsurprised, and he started to open his mouth and say more, then closed it again. 'I'll go back to work.'

The solar above the hall was crowded with beds. This had been a grand house once, but that had been long before. Now there were many years of use and wear that needed to be mended. He pushed against a shutter with his shoulder to hold it in place as he tightened screws, feeling them bite satisfyingly into the wood. Standing back, he examined his work, seeing small patches of rot in the frame. The timber would need to be replaced, and sooner rather than later, but that wasn't something he could do with one hand.

The afternoon passed slowly, each job taking longer than it should. He put the tools away while it was still light, wiping each one as best he could, before walking carefully down the stairs.

'You're welcome to stay for supper, John,' Katherine offered. 'We'd be glad for your company. Walter will be home soon.' Her look was hopeful, but she understood when he shook his head. 'I can walk back with you if you'd like. I can leave them alone for a few minutes.'

'People will talk,' he said with a smile.

'If they're not already talking there's no hope for them as gossips,' she answered, her grin wide and happy as they walked along the street. 'Half of them probably already have us married off.' She began to blush.

'Perhaps there'd be worse fates,' he teased her quietly, seeing her colour deepen as she turned her face away.

'You've been very quiet today.' A few men were making their way home from work, some idling along, other striding purposefully, smiling to be returning to wives and children.

'I just keep thinking about last night,' he explained. 'Your brother really did save my life.' He shook his head sadly.

'Will you be coming tomorrow?' Katherine asked.

'Of course,' he answered. 'I've given you my word, hadn't I?' She nodded. 'After dinner, though. There's something I need to do earlier.'

'Does it have to do with talking to the coroner?'

He smiled and said nothing.

'You don't have to tell me, John,' she told him, her voice serious. 'You don't owe me anything, and a man's business is his own. But please, remember, I'm your friend. So is Martha, so is Walter. We want to help you if we can.'

'Not on this,' he answered quietly. 'None of you can.'

'What's the matter? Don't you trust us?'

'Yes, but –'

'Never mind but.' Her voice was soft but firm and she held him squarely in her gaze. 'We care about you. I'd hoped you cared about all of us.'

'I do.'

She gave a sad frown. 'Not enough, it seems. Whatever it is you have to do, God go with you, John Carpenter.' She turned and retraced her steps, never pausing or looking back, her head held high.

He sighed, hoisted the satchel higher on his shoulder and walked on to Knifesmithgate.

'You look like you've found a penny and lost a day's wages,' Martha told him.

'I might have lost more than that.' He went through to the small room at the back of the house, placing the tools carefully in the chest, and then pouring an ale in the buttery.

'Lover's quarrel?' she asked when he sat on the stool.

'No,' he said, and then, 'I don't know.'

She put her sewing aside and folded her hands patiently on her lap. The wimple covering her hair was bright white, her gown dark red, faded by years of wear. 'I've told you before. A woman can look right through a man. If you're keeping something from her, she knows. That Katherine's a bright lass.'

'There are some things it's better to do alone.'

She considered the thought, nodding slowly. 'Perhaps you're right, but it sounds as if she doesn't think this is one of them.'

'She doesn't even know what it is.'

Her smile was kindly. 'That'll be why she thinks that, then. She truly cares about you, and if you don't know that you're a bigger fool that I took you for. She was here earlier, telling me what had happened last night.' She stared at him with her clear blue eyes. 'If it hadn't been for Walter you could have been killed, you said. Now this. She doesn't want you dead any more than I do.'

'None of you can help me with this.'

'Maybe we can't,' she agreed calmly. 'You're the only judge of that, since you won't tell us what it is. But if we know, we might have some ideas that can help. Have you considered that?' She saw his expression. 'No, I didn't think you had. It's your choice, but if I were you I'd be at Katherine's door in the morning begging her forgiveness.' She stood wearily. 'I've had my say, now I'm off to my bed.'

The silence hung heavy in the hall.

CHAPTER TWENTY

He hoisted the satchel onto his shoulder and picked up the staff he had cut the other day. Rain had fallen during the night and morning smelt fresh.

There was surprise and happiness on Katherine's face as she opened the door.

'I didn't think you were coming until later,' she said. 'Come in, come in.'

'I just wanted to leave my tools,' he told her, watching as her face fell a little. 'I also need to talk to you.' He looked down for a moment. 'And to apologise.'

She led him into the garden and took his hand, a small, fierce grip. 'The truth?' she asked.

'All of it.' He gave her everything, letting the words flood out quickly so he couldn't halt them. She listened in silence, her expression darkening, waiting until he had finished.

'You understand what the coroner's doing, don't you? He's using you.'

'I know that. But at least I'm doing something. That's better than having it eat at me.'

She sighed. 'Are you going out to the manor today?'

'I don't know where else to begin,' he admitted.

'What do you think you can do there, John?'

'Find something. I hope.'

'Listen to me. Please.' She pulled at him, forcing him to turn and face her. 'Someone attacked you in town. Can't you see how much easier it would be to do that out in the country with no one else around?'

He nodded.

'At least take Walter with you,' she said. As he opened his mouth to protest, she continued, 'I know, he's not a fighter; but he helped you well enough the other night, and he would do anything for you. People will think hard before they attack two men.'

He knew she made sense, but he was reluctant to involve the lad. 'It could be dangerous,' he said.

'Let him choose,' Katherine said and called for her brother. He appeared, chewing bread, a mug of ale in his hand. 'John needs help,' she told him.

'Why didn't you ask me, John?' he asked.

'You could get hurt. I don't want that.'

'I'll help you,' the boy offered. 'You know I'll help you.'

Katherine cocked her head. 'Well?'

He chuckled and lifted his good arm in surrender. 'We'd better start walking, I suppose.' He turned to the girl. 'We should be back by dinner. If we haven't returned by evening …' He didn't try to complete the sentence, just saw her nod quickly.

At the front door, hidden by the screens, she stood on tiptoe and kissed him quickly. 'I think you're a fool for doing this. But I thank you for telling me, at least.' She looked at the pair of them. 'God go with you both.'

• • •

On the road he told Walter what he knew and what he suspected.

'What will we do out at the manor?' the boy asked.

'We'll see what we can find.'

'What do we do if they don't want us there?'

'Then we leave,' he answered. He wasn't after a fight. 'That'll be the end of it.'

The clouds had blown away, leaving a clear, pale sky and a warm sun. They followed the charcoal burner's track that led away from the road and through the woods. As they passed the clearing where Geoffrey's body had been found he stopped to cross himself and say a small prayer, leaning on the staff. On the hill the woodcutters had gone but the trunks remained, branches stripped away, laying long and straight on the ground. Down in the valley he could see a village and a single larger house standing away from the others.

'Down there,' he said. They followed the path over the common ground where a few cattle and sheep grazed, then around the fields cut into strips, little left growing now, the earth roughly tilled.

The village looked poor, some of the cottages no more than hovels, two of them empty, the roofs pulled down inside the walls. But the manor house was prosperous, faced in good stone with thick glass in the windows, the home of a wealthy man.

Walter pulled at his arm and pointed. Two men were working in one of the fields, one guiding a bullock, the other holding a plough.

'We can try them,' John said. He led the way, calling out to claim the men's attention as he walked. They wore leather jerkins over their shirts, feet and legs bare to their braies, their skin weatherbeaten and creased. 'Is this Henry de Harville's manor?' he asked them.

The taller of them eyed him suspiciously. He was broad, with heavily muscled arms, the beard thick on his face. 'Who wants to know?' he asked, glancing at his companion.

'My name's John. John the carpenter.'

'What do you want with the master?'

'Is he here?'

The man spat. 'He's never here, that one. Visited for a day at Lammas and that was the first we've seen of him this year. Leaves it all to the steward.'

'Hugo?'

The man raised his eyebrows. 'For someone who seems to know nothing you know a lot, carpenter. There's no work for you here, if that's what you're wondering.' He nodded at the broken arm. 'Especially for someone who's not whole.'

'You've had men cutting wood up on the hill,' John said, ignoring the jibe.

'Aye.' The man offered nothing more.

'I heard there was a man killed up around there.'

'No one from here.' The man shrugged. 'Not our business.'

John nodded his understanding. 'Is Hugo here today?'

The man looked carefully at his friend, still holding the bullock. 'Gone to one of the other manors, hasn't he?' The other man nodded. 'Back in a day or two.'

'Thank you. God be with you.'

'And with you,' the man said tonelessly.

They trudged away through the village. He glanced over his shoulder to see the two men still standing, watching them. 'What did you think?' he asked Walter.

'I didn't like them.'

'Neither did I,' he said with a smile. 'I don't think they welcome strangers here.'

'What do we do now, John?'

'We go home and wait,' he said with a smile, looking at the long hill ahead.

'Wait for what?' the boy asked.

'For something to happen.'

'What's going to happen?' Walter asked, not understanding.

'I don't know yet, but something will,' he said with certainty. The men had his name and they'd pass it on to Hugo when he returned – if he'd actually gone anywhere at all. The steward would know who he was from the broken arm, if nothing else; the men who attacked him had been able to identify him easily enough.

And what might come after that, he wondered. Another attack? That was why he'd been careful not to give Walter's name, to offer him at least a little protection. He glanced around as they entered the woods, searching for any movement and keeping the staff tight in his good hand. It wouldn't do much, but at least it was a weapon. 'Pick up a rock,' he instructed the boy. 'Just in case.'

But nothing happened. They were back in Chesterfield before dinner, Walter loping off to run messages and earn money, John sitting down with the family to eat, entertained by the girls and smiling reassuringly at Katherine.

He started work, knowing she'd come to talk to him, but it was the middle of the afternoon before she arrived, bringing him a mug of ale and settling on a joint stool.

'Did you learn anything?'

He sat back on his haunches and drank before answering. 'Nothing, really.'

'Was it a waste of time?'

'I don't think so,' he replied slowly, seeing the question in her eyes. 'The steward will hear I've been out there. He'll make the next move.'

'What about Walter?'

'He didn't say anything and I didn't give his name.'

'Thank you,' she said, her voice tight. 'So what now?'

He shook his head. 'I don't know, but at least I'll be prepared for it.'

'You'd better stay alive,' she warned, trying to tease him although there was fear in her eyes. 'At least until you've finished the house.'

He grinned. 'I'll do my best.'

'I'm sorry,' she said.

'What for?'

'Making a joke of it.'

'It's better to do that than cry.' He stroked her hand, the skins of her palms as rough as his. 'I'll look after myself.'

'Is it really worth it?'

'Yes,' he said after a long hesitation, looking up at her. 'It has to be.'

'Do you think you'll change anything?'

'No,' he answered with a sigh. 'Everything will still be business as usual. But at least Will won't be buried and forgotten quite so easily. Nor Geoffrey, for that matter.'

'And you still say you're not a good man, John?'

He shook his head firmly. 'I am who I am. Nothing more than that.'

'Well, I think you're a good man.'

He stood and smiled. 'I'm a good man who has work to finish today.'

'Is that a hint?' she laughed.

'You're welcome to sit and watch me if you like,' he said. 'But I'm not a juggler or a storyteller. I'm afraid I won't entertain you well.'

'Well, if you can't do that, I'll leave you to work without an audience.' She gave a small pout, then laughed again. At the top of the stairs she turned, 'Please, John, just be careful.'

'I will,' he promised, although he knew they were nothing more than words. So much was out of his control. He put it from his mind for the rest of the day, moving steadily from job to job, enjoying the rhythm of the work and the sounds of life drifting up from downstairs. Before dusk he carefully packed the tools away. At the front door Katherine offered to walk with him, but he refused.

'I'll be fine,' he told her. 'It's still light.' But he still kept a tight grip on the staff as he walked, glancing around and listening carefully. By the time he reached the house of Knifesmithgate his heart was racing as if he'd run all the way there.

In the small room he placed the satchel in the chest, stood the staff in the corner and lay on the bed. Sooner or later Hugo would do something. He had no choice now, and after one failure he wouldn't risk another; that would just draw attention. He'd come himself, John decided, bringing help for the killing.

Carefully, he pulled the blanket across his body. The nights were cooler now. The rough wool itched against his skin, but it kept him warm. He settled back, eyes closed. He knew he should feel fear, but he didn't. He was as calm as he could ever remember being. His days of terror had passed with the pestilence, when all he could see was the dead and the haunted, and he believed that the world was about to end.

Hugo had a great deal to lose, both for himself and for his master. He'd sold green timber at the price of seasoned wood and two men had died because of it. He couldn't afford to let the truth out.

John didn't care that the coroner was using him, or that he'd receive no support or sanction. He'd lived off his wits and his skill for too many years now and survived well enough. The only thing to slow him would be the arm.

How would the game play out, he wondered? And how soon? Breathing slowly, he drifted into sleep.

• • •

The noise woke him. At first he wasn't certain he had heard anything, that perhaps he'd dreamed it. Then it came again, the small scrape of wood against stone and he knew it was the back door, the one he'd fixed during his first days here. For once, it seemed, he hadn't done his work well.

He slipped out of bed, taking the knife from its sheath, hardly daring to breathe, and let his eyes adjust to the darkness. He moved slowly to the door, ears pricked for every tiny sound. Behind him the shutters were closed tight, no slivers of light coming through. His fingers felt for the latch, glad he'd oiled it after moving in, feeling it rise silently. Then he pulled the door open inch by inch, just wide enough to slide through.

The flagstones were cold against his bare feet. He stood, waiting, straining to hear a step or a breath. Finally it was there, in the hall, the faint click of a heel against stone, and he moved silently along the passage to the corner.

As he stared he slowly began to pick out a shape by the table. A man, standing still, was turning his head slowly. John drew back slightly, enough so he could keep the man in view but not be seen himself, the knife held down at his side.

When the man finally moved, he seemed to glide over the floor, his steps sure and soundless. He circled the table then started back towards the passage. John pressed himself hard against the wall, sensing the man come closer, not even daring to look towards him.

Then he lifted his leg slightly, tensing his body. He felt the man hit against it and go sprawling loudly on the floor. John fell to his knees on the man's back, forcing the breath out of him, and held the blade against his neck, giving just enough pressure on the point to prick the skin.

'What's happened?' Martha called from upstairs.

'Come down and bring a candle and some rope,' he shouted back, surprised at the calmness in his voice.

The man was quiet, careful not to struggle against the knife, his eyes wide open, keeping silent.

Martha was in her long shift, her grey hair loose, the tallow candle smoking and casting a wide circle of light. 'What is it, John?' she asked before she saw John pinning the man to the ground. 'Jesu. Who is he?'

'I don't know, but he was in the house.' He could make out the man's features now. His jaw was set firm, his eyes dark, with brown hair cut short on his skull. John pressed the knife harder against his neck, watching a few more drops of blood run. 'What's your name?' The man didn't answer, just kept staring ahead. The light flickered then burned brighter. 'Tie his wrists behind him,' John told Martha. He kept the blade in place.

'He won't struggle. Make the knots tight. He's good, I don't want him escaping.'

When she had finished he searched the man, taking a long dagger from his belt. He removed the man's boots, letting a hidden knife clatter to the floor, then stripped off his hose.

'Why are you doing that?' Martha asked him.

'He's not going to be able to run far like that,' John grinned. 'Tie his ankles and then hold the knife on him while I dress.'

Once clothed, he used the candle on the rushlights in the hall and then dragged the man in.

Martha sat on the bench, shivering. 'What are you going to do with him?'

'As soon as it's light I'll take him to the coroner. Let him decide. Do you know his face?'

She shook her head.

'You go back to bed. I'll sit with him.'

'What?' she yelled. 'Do you really think I could sleep now? I don't know if I'll ever sleep again.' Martha shook her head in disgust. 'How did he get in, anyway?'

'He slipped the latch on the back door.' He laughed lightly. 'You should be glad I didn't mend it too well or I'd never have heard him. I'll put a proper lock on in the morning.'

'Is he a thief?' Martha wondered.

'That's a good question.' He knelt, bringing the tip of the knife close to the man's neck once more; the man didn't flinch. 'Well, what are you? A thief, or something more.' He just turned away, his mouth firmly closed. 'He's not going to tell us. We'll see what the coroner and the bailiffs can get out of him.' John stood. 'I'll get us some ale then you dress if you're not going to rest. You look like you're chilled.'

She looked up at him, her face empty and pale. 'That's not cold, John. I don't mind the cold. That's fear.'

He made her drink a little and then persuaded her back upstairs, out of the way. The man hadn't moved, hadn't spoken – had barely seemed to notice their presence, just lying there in his bonds. This wasn't a common thief, he thought, not a latchlifter out for what little he could steal. This was a killer.

John sat, staring at the man. He hadn't expected Hugo to act quite so quickly, or like this. Still, it told him that the steward hadn't been too far away when he had visited the manor that morning, and that he was resourceful and ruthless.

Upstairs he could hear Martha crying softly. He'd brought this on her, this threat on herself and on her house. He was certain that the man in front of him would have murdered her if necessary and never given it a second thought. She knew that, too. Perhaps he needed to find somewhere else to live, to give her back her peaceful life she treasured.

He was still sitting there as dawn arrived and the thin band of light on the horizon widened. Outside there were a few early voices, hushed, vague sounds that carried. Finally he stood up and sliced through the rope tying the man's ankles.

'Up,' he said. The man obeyed without look or question, slowly easing himself to his feet.

CHAPTER TWENTY-ONE

John marched him down the streets, the man with his legs and feet bare, wrists tied behind his back, a black cote hanging low over his braies. People stopped to stare, looking quizzically at each other.

He kept the knife in his hand, walking two paces behind the man, watching him carefully for any signs of flight and speaking only to tell him which way to turn. It was humiliation, and John was doing it deliberately. Another hour and this would be the talk of Chesterfield; by the end of the day word would have passed out among the villages. Let Hugo hear that another attempt had failed, that his assassin had been beaten by a man with a broken arm.

• • •

'What have you brought me, carpenter?' de Harville asked as he came out to the stables, pulling the robe around him, keeping the fur close against his neck. Brother Robert limped behind him, frowning at the pain in his leg.

'He broke into Dame Martha's last night.'

'Did he now?' The coroner walked around the man who kept staring ahead, his mouth a thin, tight line. 'A thief?'

'A killer.' John took out the two knives and threw them down on the straw.

De Harville raised his eyebrows in mock admiration. 'A man comes to kill you and you overcome him with one arm. You must live a charmed life, carpenter. What do you think, brother?'

'Why would he want to kill you?' the monk wondered.

'He hasn't said, he hasn't uttered a word. Didn't even complain when I brought him down here like that.'

'No?' the coroner said. 'Perhaps the bailiffs can loosen his tongue a little. You found him in the house?'

'In the hall.'

'Do you know him, Robert?'

The monk shook his head slowly. 'He has a familiar look, but no, I can't say I could give him a name.'

'Find two of the bailiffs. Have them take him to the gaol and question him there.'

The monk hobbled away. De Harville stared at the man. 'He looks familiar to me, too, but I can't place him.' He shook his head. 'No matter. The bailiffs will have him talking soon.' He turned to John. 'How did you take him?'

'Just luck, Master, and surprise.'

'Luck and surprise seem to be your friends, John Carpenter. I'll expect a lot from you once you're my steward.'

'Yes, Master.'

The brother returned with the bailiffs, a pair of large men with brutal faces and scarred hands.

'Take him away,' the coroner ordered. 'Find out what he has to say.' They watched the man being led away to the gaol.

'How many times is that, carpenter? Three if we include Mark?'

'Yes, Master,' he answered simply.

'It seems as if a number of people here haven't taken to you.' He paused. 'This one looked as if he knew what he was doing.'

'He did. I told you, I was lucky.'

'Perhaps a little more than that,' de Harville said thoughtfully. 'You handle yourself well, even with that.' He nodded at the arm in its sling.

'If you travel you learn how to look after yourself.'

'Perhaps.' He glanced over at the monk. 'What do you think, brother?'

'You believe Hugo sent him?' Robert asked.

'I do. I went out to the manor yesterday. They said Hugo was away.' He shrugged. 'But they could have been lying.'

'What did you learn out there?' the coroner asked him.

'Nothing. They've felled quite a few trees; some are still waiting to be hauled away. That's it.'

De Harville remained silent for a long time, pacing around the stable, stopping to stroke the horses and whisper soothingly to them. John and the monk looked at each other, their expressions blank. 'So what do you do now, carpenter?' he said finally.

'I don't know, Master.'

'Watch out for Hugo,' the coroner advised. 'He's a clever man.'

'I've seen that,' John said wryly.

'If you're going to be of any use to me in this, I need good evidence.'

'I understand that, Master.'

The coroner stared at him, confusion and frustration on his face. 'You don't make any sense to me. I keep underestimating you.' He hesitated. 'There's more than luck in taking someone like that. You saw his eyes, they're empty.'

'Perhaps the bailiffs will find out he's working for Hugo.'

The coroner shook his head. 'They'll hurt him, right enough, but I doubt he'll say much. He'll be sent to Derby to stand trial.'

'And hang?'

'That depends who supports him. If it's my brother he'll vanish quietly before it ever comes to court.'

'So all this is for naught?'

'Most likely,' he said with a slow nod. 'Whoever that man is, he's being paid well to keep his mouth closed. That should tell you something.'

'How's Dame Martha?' Robert asked.

'Terrified.' The monk nodded sadly. 'She might enjoy some peaceful company today.'

'Go and see her, Brother,' the coroner suggested. 'Pray with her. She's a good woman.'

'Yes, Master.'

'What am I going to do with you, carpenter?'

'I don't know.'

'Neither do I,' de Harville said with a small laugh. 'But you seem capable of making things happen by yourself. Where will I see you next? Bringing me Hugo, or will I be examining your body?'

'Pray God I'll be alive.'

'I hope so, I have plenty for you to do out at Unstone. For now, you seem to be managing.' He swept back into the house.

'I'll come and see Dame Martha later,' Robert told him. 'The master's right, it's Christian work.'

'I'm sure she'll be grateful.'

'Go with God,' the monk said. 'I pray He keeps watching over you.'

• • •

At the house he poured ale and took a mug up to the solar. Martha was dressed, sitting in bed with the coverlet pulled around her. Her eyes were red from tears, the skin of her cheeks pale.

'Here,' he said gently. 'I brought you this. He's in the gaol now and they'll send him to Derby. You're safe, I promise.'

She turned to face him, her mouth mournful. 'Why, John? What did he want?'

'He wanted to kill me.' He reached across and pressed her hand gently. 'They're going to have to do better than that to succeed.'

She began to cry again, dabbing away the tears with a piece of linen. 'He was in my home.'

'I'll make sure no one else can get in.'

'I'll never be able to forget he was here.'

'I'm sorry,' he told her gently. 'It's my fault.'

She sat up straighter, her face suddenly alive. 'Your fault?'

'If I hadn't started looking into all this …'

'No,' she said forcefully, the blood coming back into her face. 'I don't blame you. I'm scared, John, I'm not stupid. What you're doing takes courage.'

'He could have killed you.'

'And he would have killed you. Think about that, John Carpenter.'

'I have, believe me.' He squeezed her hand a little more. 'Brother Robert's coming over to see you later.'

She laughed. 'How did you persuade him to do that?'

'The coroner ordered it.' He grinned. 'The brother will do his duty.'

'John,' she told him slowly, 'I don't understand what's going on here, but please don't worry about me. Do what's right.'

'Thank you.' He stood. 'I'll make sure the house is secure.'

He worked carefully, checking every entrance and window until he was certain they couldn't easily be forced. Anyone would have to break down the door to get in and the noise would wake half the town.

Martha was in the hall, working on her embroidery. Her fingers moved slowly, but her touch was unsure, shaking, and she kept having to pull out stitches, muttering in frustration to herself.

He fitted the satchel on his shoulder.

'I can stay if you need,' he offered.

'You go,' she said with a smile. 'I'll be fine. Robert will be here before dinner, if I know him well. That man was always led by his belly.'

• • •

At the house on Saltergate Katherine drew him in quickly and took him straight out to the garden.

'Who was he?' she asked bluntly.

'I don't know. He wouldn't say anything.'

'He came for you, didn't he?' Her eyes were on him, daring him to lie to her.

He nodded. 'He was there to kill me.'

'He didn't hurt you?'

'No. I was able to take him by surprise.'

'How's Martha?'

'She putting on a face as if she's fine, but she's shaking inside.'

'I'll go and see her later,' Katherine told him.

'The coroner's clerk is going to pray with her.'

She snorted. 'She needs a woman there, not a monk.'

He smiled. 'I'm sure she'd be happy to have your company.'

'Do you think you can win in this?' Katherine asked.

Win, he thought – he wasn't even sure what that meant. He had believed that winning was finding Will's murderer, but that had been done and now Geoffrey was dead as well. Some would find God's hand in that, the divine justice. And now? Whatever he did, the oak would still be used on the spire. The diocese had paid for it and they wouldn't spend more. Few would care what would happen; the results, the twisting and the warping of the timber, would be years away, when the children of today's children were grown and no one could recall what had happened. 'I don't know,' he answered eventually and stirred. 'I should get to work.'

'You're not getting away like that, John.'

'I didn't think I could,' he admitted wryly.

'I need some honesty from you.'

'Honesty?' he asked in surprise, 'I've told you what I know.'

She reached out and placed her small fist on his cote over his heart. 'I want the truth of what's in there.' He didn't know how to answer. He felt the warmth of her palm and the firm pressure against his chest. His heart was beating a little faster. 'I've made it plain what I feel, haven't I?' she said.

'Yes.' His voice surprised him, hoarse and quiet, all the confidence gone.

'But you've said nothing of what you're thinking. I need to know, John.'

'I don't know what to say to you.'

'No?'

He shook his head. 'I can't give you any sweet words.'

'I don't want sweet words,' she told him with a shake of her hair. 'I just want your truth, John. Give me that.'

He looked at the ground. Finally he pulled her to him and kissed her mouth, his lips staying on hers until they couldn't breathe any longer. 'Is that honest enough for you?'

She grinned happily. 'It'll do for the moment. Now you can get to work.'

He lost himself in his tasks, concentrating on each job, doing it as well as he could and taking pride in his labour. She came to him often, bringing ale and a few words, and he could remember the taste of her. There were things he had wanted to say but for now he knew it was better to remain quiet. He liked the girl, so spirited and different, but there was a long distance between that and what she hoped to find in him. Alone, there was no one to betray him, no one to ask him where he'd been. He had given his heart once. He was in no rush to do it again.

He finished before twilight, packing up and leaving while Katherine supervised the girls, slipping out with a quick farewell before she could come after him. He kept his hand on the hilt of his dagger all the way back to Knifesmithgate, his body tense.

It was only when he locked the door behind him that he could feel his body ease, noticing that his hand was shaking and his breathing ragged.

'It scared you, too, didn't it?' Martha said, watching him. She seemed brighter, more alive than when he had left.

'Yes,' he admitted. 'It did. Has Robert visited you?'

'He stayed two hours.' She smiled. 'You should have seen him at first. Nervous as a cat wanting to know he could escape. God only knows what he thought I was going to do to him. But we began talking about the way things were like when we were young.'

'You look all the better for it.'

'I am.' She flexed her fingers. 'He remembered things I'd forgotten, like the time he fell in the river when we were playing and his mother thrashed him red raw for coming home wet. As soon as he mentioned it I could see him clear as I see you now, walking up Soutergate dripping and crying because he knew what was going to happen.' She sighed. 'He took me out of myself and that's the best thing he could have done. I still won't sleep well for a long time, but at least he sent the black dog from my mind.'

'I'm glad.'

'What about you? Have you thought what you're going to do next?'

'No. There's not much I can do, except wait.'

'That's never easy, is it, lad?'

He shook his head. 'If I'd known all this would come into your house I'd never have done it.'

'You're doing something right,' she told him. 'I'd rather that, no matter the troubles it brings with it. Young Katherine would, too. She needs someone who believes in things.'

'She doesn't need someone who could die tomorrow.'

'What's tomorrow?' Martha asked. 'I've been on this earth long enough to know that tomorrow's just a dream. It might not happen for any of us. Just think back a few years and you know that yourself. God places us here to live, John. If you don't do that you're not serving Him well.'

'Maybe,' he acknowledged with a frown.

'You grow old enough you'll see that I'm right,' she told him confidently. 'Don't let anyone say wisdom comes with old age. The only thing it brings is acceptance.'

'Are you trying to distract me?' he asked with a smile.

'I was doing a good job of it there for a minute, too,' she laughed. 'Pour us some ale. I daresay sleep will take a while for us both tonight.'

'We're safe in here. I made sure of that.'

'Maybe we are.' She tapped a finger against her skull. 'It's in here that we're not.'

CHAPTER TWENTY-TWO

He kept the knife under his pillow, his fingertips reaching up to touch it and feel the reassurance of the handle. It was a broken sleep, no real rest at all, full of dark dreams, of things waiting just beyond the horizon and dangers that he couldn't quite see. Twice he sat up, sweat chilling on his skin, believing he'd heard something before realising it was just the night mare galloping through his head.

By dawn he was up and finding his awkward way into his clothes, fitting the sling over his head and putting his arm into it. It itched under the cast at times; sometimes so much that he wished he could take his nails to the skin and rub it raw. But it hadn't given him any pain for days. Maybe it would set properly and he would have the full use of both arms. Just a short while ago that had seemed to be the only thing in life that mattered. Now, knowing he would never be hired back at St Mary's, it seemed curiously unimportant.

• • •

On Sunday he escorted Martha to the church, letting her hold onto him as they walked down the path to the ringing of the bell. He glanced up at the tower, noticing they'd done no more work on the spire. Nor would they until spring, he guessed. Over against the wall of the yard were the piles of timber, covered by canvas, just as he had seen them a few days before.

She hung close on his arm as they entered the church porch and into the nave.

'Let them all think I'm weakened,' she whispered with a sly grin. 'At least it'll give them something to talk about.' He delivered her to the goodwives and widows, their tongues chattering as they fussed about her. He began to move to the back of the church, towards the workers and the single men, then changed his mind and joined Walter, Katherine and the rest of their family. The girls crowded close, eager to tell him all they'd been doing, while Katherine smiled gently.

'Good day, Mistress,' he said, giving her a bow.

'Good day, Master.'

'John,' Walter asked with concern on his face, 'is what they said true? That someone came to kill you?'

'It's true enough,' he said.

'Did he hurt you?'

'No.' He glanced at Katherine. 'He didn't hurt me.'

'Good, I'm glad about that,' the boy told him with a smile. 'I don't want you to be hurt.'

He dawdled with them after the service, Janette and Eleanor running hither and yon in the churchyard, around and between the piles of stone that lay here and there, jumping and laughing.

'Has anything more happened?' Katherine asked. She moved nearer to him, so close they almost touched. A few of the older women who'd remained looked on with scandalised horror while the girl stared back with amusement.

'Do you enjoy doing that?' he asked her.

'They like to cluck like hens, so I just wanted to give them something to cluck about. At least they won't have to make it up. Do you know what they're saying about you?' He shook his head. 'If you believe the gossips, you overpowered two men in Martha's house and led them naked as the day God brought them into the world to the coroner.' He laughed loud as faces turned to him, outraged that anyone should find humour so close to the Lord's house. 'It's the truth, John, I heard someone saying it at the market yesterday. She claimed she'd seen it with her own eyes.'

'Believe me,' he said, shaking his head at the tale, 'one was more than enough. And no, there's been nothing more.'

'Janette,' she cried. 'Eleanor. Come on, it's time for us to go before your gowns are covered in mud.' She turned to him. 'Would you walk with us? Stay for dinner if you like.'

'I'll gladly go with you, but I'm going to eat with Martha. Brother Robert is coming by later, but I'll give her company over her meal.'

'The monk's back again?' Her eyes twinkled at the nugget of gossip.

'They talk about when they were young together.'

'Then maybe you can spend time with my brother this afternoon,' she suggested. 'I think he's jealous that I see more of you than he does.'

He glanced up at the sky, the high clouds, the breath of a chill in the air.

'Aye, that would be good.'

• • •

The meal was just bread and cheese, but she'd pulled the loaf out of the oven just before they left for church, and it was still warm in the centre as he ate, the rough texture of the wheat sweet on his tongue. Washed down with freshly-brewed ale, it was as good a feast as he had ever tasted.

By the time he and Walter set out on the road the day had cooled a little, the wind picking up out of the west, enough to rustle the leaves in the branches and send the first few tumbling. Autumn was close. They were walking north, following the path towards Dronfield, the one that had first brought him to Chesterfield.

They'd covered little more than a mile when he heard hooves in the distance. He looked back to see who was riding up, ready to move aside for the horse.

'John,' Walter whispered urgently, 'I know who that is. It's Hugo.'

'Run back to town. Go straight to the coroner. I'm the one Hugo wants; he'll leave you be.' He turned to the boy to see him looking at the rider.

'No, John,' he said. 'You're my friend. I'm going to stay here with you.'

'God's blood.' He growled and tried to push the lad with his good hand. 'Go!'

Walter stood his ground stubbornly and shook his head.

'Then take my staff.' He thrust the wood at the boy. The horse was closer now, easing back into a canter. The man in the saddle was gazing intently at them. John had seen him before, talking to the new master carpenter at the church. He had long hair that waved free in the breeze and he was dressed like a lordling, wearing a heavy robe with a fur collar, brilliant red wool hose and high boots that shone as the light caught them. A sword in its scabbard bounced at his side.

As he approached, John moved in front of the lad, keeping his hand resting on the hilt of his knife, watching as the man reined in the horse a few feet down the road.

'You're John the carpenter.' His voice was a haughty drawl, as if even speaking to someone lowly was an effort.

'You already know that, it seems.'

'Who's he?' Hugo nodded at Walter.

'No one to concern you.'

'You were out at my manor, carpenter. What did you want with me?'

'Your manor?' John asked in surprise. 'I was told it belong to Henry de Harville.'

Hugo raised his head and tightened his grip on the reins. It was only a slight movement, but John noticed it. 'I'm his steward. I look after it in his absence.'

'That's what I thought.'

'It'll serve you well to keep a civil tongue in your head, carpenter,' the man said.

John smiled. 'When I'm talking to my betters, you mean?'

'That's exactly what I mean.'

'When that happens, I'll do it.' He smiled. 'But you're not my better.'

Hugo frowned. 'You don't think so, carpenter?' He spat after the last word.

'Your master's brother asked me to be the steward of one of his manors.'

'Then your master's a fool.'

John shrugged. 'Possibly, but at least he'll have an honest man as his steward.'

'You seem intent on accusing me.'

'You seem intent on trying to kill me for it,' John said calmly.

Hugo raised his eyebrows. 'More accusations, carpenter?' He glanced over at Walter. 'Are you listening, boy? I might take your friend to the law for the slander he's spouting.'

'I'm sure your master would like that,' John said, his voice calm and steady. 'His name read would out in another court. You came looking for me, so you must have a reason.'

'I'm offering you a last chance, carpenter. You seem to think that the oak from the manor shouldn't be used on the church.'

'It can be used,' he said. 'Just not yet. It needs two years or more to dry out.'

'The master carpenter disagrees. Who do you think knows more?'

'The one who's not being paid to lie.'

'And yet another accusation.' Hugo shook his head sadly.

'Seasoned oak fetches a pretty price, steward. Is that what the diocese believes it's bought?'

'By the time that wood is used it will be dry. Ask the master carpenter.'

'And should I jingle his purse to see how much you've paid him to say that?' John wondered. 'Perhaps your master doesn't know what you're doing with the trees he owns.'

'My master trusts me,' Hugo said haughtily.

'He'd hardly be the first man to trust and be cheated.' John shrugged. 'I daresay your coffer's full. How many manors do you run for him?'

'Three,' Hugo answered proudly.

'Ample chance for profit there. It would be interesting to see how he'd react to a letter saying what his steward was doing in his name.'

'You can write, carpenter?' Hugo smiled, his mouth twisted. 'You're a man of many talents.'

'My master has a clerk.'

'Are you threatening me?' Hugo moved his arm to his sword.

'I don't threaten,' he said quietly. 'You must be a very fearful man, steward.'

Hugo laughed. 'Me? Who should scare me? You?'

'Why else would you send men twice to kill me?'

The steward cocked his head. 'Who claims that I have?'

'I do.'

'You want to blacken my character completely, don't you? I'd advise you to think before you speak – about everything.'

'Before you silence me?' John asked wryly.

Hugo shook his head. 'No one would listen to a carpenter.'

'Perhaps you should pray that's true.'

'I could kill you myself, out here, right now. And the boy. Who do you think would care? What do you think your coroner would do?'

John said nothing for a long while, listening to birds cry in the woods up on the hill. Finally he stared at the steward. 'The men you sent couldn't kill me. What makes you think you could do the job? It might be you who ends up a corpse.'

Hugo showed his teeth. 'Then you'd have to answer to my master. People know I've come looking for you today. And my master is a powerful man.'

'Powerful enough to be accused of cheating the church?'

'Powerful enough to crush you and your master if he needs to.'

John knew it was true; he'd learned that much from the coroner. But he wasn't going to be cowed by words and warnings.

'You'd still be a dead man.'

'I'd wait for you in purgatory, carpenter. You'd be joining me soon enough.' He gathered up the reins. 'I've said what I came to say.' He offered a small, mocking salute, turned the horse and rode away.

'What did he mean, John?' Walter asked after the figure had crested the hill and disappeared. 'What was he saying?'

'I think he's a very scared man.'

'Why?' The boy looked confused. 'He didn't seem very scared to me.'

He took the staff back from the lad. 'Not everything's always as it seems. Do you still want to walk?'

'Yes, of course,' Walter told him. 'But why do you think he was frightened?'

'He was offering me a last chance to keep quiet about the wood.'

'Is that good?'

'Yes,' he answered thoughtfully. 'He's worried that people might start to listen.'

'What are you going to do, then? Are you going to stop?'

John smiled. 'I'm going to speak even louder. Come on, we can make it to Dronfield and back before the light goes.'

• • •

He sat on his bed, sipping at the mug of ale. He could hear Martha moving restlessly in the solar above, reluctant to sleep for the dreams and worries that would come when she closed her eyes. For all her strong words he had seen the flickers of fear in her gaze and the way her hands shook. She had hidden them quickly, but he had noticed.

None of Hugo's words had terrified him. The man dressed like he had money but underneath he was no different from a carpenter. He was just a man who'd allowed his greed to go too far and who was trying to protect himself. He'd hoped to intimidate with his threats, but all that lay behind them was emptiness. And now Hugo knew he was going to be the coroner's steward he had to be more careful. Henry might have important friends but his brother still exercised some power in Chesterfield.

He'd told Walter he would speak louder. It sounded fine when it fell from his lips, but who else could he tell? Who would listen, who would care? He rubbed a hand over the rough bristles of his chin. In truth he had no idea what he could do. He needed proof or testimony and that would be difficult to find.

He sat for a full hour, the shutters open to let in the moonlight. The steward wouldn't send any more men, at least for now. He would wait, bide his time to see what the carpenter did. Finally, John placed the mug on the floor and slipped under the blanket. He felt safe enough for the present but he still kept the knife under the pillow.

• • •

Katherine was full of questions, sitting with him as he worked, ignoring the girls playing in the hall and other woman who simply sat in her chair and stared blankly at the world.

'Walter thought he was going to try and kill you.'

'I told your brother to run, but he wouldn't. He insisted on staying with me. There's bravery in that lad.'

'He looks up to you, John. He'd defend you to the death if he had to,' she told him.

'Praise God it didn't come to that.' He pointed across the floor. 'Can you hand me that nail?'

She bent to pick it up. 'Walter said you thought Hugo was scared, but he didn't know why. Was he?' she asked carefully. 'Or were you just trying to comfort my brother?'

He put down the hammer. 'No, he's scared, right enough. He wouldn't have taken the trouble to find me otherwise. And he wouldn't have been all bombast and threats.'

Katherine pursed her mouth in thought. 'That doesn't sound like fear.'

'If he'd really wanted to, he could have killed us both yesterday. He had a sword, he had a horse: we couldn't have outrun him. He's sent men out twice to try and murder me and my luck has held. What he was really saying was that if I did nothing, he would do nothing.'

'A truce?'

He considered the word, frowning. 'A stalemate, more like.'

'Are you going to do what he wants?'

'No.' He shook his head firmly. 'I'm not.'

'Can you trust him?'

'Probably not,' he grinned. 'But if that's what he chooses, I'm ready for him.' He patted the knife tucked into its sheath.

'John, please, don't sound so cocksure,' she begged quietly.

'I'm sorry.' She was right; it had been a stupid, vain remark. He could die as easily as anyone else and it would do good to remember that. He glanced down at his good arm, tensing the muscle and imagining the life gone from it. 'I'm sorry,' he repeated.

'What can you do to bring this Hugo down?' Katherine asked.

He gave a long, sad sigh. 'I don't know. I've been puzzling over it. Someone who'd testify against him or some proof. But who'd be willing to do that?'

She smiled at him. 'I have faith in you.'

'More than I do myself sometimes.' He brightened. 'But for the present I still have plenty to keep me busy here. That's work enough for now.'

He found real joy in each of the tasks, however small. He could concentrate on them; let his hand work in the way God had intended, watching things take form as he used his tools.

There would be ample to keep him busy on the manor; so the coroner had promised him, and he hoped it was true. That and all the hundred other things he'd need to learn would fill his days. There would be no time to think of other things, every hour of daylight would be filled.

He rasped an awkward, sharp corner of metal on a hinge, rubbing away the rust to show the brightness underneath, working it until it was smooth and he could run his fingertip over it. He tested the door, checking it opened and closed as smoothly as it should, and then tightened up the screws for one final half-turn so they'd remain securely in place. He sat back, satisfied, picking up the mug and taking a long swig of ale. Another day and he'd be finished in the solar. For a moment he imagined Katherine up here in the evening, settling down in the bed with her two younger sisters, and he tried to picture her face as she slept, all the cares and responsibilities gone, a small, sweet smile on her face.

He stood and gazed out of the unglazed window. He could just make out the top of the tower at the church, one of the timbers that poked out to the sky swaying in a gust of wind. Maybe Martha was right, maybe God truly did have a plan for him. He'd seen the broken arm as something awful, but perhaps there had been a divine hand behind it.

He held each tool in turn in his left hand, wiping all the metal with the oiled cloth in his right before slipping them back into the satchel. The chisels were growing blunt; he'd need to use a whetstone on them soon, once he had two working arms again. If Walter was willing, it would be a good, useful task for the lad.

He glanced around the room, making sure he'd put everything away and not left any tools. They were his fortune, although God knew the one time he had forgotten one, when Walter had come after him, it had saved his life. With a final glance he settled the satchel on his shoulder and eased his way down the stairs to the hall.

Katherine was out somewhere, the girls gone with her. Only the old woman in the chair remained. As he passed her she raised her head. In a voice as ragged as a raven's caw, she said, 'You have a curse on you. The devil gave you that arm.'

'Mistress,' he began, not sure what to say to her. The woman's face was agitated, her mouth moving but no more words coming out, her fingers drumming wildly on her lap. He moved closer to help, but she lashed out at him with her arm. Then her eyes closed and she seemed to fall asleep.

He'd barely opened the door when the girls rushed in, laughing with delight over some little thing, followed by Katherine carrying a basket of wet linen, her face flushed from the walk up Soutergate from the river.

'Your mother …' he began, and saw her eyes widen. She dropped the basket and dashed in the door, kneeling by the chair, feeling the older woman's brow and neck.

'Mama,' she said quietly, her voice desperate. 'Mama.'

'I'll go for the apothecary,' he offered. Katherine kept her fingers against the woman's neck a few more moments, then lay her head against the woman's breast. The girls stood hushed at the other end of the room, watching the scene, not understanding what was happening.

'There's no need.' He walked over and placed his hand lightly against Katherine's back, feeling the small shudders going through her, each one growing longer and deeper until the sobbing began. She clutched at her mother's gown, bunching the material in her small fists. Her tears were flowing fast, her breathing was ragged.

He motioned to the girls with his head. 'Come on with me,' he told them quietly. 'Let's leave your sister and your mother together for a little while.'

Janette and Eleanor were a loud gaggle of questions as soon as they were out of the door, wondering what had happened and why their sister was weeping. Once they were in the house on Knifesmithgate, Martha coming through from the buttery, wiping her arms on a piece of linen, he sat them down on a bench and knelt in front of them.

'Your mama's died,' he told them, looking each one in the eye, his voice as gentle as he could make it. He heard Martha's swift intake of breath. 'You know she wasn't well, don't you?' They both nodded shyly, eyes wandering around the unfamiliar room. 'She's at peace now, she'll be with God.'

'Why don't the pair of you come with me?' Martha told the girls, holding her hands out to them. 'Let's see what we can find in the garden, shall we?' She glanced back over her shoulder, offering him a small, pained smile.

Death was a woman's time, he thought. For the grief and the wailing, for the washing and preparing of the body, for all the emotions and the sadness. He could go and sit with Katherine, but she needed this time alone. He could help Martha with the girls, but she'd be much better without him around. He poured a mug of ale and stood by the table. 'You have a curse on you' she had said. Her last words, the first he'd ever heard her utter and dark ones, coming from a place no one else could see.

• • •

They held the funeral two days later. Martha and some of the other goodwives had helped ready the corpse, washing it and dressing it in the long linen winding sheet. John marked out the boards for the coffin and cut them with Walter's help, showing the boy how to nail them together, nodding his approval as the boy worked. He stood at the graveside between Walter, his face fixed ahead, his gaze empty, and Katherine, her eyes rimmed red. Martha had charge of Janette and Eleanor, holding onto their hands and whispering in their ears. A few others attended, giving their responses to the priest as a bitter wind swept through the churchyard, the laughter and chatter of the workmen a backdrop to everything.

He hung back when others went to drop small handfuls down on the wood. She wasn't his family; he hadn't known her at all. When everyone had finished, Katherine knelt, picked up a clod and placed it in his hand. 'Please,' she said, her words so soft that the breeze threatened to whip them away, 'you were with her when she died.'

He stepped forward, holding out his hand and crumbling the dirt through his fingers, watching it fall before turning and walking to the others. As they passed through the lychgate he looked back to see the gravediggers already at work, a flagon of ale sitting on the ground beside them.

• • •

For two days he stayed away from the house on Saltergate. He wanted to give them time to mourn, to find a little peace in their new lives. He barely left the house, moving from bench to stool to bed, wandering in the garden, unable to settle or rest properly. At night his dreams were full of the woman's face as her eyes closed, her final words filling him. In the mornings and at night he prayed for her troubled soul, hoping she had finally found grace.

On the third day he knocked on the door, finding Katherine with no smile of welcome, but with half-moon smudges of sleeplessness under her eyes. He drew her close, holding her as she cried, feeling her grab at him until the tears had all passed.

There was a pall of sorrow over the place. The girls played some silent, private game, one of them going into the garden and returning with a flower that she arranged carefully with the others, before the other girl did the same.

He went out to the cookhouse, the fire there warm after the crispness of the morning. Like every other place in the house, it needed work. Katherine had followed him, watching him as he settled chisel against wood, delicately shaving off a corner and feeling the smoothness of the wood.

'Talk to me,' she begged. 'Please. Something pleasant.'

He leaned back and started to speak, telling her of York, of the magnificence of the Minster, the way the streets were so crowded that each journey from one end of the city to the other took a full hour. He described the houses in the Shambles there, the way each storey jettied out over the one below it, until at the top a man could reach out and shake hands with his neighbour across the street. Her face began to lighten and the sadness clear from her eyes as he recalled the priests and friars who populated the place, some venal, some holy, and the churches scattered like stars all across the city.

'Thank you,' she said finally, giving him a wan smile. 'I feel like there's been too long without any joy in the house.'

'How's Walter?'

'He went and worked after the funeral. He's been gone every day, coming home late and not saying much. Even the girls have been quiet. I know their game has something to do with mother, but they won't tell me what.'

'Death's a hard lesson when you're young,' he said, remembering his own childhood. 'And what about you?'

'I look after them all, the way I always do.' She opened her mouth to say more, shook her head, then asked, 'You love this work, don't you?'

'Aye,' he agreed. 'There'll be plenty of it at the manor, too, from what the coroner's told me.'

'You've made up your mind, then?'

'It's too late in the year to take to the roads and start looking for anything else. No one will be building during the winter. Besides,' he added with a small sigh, 'the idea of a home's becoming more appealing.'

'You've always lived in towns and cities?'

He nodded. 'It's where the work is.'

'You'll find it lonely out there, John.'

'I'll be so busy that I won't notice. There are repairs, things to learn, new tenants to find.' He shrugged and winked. 'Besides, I'll be here every Saturday for the market. You won't be rid of me so easily.'

'I'll look forward to that,' she told him with a weak smile. 'I should let you work. The girls will wonder where I am.'

• • •

The jobs in the cookhouse took all day. He wished Walter had been there to help, with his eagerness and desire to please and his patience that never seemed to end. Finally he finished, less than happy with a few things, but knowing he'd done some good.

He was in the hall, ready to take his leave, with the satchel hoisted on his shoulder, when Walter came home. He was frowning, his head down. John hadn't seen him since the funeral, and he seemed weighed down, bothered by something.

'Hello, lad. It's good to see you.' The boy smiled vaguely at the words, but they didn't seem to touch him. John looked questioningly at Katherine, who shook her head. 'Come on,' he said. 'Walk with me, you can tell me what you've been doing.' He put his arm around the lad's shoulders and ushered him out of the door. 'Something's troubling you.'

'Yes, John,' Walter said in surprise. 'How did you know?'

'It doesn't matter. Is it about your mother?' The boy shook his head. 'What is it, then?'

'I was thinking about what you said.'

'Me?' he asked. 'What did I say?'

'About how you needed proof against Hugo. I didn't like Hugo.'

'Neither did I, but proof won't be easy to find.'

'I know. I've been looking and asking. I thought it would help you.'

'Just be careful,' he warned. 'If people know you're doing that, it could be dangerous.'

'I am, John,' Walter insisted. 'I've been at the churchyard. I listen a lot when people are talking. They don't notice me.'

'Still, watch yourself.'

'I will,' the boy promised. 'They said there's more wood coming tomorrow.' That made sense, he thought. They'd seen the trees when they went out to the manor. This would be the last load of the year, most likely, ready to be cut and stored until spring. 'I know the carter. He's called Phillip. He always talks to me when he sees me. I can ask him if you like. Do you think he'd know anything, John?'

'He might.' That was possible, although he doubted a carter could help much; his only job would be to transport the timber. 'You just make sure there's no one else around when you speak to him.'

'I will, John.'

'Do you want me to go with you?'

The lad shook his head adamantly. 'He knows me. I want to do this by myself.'

'Thank you,' he said. 'Be careful, and tell me what you learn.'

'I will,' Walter answered, smiling fully for the first time.

'God be with you.'

John watched as the lad loped away, feeling ashamed. The boy had just lost his mother, but he was doing something. Meanwhile, he'd contented himself with working on a house, putting the other problem aside quite prettily as if it no longer mattered. With a heavy heart he completed the short journey back to Knifesmithgate.

• • •

All the next day he stirred whenever there was a sound, setting his tools aside to listen in case Walter had returned. He'd explained to Katherine what the boy was doing, trying to calm her fears.

'The odds are that the carter won't be able to help,' he assured her. 'I told him to be careful and take the man aside to talk to him.'

But he could see the worry creasing her face, and twice he heard her start to shout at the girls, stopping herself short after a word or two. It was late in the afternoon when the lad appeared, his face beaming like a summer sun, all the cares vanished from his face. Katherine held him close for a moment, before she stepped back.

'You look happy,' John said. 'Did you see him?' The boy nodded. 'What did he have to say?'

'He doesn't like Hugo, either. He says it's always difficult to make him pay.'

John laughed. 'Somehow that doesn't surprise me. I can see him keeping his purse closed.' He was eager to hear more, but he could wait and let Walter tell it all in his own time.

'Phillip says he knows about Hugo selling the wood, John.'

Suddenly he was alert. 'What does he know?'

'He said …' The boy pursed his lips, trying to remember. 'He said he heard Hugo talking to the master carpenter. Not the new one, the one who died. Is that right?'

'Will. Yes.'

'He said if he didn't accept the wood, he could expect trouble. But the master carpenter said it wasn't good enough.'

'What else did he hear?'

'He says that Hugo and the new master carpenter are friends. He's seen them together at the manor.'

'You've done very well,' John praised him. 'Very well indeed.' He thought for a moment. 'Do you think Phillip would testify against Hugo?'

'I didn't ask him,' His face fell. 'Did you want me to?'

'No, you've done more than enough.'

'He's going to be back tomorrow,' he said. 'I can ask him then, if you want.'

'You just be careful,' Katherine warned him, 'I don't want anything happening to you.'

'None of us do,' John agreed. 'Would you like me to come with you tomorrow?'

'Don't your trust me, John?' Walter's voice was hurt.

'I trust you with my life,' he answered honestly.

'Let him, Walter,' Katherine said. 'He knows what to ask, that's all. John's right. No one could have done better than you; he just wants to help you, that's all.' The lad's eyes were wide, his face glowing.

'Do you want to help me, John?'

'I'd be proud to, but I don't think I'm welcome at the churchyard anymore.'

'We could see Phillip on the road,' the boy suggested brightly.

'Yes,' he agreed with a nod. 'That's a good idea.'

'He said he'd be in early tomorrow.'

'Then we'd better be ready for him.' He lifted the satchel higher on his shoulder. 'I'll call for you a little after dawn.'

• • •

'You've got a sly smile on your face,' Martha told him, an edge of curiosity in her voice. 'Something good with Katherine?'

'Maybe something good about Hugo.'

'Oh?' She sat back on the bench, her blue eyes bright and expectant.

He explained what little he knew, realising how fragmentary it seemed in the telling. 'We're going to talk to the carter tomorrow.'

'You underestimated Walter, didn't you?'

'Aye,' he admitted a nod. 'I did. There's plenty to him.'

'There is to most people if you look, John,' she chided him lightly.

'I never thought to ask him to help,' he said.

'But he did it anyway.' She looked at him. 'That lad thinks the world of you.'

He sighed, shaking his head in bemusement. 'I don't know why.'

'I do,' Martha said. 'His father …' She sorted the words in her mind, picturing the man who was long since buried. 'He was as good a soul as you'd care to meet. Worked hard at his trade, looked after his family. He put money aside, that's the only reason they still have that house. But he died too young. Walter would only have been four or five. His mother tried to make up for it, but then she had the palsy and she was never the same, God rest her soul. He needs someone and he found you.' She cocked her head. 'Like it or not, what with Katherine and Walter, you're part of that family now.'

'I don't want him risking anything for me.'

'It seems to me he's decided that for himself. Pleasing you is important to him. And he's done a good job of it.'

'Aye, he has that. I told him so, too.'

'That's all he needs, John. That's everything.'

• • •

The dew was heavy on the grass as they stood by the mile marker outside Chesterfield on the Bolsover road. He had his hood pulled up over his head, watching his breath steam in the air, his good hand tucked under his sling to keep it warm. He'd need new hose before winter, thicker and better woven, something to keep out the cold. Time passed slowly with nothing to fill his mind. Walter barely seemed to feel the chill, moving from foot to foot, running to the crest of the hill to see if he could spot the carter in the distance.

Finally he returned, smiling wide. 'He's coming, John. I can see him.'

Even then it took a good half hour for the cart to reach them, drawn by a bullock that paced with aching slowness along the road. The tree trunk had been cut in half but even so it hung far behind the wagon, lashed down with heavy ropes to hold it in place.

'Hello, Phillip,' Walter said brightly.

The carter nodded at the lad. He was a small man with thick arms, moving the reins to keep the animal moving steadily. His gaze flickered suspiciously around. 'Who's he?'

'This is John,' the boy explained. 'I told you about him yesterday.'

'God's blessing on you,' John said.

'Aye, and on you,' the man replied. 'You're a friend of Walter's?'

'He is,' the lad said.

'You want Hugo, Walter said.'

'If there's evidence against him.'

'I hate that bastard,' Phillip said flatly.

'What's he done to you?' John asked.

The carter snorted. 'He'll pay you when he's good and ready, and never the amount he first promised. He doesn't care if your family's near starving for want of a few coins.'

'Why do you work for him, then?'

'Because even something's better than nothing out here,' he answered plainly. 'I'd rather the promise of a penny than nothing when there are hungry mouths at home.

'If you hate him that much you could see him gone,' John suggested.

The carter considered that as the animal plodded on. 'I can tell you what I know,' he said finally. 'You can make of it what you will.' He glanced at John.

'Aye.'

'I saw him up by the church a few weeks back, arguing with the one in charge there, the master carpenter. The old one.'

'Will.'

'That's him,' Phillip said. 'I'd brought a load of wood, like this, and he said he wouldn't accept it. Said the old stuff had been good but this was useless for building. Hugo was there and told him it had been paid for, but your Will was saying they'd paid for seasoned wood.' He glanced over questioningly and John nodded. 'Hugo said if he didn't take it he would make sure there was trouble and mentioned Henry de Harville's name – that made your friend stop. A few days later he was dead and there was that new man in charge, that Joseph. There was no problem with the wood after that.'

'You told Walter you'd seen Joseph at the manor?'

'Right enough,' Phillip nodded. 'Twice?' He stopped and corrected himself. 'Nay, three times now. Laughing together so you'd think they were the best of friends.'

'What were they saying?' John asked.

'I wasn't close enough to make anything out. But,' he added with a dark grin, 'I did hear one of the other men say we wouldn't have a problem anymore.'

Was it enough, he wondered? Probably; it was certainly damning. Then another thought came to him. 'Do you know anything about a man named Geoffrey? He was murdered on the manor, up in the woods where they were felling the oak.'

'Everyone was talking about that.' Phillip cleared his throat and spat. 'First time I can ever recall someone being killed out there. But that's all. Mind you, Hugo was out the evening before. I saw him walking on the road when I was going back to Bolsover. Thought that fine horse might have thrown him.'

John remembered when he and Walter had gone to see where Geoffrey had been killed. The woodcutters had said the steward had been out in the woods. 'Would you testify to what you've told me?' he asked the carter.

The man was silent for a long time, flicking his whip over the bullock as the cart strained along under the weight of the timber. 'What'll happen to the steward?'

'From what you've told me, he'll likely be sent to Derby to stand trial for murder. Come down and talk to the coroner after you've delivered this.' He patted the oak, feeling the age of the wood, the way it could be used in time, made into something beautiful and lasting.

'Not today,' Phillip said adamantly. 'I've got to go to Wirksworth and back yet. That's money. Your coroner's just going to have to wait.'

'When?' He wanted to shout the word, but he held his voice down, making it into a gentle question.

'Sunday,' Phillip replied. 'We come in here for the service. I always stay after to say a prayer for my mother, after everyone's gone.' He spoke the sentence quickly, as if it was embarrassing to reveal so much. 'I'll meet you in the porch after that and I'll tell your coroner everything I've told you.'

'Thank you,' John told him.

'You'd better not be lying to me,' Phillip warned. He turned to Walter. 'Can I trust his word?'

'John wouldn't lie,' the boy said, his jaw set firm. 'Would you, John?'

'I'm telling you the truth,' he told the carter, seeing the man nod his acceptance.

'I'll be there on Sunday, then. You just make sure your coroner arrests Hugo.' He looked ahead. 'Soon be at the church now.'

The tower was tall on the horizon, standing at the top of the hill, the first few boards of the spire visible.

'We'll go,' John said. 'It's probably best if you're not seen talking to us. God be with you, Phillip.' And keep you safe, he thought.

They stood, watching the cart slowly rumble up the road, going no faster than a man's slow amble.

'I need to see the coroner,' John said and turned to the boy. 'You've performed a wonder finding Phillip. Thank you.'

Walter smiled broadly. 'All I wanted to do was help.'

'You've done that, right enough. Maybe more than you'll ever know. I'll make sure the coroner knows that, too.'

• • •

De Harville was out in the stable, watching the groom prepare the roan. He was wearing a short green riding cloak trimmed with fur, a cote of the deepest burgundy and black hose, his boots polished to a high shine.

'You'd better be quick, carpenter. I'm going hunting. No, not that like,' he rebuked the groom. 'Tighten the girth properly. I don't want to slip off the damn horse.'

'You wanted evidence against the steward,' John said and watched the coroner turned sharply.

'What have you found?'

He explained what Phillip was willing to say. De Harville stroked his cheeks thoughtfully. 'Take the animal out in the yard and wait with him,' he ordered the groom, 'I have business here.' He waited until the door had closed, just a half-light coming through the high windows. 'He'll swear to this?'

'In the church.' He hesitated. 'Is that enough for you?'

The coroner gave a wolfish grin. 'More than enough. You've done well, carpenter.'

'Not me,' he corrected. 'Walter.'

'The boy again?' He eyed the lad. 'I'll have to look into employing you.' Walter reddened as he smiled. 'As soon as I have the testimony I'll issue the warrant for Hugo.'

'He might not come easily.'

'That's what the bailiffs are for,' de Harville said dismissively. 'You've seen them, they're big men.' He started to walk away, turning at the door. 'By the way, what's your Dame Martha done to Brother Robert?'

'Done?' He didn't understand the question.

The coroner laughed. 'The monk's happier than I've seen him in years. Has she bewitched him?'

John smiled. 'I think she's just been reminding him of a time when they were young together.'

De Havrille shrugged. 'Whatever it is, it's made him happy. I'll see you at the church on Sunday. God keep your carter until then.'

CHAPTER TWENTY-THREE

Martha clung tight to his arm as they walked along the flagstone path to the church. There was a chill in the air, a deep breath of autumn on the wind. The leaves were already beginning to change their colours, going from green to gold, some already taking on a deep red lustre. He glanced across, seeing the neat piles of earth marking the graves of Will, Mark, Geoffrey, Katherine's mother – all the people who'd died since he arrived in Chesterfield.

'Are you sure you know what you're doing?' Martha asked, her face anxious as she looked at him. 'Going against that Hugo could be dangerous.'

He had thought about little else. The nights had passed with desperate slowness, sleep no friend to him. It was a time for dark imaginings, of the worst that might happen, when all manner of thoughts flew through his mind.

He prayed that Phillip would be there, that he hadn't changed his mind. In the nave he escorted Martha over to the other women. She squeezed his hand lightly.

'I'll see you when you come home. God grant you what you need, John.'

He looked around as he moved to join Katherine and Walter, both of them smiling and moving apart so he could stand between them. Finally he saw the carter with three women, one his age, the others his daughters, both with the look of their father in their faces. The man looked straight ahead, eyes on the altar, his lips moving in prayer.

'Can I be with you after?' Walter asked.

'Of course you can,' he said. 'This wouldn't be happening without you.' He turned to Katherine and bowed slightly. 'Good morning, Mistress. You're well?'

'I'll be better when this is all done.' She kept the smile on her mouth but he could see the worry in her eyes.

'Soon enough,' he promised, and hoped his words were true. All around, people were talking before the service began, low buzzes of gossip that flew around the building. He could feel his broken arm starting to itch inside its cast but put it to the back of his mind before it could torment him. He felt the light stroke of a finger against the back of his hand and turned to see Katherine gazing straight ahead, smiling impishly.

Silence fell as the priest appeared, followed by a deacon who reverently placed the Bible on the altar. The priest spoke his Latin so quietly it came out as a mumble, looking down at the floor, only able to be heard when he made the readings and led the congregation in the creed.

John mouthed the words of the Gloria, then joined the others, waiting to kneel for the Eucharist. He took the small scrap of bread on his tongue and the tiny sip of wine, swallowing them before he said 'Amen' and the priest made the sign of the cross over his head. He stood, moving his good hand to the four points of his chest without thinking, making silent prayers for his mother, dead so long she was no more than a name, and his father, the man's gentle face springing into his mind.

He half-listened to the words, joining in with 'Thanks be to God', then watched the priest leave, the deacon behind him, the Bible clutched close to his chest. People were quick to leave, the church emptying in moments. He looked at Walter. 'We should meet the coroner.'

Katherine left with the girls, looking back over her shoulder with a fearful glance. He saw Phillip's wife and daughters go. Martha smiled as she passed him in the porch. Small groups gathered to talk outside, and soon there was only the pair of them, the coroner and the monk left.

'Where's your man, carpenter?'

'He likes to pray inside after the service when it's quiet.'

'Then let's hope he doesn't need to talk to God for too long.' He pulled the robe closer around himself.

'Give him time, Master,' Brother Robert told him.

De Harville turned away and started pacing impatiently around the small porch, the sound of his boots sharp against the stone floor. The few still left in the churchyard drifted away to their homes, leaving just the silence of Sunday.

'Go in and get him, carpenter,' the coroner barked eventually. 'He's had enough time.' He raised his hand before the monk could object. 'Go.'

He eased the heavy door open, hearing it creak on the great iron hinges, and entered slowly. The church seemed hushed, light from the tall windows showing the motes of dust in the air. The flames from a pair of candles flickered on the altar.

He looked around expectantly but saw nothing of the carter. Stepping slowly and lightly he walked down the centre of the nave, peering into the corners where the shadows clung, moving towards the crucifix at the east of the building. His throat felt dry. He reached for his knife but the sheath was empty; men didn't bring weapons to service.

He heard a small sound, someone struggling for breath, and stopped, listening intently. There, over by the small chapel of St Mary in the corner, he saw a shape on the floor.

'Master! Brother!'

He dashed over, seeing Phillip lying before the statue of the Virgin, blood pooling under him and edging out in a small lake across the flagstones. 'Phillip,' he whispered, seeing his eyes flutter. Gently he lifted the man's head, turning it, hearing the footsteps. 'Over here,' he shouted.

De Harville and the monk pushed him aside, gently turning the carter onto his back. Blood soaked his cote from a cut deep in his belly. The coroner glanced at Robert, who gave a small shake of his head.

'Who did this?' de Harville asked urgently. Phillip opened his mouth, drawing in breath to speak.

'Hugo.' The word came out as a hiss.

'Robert, you look to him,' the corner ordered, standing. 'I'll raise the hue and cry.' He blew out a long breath. 'Well, carpenter, do you want to go hunting?'

'Yes,' John answered without hesitation.

• • •

He left the church, thinking rapidly, with Walter at his heels.

'Where are we going to look for him, John?'

'He'll be going to the manor. But I want you to stay here.'

'Why?' the boy asked simply.

'Because it's going to be dangerous. I don't want you hurt or killed. I couldn't face your sister if that happened so soon after your mother.'

'But –'

John shook his head.

'No,' he said firmly. 'I know what you want, but he's going to be desperate. Please, Walter, do it for me.'

The boy nodded sadly and started to walk away, his shoulders slumped. John felt a moment's guilt, ready to call him back. But this could be saving the lad's life. Leave it like this, he told himself, leave it like this.

He ran along the road to Bolsover, each step jolting his arm. He knew what could happen if he tripped and tumbled hard once more onto his broken arm, but he forced it away from his mind.

He was breathing hard when he saw the horse at the side of the road and slowed as he approached it. It was the animal Hugo had ridden when they'd met, a big, lovely beast that eyed him nervously now, limping as it shied away. Lame. He petted the animal, stroking its mane and looked for any sign of the steward.

There was nothing to see, but the twists and turns of the land hid so much. He started to run again, going to the top of the hill and peering down into the valley. He could see a figure scrambling across a field, pausing to look back then moving on again towards the woods where Geoffrey had been killed.

He followed, keeping Hugo in view. He loped steadily, not dashing, but slowly gaining some ground. Soon enough the others would arrive; armed men who'd be able to subdue the steward and take him back to Chesterfield.

At the bottom of the hill he had to slow his pace as he climbed. The steward had vanished into the woods.

He was panting by the times he reached the trees, pausing for a moment to try and find the path Hugo had taken. Finally he spotted the grass trodden down and started walking slowly, glancing around every few paces, listening for any flutter of wings or unusual sounds.

John stopped in the clearing, seeing where Geoffrey had been killed, imagining Hugo creeping up behind the man and slitting his throat. He cast his eyes around, finally selecting a fallen branch and hefting it with his good arm. It was hardly a weapon at all, but it was better than nothing.

Hesitantly he moved on, going back into the trees. If he carried on this way he would come out above the manor. With luck, some of the men would already be there. If not, he might be able to stop the steward leaving until they arrived and could make the arrest. He tried to move quietly, but he was no countryman. With every step he blundered on a twig or heard a cone skitter off through the undergrowth.

He could see the clear slope ahead of him and the ruts where the trees had been dragged away when he felt something behind him. He tensed, turning quickly and brought up the branch. Hugo was there, three paces behind him, just out of reach. His sword was drawn and the haughty, mocking smile played across his mouth.

'The coroner sent you out alone, did he, carpenter?'

John's mouth was dry, his eyes on the man's hands and feet. They'd tell him what was coming next, not the words from his mouth. 'There's me, and there's the men,' he said. 'I daresay they'll find you before you can go too far. Especially after your horse went lame like that.'

'Where did you think I was riding? Back to the manor?' He barely paused for an answer. 'Of course you did. That's what you're meant think.'

'You won't get far on foot.' John advanced half a pace; anything to keep the man on edge.

Hugo swung the sword lazily. 'I only go on foot when I have to, carpenter. There's another horse hidden and its saddlebags full. By the time the men understand I've gone, I'll be half a county away and Henry de Harville will be a much poorer man.'

'And I'll be dead.'

'Oh yes,' the steward told him with relish. 'Tell me, did you really think I wouldn't find out about the carter? It's a very small world out here.'

'Why did you kill him in the church?' The longer he kept the man talking, the more chance of the posse arriving.

Hugo shrugged. 'It started with a murder there, it seemed only right to end it with another. No matter where it had happened, someone would have been looking for me.'

'He named you.'

'He was still alive, was he?' He shook his head. 'No matter. Are you ready to die, carpenter?' he asked casually and lifted the sword. 'You might as well put that branch down. It won't make any difference in the long run.'

John smiled. 'We'll see.'

The steward took a pace forward, extending his sword, offering it as a target. John poked the branch at it then had to step sharply back as the blade moved quickly towards him.

'I'm not going to toy with you. I'm going to make it quick.' Hugo feinted to the side then brought the sword down hard, jarring the branch from John's hand. 'Just as simple as that.'

He stood there, the broken arm held against his chest by the sling, the other arm outstretched. Slowly, he smiled, not moving. 'Do what you want,' he said.

The steward raised the blade, his grip tight on the hilt, ready to end things. John looked him steadily in the eye, his face placid and accepting. Then he heard the sound, something that whistled in the air, and Hugo was face down on the ground, the sword thrown from his hand.

John looked around, crouching and picking up the weapon. He put his hand against Hugo's neck, feeling a movement under his fingers, then saw the wound on the back of the man's head, his skull sticky with blood. He removed the dagger from the steward's belt and checked his boots for another blade before standing again.

'You can come out now,' he shouted, looking around and waiting.

Walter emerged from behind a tree, the slingshot still in his hand. His eyes were a mix of thanks and terror as he moved forward.

'Is he dead, John?' he asked fearfully.

'No. He'll live long enough for them to hang him.'

'He was going to kill you, wasn't he?' The words flooded out of the boy's mouth. 'I thought he was, that's why I threw the stone.'

'Yes, he was.' He could feel his heartbeat gradually slowing. He smiled and shook his head in wonder. 'That's twice you've saved my life now. Thank you.'

Walter was grinning.

'Why didn't you want me to come, John? I wanted to come. I followed you.'

He let the sword drop and clapped the lad on the shoulder. 'Because I can be very stupid sometimes.' He let out a long, slow breath and sat on the ground close to Hugo, leaning forward and breathing deeply before he looked up. 'Thank you,' he said again. The exhaustion was sweeping through him. He was bone weary, his head a muddle of thoughts that made no sense. 'Can you go and find the men?' he asked. 'I'll stay here with him.'

'Yes, John,' the boy said eagerly. He heard Walter loping away, the sound slowly fading. The steward still hadn't moved. He closed his eyes and let the imaginings trickle through his mind like sand. He'd been ready to die. He'd accepted it, simply waiting for the cut. It hadn't scared him. He'd stood his ground, prepared. And God had released him, decided that it wasn't his time yet. He raised his good hand, surprised to see it steady, not shaking.

He eased himself back to his feet, hearing birds calling to each other in the trees. Somewhere out of sight men were shouting.

CHAPTER TWENTY-FOUR

It was the soft grace of an autumn morning, with mist lying along the river valley. The air steamed his breath as he stood outside the bone-setter's house.

The last of summer had fallen away quickly, bringing crisp nights and rainy days that churned up the roads. He'd spent the time quietly, completing all the work he could do on Katherine's house, revelling in her company whenever she brought him ale and they could snatch a few minutes together. On Sundays he walked with Walter, careful to avoid the Bolsover road and the dark memories it would bring.

In the evenings he sat with Martha, exchanging tales. She would talk of the past, of the place Chesterfield had been when she was a girl, and he would tell her more of the towns and cities he had seen, enjoying the wonder in her eyes and her laughter at some of the strange characters he had met.

And so the time had passed.

The men had taken Hugo. The coroner had found the horse and the money the steward had hidden away and confiscated both for the Crown, a handsome small fortune to add to the King's coffers. Now he waited in the gaol to go to Derby and hang, convicted by the carter's dying words.

It had all given the coroner more in the case against his brother. But, the lawyers told him, there was no knowing when it might be heard. The following year, perhaps, or the one after that; Henry de Harville had the money and the influence to keep bringing delays.

• • •

John knocked on the door, escorted in by the old servant and left to wait in a room full of bottles and unguents with their strange smalls, the walls full of charts he couldn't begin to comprehend.

The bone-setter came in, a smile on his placid face.

'Well,' he asked, 'are you ready to have your arm back?'

'I am,'

'Take off the sling. Have you had any problems?'

'Just itching.'

'That's normal, it's good,' the man told him, feeling lightly along the dirty cast and nodding to himself. He reached for the scissors and cut the stiffened linen carefully. His hands peeled it away, bringing the bark of the splint along with it. His flesh was as pale as if it had never seen the sun. 'Keep it still.' The bone-setter stroked the flesh, checking it carefully. 'Lift your arm,' he ordered.

He obeyed, the sensation of seeing and raising the arm strange. It looked thin, withered, something that wasn't quite his.

The man held out a small block of wood. 'Take hold of this.' He grasped it, letting his fingers tighten around it before raising it above his head. The bone-setter stood back and nodded. 'It seems to have healed well. Be careful, though,' he warned. 'You haven't used it; you've lost much of the strength in your arm. You'll have to build it back up slowly. Do you understand?'

John nodded, flexing his hand and moving the arm with all the wonder and joy of a child discovering something new. He stood, happy to dig into his purse with his left hand and pick out the coins for payment. Carefully, he eased his arm into the sleeve of his shirt, then his cote, watching himself button the garment.

He didn't return directly to the house on Knifesmithgate. Instead, he went to the church, slipping inside and kneeling, offering his thanks for the use of his arm.

Work had already fallen away here for the winter, just a few men remaining, the others all gone, most taken to the roads, some finding what they could around town. The master carpenter had vanished as soon as the news about the steward had spread, leaving as quickly as he'd arrived.

The wood remained, stacked in piles against the wall, covered by canvas.

In the end nothing would change. Spring would come and the wood would be used for the spire, seasoned or not. The Diocese had spent the money, the timber was there. They wanted the spire raised to God's glory, to have it climb to the sky by the end of the next summer. The final word had come from the Bishop himself. The jingle of coins had a loud voice.

He walked by the graves, wondering what it had all been worth. In the end he had achieved little. In a year or two few would remember anything about the wood. The church would have its glory, the spire rising to the sky, visible for miles, a sign to the faithful. He sighed and shook his head as he left.

• • •

Walter was sitting on the joint stool, Katherine sharing the bench with Martha. The girls were playing with a pair of carved wooden dolls taken from an old, dusty chest in the corner.

'Well?' Martha asked, her clear eyes on his face.

'He says I'll be fine' He raised the arm, grinning. Katherine ran to him, and he hugged her close, for the first time able to properly wrap his arms around her. She pulled back, blushing, with a joyful smile. 'What do you think, lad?' he asked Walter.

'Does this mean you'll be leaving, John?'

'I'll only be a few miles away, don't worry. You'll see me every week. 'And,' he added brightly, 'sometimes I'll need help on the manor. Would you like that?'

'Yes, John,' the boy answered eagerly. 'I'd really like that.'

'Since you've two good arms again you can bring the wine and cups from the buttery,' Martha told him. 'You might as well make yourself useful again.'

'Yes, Mistress.'

They drank a toast to his health, Walter grimacing at the harsh taste.

'I'll miss having you here,' Martha said.

'I won't be far away.'

'I'm an old woman, I can't travel out there.' Her eyes were twinkling.

'You won't be rid of me like that.'

'You'd better keep that promise,' Katherine warned him. 'I'll be expecting you every Saturday.'

He gave her a small, elegant bow and finished his wine.

'I should go and see the coroner.'

• • •

The man was sitting by the table, the monk close by, thumbing through several closely-written pages. He glanced up as John entered.

'Well, carpenter,' he said lazily, 'two working arms again?'

'Yes, Master.'

De Harville cocked his head and smiled. 'It seems strange to see you like that. I'd grown used to the broken wing.' He shrugged. 'Are you ready to work?'

He stood straight. 'I am.'

The coroner stood up and paced across the room to stare out of the window. 'If I find you've been dishonest I'll turn you out and prosecute you.'

'I won't cheat you.'

'No, I'm sure you won't.' He turned to the monk. 'What do you think, Robert? A good new steward?'

'Aye, Master, very good indeed.'

De Harville smiled. 'Bring your things and be here first thing in the morning.' He held out his hand. 'Welcome, carpenter.'

About the Author

CHRIS NICKSON is the author of the Richard Nottingham series (Severn House), in addition to being a well-known journalist. He lives in Leeds.